"Say it," Damon commanded

"Say what?" came the whispered question.

"Say my name."

Dale's eyes came up slowly to focus on his wide mouth, to notice the tensing in his jaw. "Damon," she said, somewhat mesmerized. He slowly smiled.

"That's better." And then he kissed her. His firm mouth covered hers, possessing it, staking an immediate and undeniable claim.

Dale tried to pull away, but his lips held her captive. She felt his tongue flick across the surface of her lips, wanting her to respond and give him access. She did.

Damon deepened the kiss. There was an unconscious urge to place her arms around his neck. But she couldn't, and her hands lay in her lap, clenched tightly....

Neither spoke right away as they searched each other's faces. Dale watched him in growing awareness and fascination. It finally occurred to her that she was being gently seduced....

ABOUT THE AUTHOR

Sandra Kitt and her husband currently live in
New York City, where she is the librarian for a
major museum. Aside from her writing,
Sandra is also a free-lance graphic designer
and has had several pieces used as greeting
cards for UNICEF.

Books by Sandra Kitt

HARLEQUIN AMERICAN ROMANCE

43—RITES OF SPRING
86—ADAM AND EVA
97—PERFECT COMBINATION

These books may be available at your local bookseller.

Don't miss any of our special offers. Write to us at the
following address for information on our newest releases.

Harlequin Reader Service
P.O. Box 52040, Phoenix, AZ 85072-2040
Canadian address: P.O. Box 2800, Postal Station A,
5170 Yonge St., Willowdale, Ont. M2N 6J3

Perfect Combination

SANDRA KITT

Harlequin Books

TORONTO • NEW YORK • LONDON
AMSTERDAM • PARIS • SYDNEY • HAMBURG
STOCKHOLM • ATHENS • TOKYO • MILAN

Thomas A.—who is always fair

With thanks to Dr. Kenneth Cohen,
for his technical assistance and sense of humor

Published April 1985

First printing February 1985

ISBN 0-373-16097-6

Printed In Canada

Chapter One

There was an incredible sense of excitement in the air. It mixed with the humidity and mild temperature and felt like something about to explode. Dale felt it as soon as her cab swung off the airport highway and headed toward the old sector. The streets seemed crowded with people, all seemingly in high spirits.

Dale pulled the loose knit of her sweater away from her body and waved it back and forth, fanning dry air against her damp skin. When she'd left home that morning, the temperature was thirty degrees, and there were two feet of snow on the ground, so she'd completely forgotten about the steamy climate that was more usual in New Orleans at this time.

"You just made it," the middle-aged cabdriver said in a froglike voice, his teeth clamped tightly around a stubby cigar.

Dale's eyes caught his in the rearview mirror. "I beg your pardon?"

"I said, you just made it! Course, you missed the weekend, but tomorrow's the big day!"

Dale frowned, trying to remember what national or state holiday was being celebrated. "It's a little early for Washington's Birthday," she offered with a shrug. The driver looked at her as if she were crazy.

"Come on, lady! Are you kidding me or something? Don't you know tomorrow is Fat Tuesday? Where you from, anyway?"

Dale's frown deepened. "What's Fat Tuesday?"

The driver shook his head sadly. Maybe she was foreign. Maybe from Canada. "Haven't you ever heard of Mardi

Gras?" he asked in disgust. "Don't you know about the costume balls and the parades?"

Dale smiled in understanding now. She had forgotten about the famous Mardi Gras, the partying and celebrations having begun in New Orleans more than a month earlier. "I'm sorry to say I'm not in New Orleans for Mardi Gras this year," she said.

The driver looked at her with frowning speculation. Maybe someone was ill and she was just visiting. That was the only explanation. It would take something that serious or a declaration of war to prevent people in the city from dropping everything and joining in the fun. As it was, the local government practically came to a full halt, even its officials took part in events that had been a year in the making.

The driver sighed and rolled his mutilated cigar to the other side of his mouth. She didn't look particularly sad, but then you can never really tell with Yankees. He knew she was from the North because of her speech and because she was dressed for winter, wearing boots.

The cab pulled onto St. Charles Street, with its famous old mansions and the still-functioning cable cars. The driver's eyes shifted once more to the mirror, and he examined more carefully what he saw reflected from the back seat.

The young woman had shoulder-length wavy hair the color of caramel. It was brushed back off a high forehead and secured over her ears with plain tortoiseshell combs. Her large round eyes were light-green—jade—and her softly rounded chin hinted of a shallow cleft or dimple on its surface. The green eyes suddenly caught him staring in the mirror.

"We're almost there," he stated with a nod. Dale merely smiled and turned to look out the window again.

He concluded that she wasn't model pretty but certainly pretty enough to look at. Maybe she was visiting friends. She seemed much too quiet and ladylike just to be there all alone. New Orleans during Mardi Gras was as close to a riot situation as you could get without actual violence. Satisfied that he had his attractive lone traveler pegged correctly, he devoted the rest of his attention and time to driving through the French Quarter.

At twenty-nine, Dale Christensen looked a good deal younger and less seasoned than her age would normally dictate. Her complexion was clear and her face rather youthfully open, adding to the general misconceptions about her that she'd been fighting since she was seventeen. Her eyes always held an expression of perpetual curiosity and wonder, all in all giving the impression of someone who needed to be protected. Her wholesome, healthy looks, therefore, were the nemesis of her life.

Those who knew her often thought her youthful appearance was her adolescence and teen years locked in place, perhaps waiting for a chance to express themselves, awaiting the drive and ambition and determination in her to burn itself out a little so that she could, indeed, be young. Even as she rode in the cab, she wondered how she allowed herself to be talked into making a trip that was interfering with her work and that she was sure was pointless. At that very moment, she could be at afternoon rounds.

The cab at last pulled up in front of the Fairmont Hotel, and Dale climbed out feeling wrinkled and cramped. She quickly took in the pleasing architectural details of the hotel entrance while her driver removed her bags from the cab trunk and put them on the curb at her feet.

"Now you be careful and enjoy your stay," he advised. "And don't forget to see the parade tomorrow. It'll be some experience!"

"I don't think there'll be time. I'm supposed to be at a meeting tomorrow."

Shaking his head, the driver got back into the seat of his cab. "Don't bet on it, lady. You might be the only one there!"

Dale frowned as the cab pulled away. Then, finally, she gathered her belongings and made her way into the lobby with a slight limp. She managed about three or four yards when she was stopped by the overwhelming numbers of people generally milling about. Dale was just considering how she could possibly make it to the registration desk when she was approached by a young uniformed bellman.

"Are you checking in or out?" he asked briskly.

"In."

"Okay," he said, presenting her with a number of forms.

"If you fill these out, I'll take them to the desk and try to hurry things along."

"I didn't think it would be so crowded. Are there a lot of conventions this week?" she asked, looking around her in amazement.

"About three or four. But there's not going to be much business done." The young man chuckled as he pulled out identification labels from a pocket.

"Why not?"

He squinted at her. "Lady, don't you know this is Mardi Gras?"

"Oh, yes. How foolish of me," Dale said dryly with a smile. She sighed, sure now beyond a doubt that the trip was going to be a waste of her time.

"Your name, ma'am?" he asked, felt-tip pen poised over a label.

"Dr. Christenson."

"Okay, Dr. Christensen. I'll take your luggage to the room-assignment desk. Soon as you get assigned a room, they'll send everything right up."

"Great. Shall I come with you?" she asked, dubiously eyeing the mob through which she'd have to walk.

"No. You just sit for a while. When you finish with those cards I gave you, bring them to me over there." He pointed to a small desk next to registration. "I should have your room key by then."

"This is very nice of you," Dale said gratefully. "I've never heard of this kind of service before."

"Oh, we don't do it all the time, ma'am. It's only because—"

"It's Mardi Gras," Dale filled in, nodding in understanding.

"That's right, ma'am." He grinned, backing away. "Just wait until you see the excitement tomorrow!" And he was lost instantly in the crowd.

"I don't think I'm going to have much choice," Dale murmured in amused exasperation, and then looked around for someplace to sit.

The noise was deafening, what with yelled greetings, surprised laughter and screamed complaints. A weariness began to settle on Dale, and she thought wistfully of the quiet and solitude her room would provide, if she ever got one. But right now there didn't seem to be a vacant chair anywhere.

Dale spotted a metal floor ashtray near a pillar off to the side and, seeing its potential, walked over to it. It had not been used yet, so she folded her coat over the top and sat with a sigh on her improvised chair. She brushed a hand over her damp face and swept back over her hair, feeling the loose tendrils beginning to curl and frizz in the humid air. She filled out the registration forms, and when she finished, she gathered her bag and coat and stood up, prepared to follow the young bellman's instruction. As she walked back across the lobby, she spotted a tall, handsome young man in an ill-fitting new blue suit tightly holding the hand of a petite brunette. She was wearing an equally new flowered dress. A smile flashed over Dale's face. Newlyweds, she surmised.

The couple moved suddenly, and she found herself staring eye to eye with a man who'd obviously been staring at her. Dale's rounded chin raised defensively, and in that moment she filled most people's errant assumptions of her—a young, pretty-enough woman faced with a situation she wasn't used to handling. But her embarrassment passed quickly. The man, not bad-looking, was scouting for an available female. Dale gave him what she hoped was a scathing look of disgust. The man shrugged good-naturedly and turned away to find greener pastures.

So far, Dale had to admit, she wasn't finding the travel business much fun. Impatient to get settled, she aggressively began approaching the desk pointed out to her earlier by the young bellman. She murmured apologies and tugged her shoulder bag and coat with her through the tight pressing of people. Dale turned sideways to use her shoulder and was pushed unexpectedly from behind, propelling her forward and into the arms of a man equally unprepared for the contact. The surface she landed against was rather broad and hard.

"I—I'm sorry!" Dale murmured, aghast, as a pair of hands grabbed her arms firmly to steady her. Immediately, Dale tried to pull back, only to find that a brass button on the man's blazer jacket had lodged itself in the threading of her sweater. She stood rather embarrassingly locked chest to chest with a perfect stranger.

Dale looked up, prepared with another apology, and met a pair of inquisitive fawn-brown eyes searching her flushed face. She was completely arrested by the dawning look of interest and amusement in his features as a mobile, wide mouth quirked at the corners.

"Well! This is the most original encounter I've had in a long time." The voice was a low, soft, modulated baritone.

Dale began tugging in agitation at her sweater, trying to disengage it from his jacket. Her forehead just reached the man's chin, close enough for her to feel his chin brushing her hair.

"You could help a little!" she mumbled with a mixture of exasperation and unsettled nerves, twisting at the stubborn fabric.

"Of course!" he agreed readily, and his hands came up to meet hers.

Dale stiffened as the soft padded sides of his hand brushed over her chest in unavoidable contact. But her eyes were curiously drawn to the large, handsomely shaped hands, immaculately clean with trimmed, even nails. There was a silky layer of dark hair on his knuckles and wrists below the cuffs of the blazer.

"N-never mind. I'll manage!" Dale growled, more disturbed than ever.

"I was only doing what you asked!" he said, his voice quavering suspiciously. Dale gave him what was meant to be a quelling look, but the man only grinned broadly.

She was annoyed not only with the man but the button, the hotel, her shaky hands and her inability to control any of it. All the while Dale grimaced over her task, the bodies around them prevented even a micron of operating space to develop between them. In any case, only Dale seemed inclined to want to get them separated as soon as possible. The tall, athletically built gentleman stood still and let her struggle alone. He bent forward just enough to sniff the clean shampoo fragrance of her hair. It had a wild flyaway look that made him want to touch it to see how soft it was. Her rounded breasts pressed suggestively into his chest.

Dale was shoved again, and the button lodged deeper,

her chest flattening to him. She stopped moving and raised her eyes to his, her cheeks tingeing pink. Dale felt her body tense as he slid his arms around her waist to hold her. Her hands braced on his upper arms. "Wh-what do you think you're doing?" she asked, bewildered, trying to keep the hold from being too intimate.

"Just hang on a moment," he said and, holding her to him, moved his body easily sideways through the crowd to a pillar some distance from the desk. Dale was forced to move with one of her legs sliced between his and didn't allow herself to consider what he must be thinking.

"Okay, what now?" he asked in good humor once they were alone.

"Hold these!" Dale said, thrusting her coat, bag and cards at him. Hands now freed, she meticulously worked at the sweater for a long moment, and the button at last came free. She let out a tight breath of utter relief. She didn't look directly at him as she reclaimed her things. "I—I'm very sorry that happened," she said earnestly.

"I'm not," he drawled, his sparkling eyes again taking liberties over her slim body. But when he saw the uncomfortable flush in her cheeks, he relented. "Look, it was just an accident. I hope I didn't ruin your sweater. Are you staying here?" he asked, diverting her attention.

"If I ever get checked in, yes!" she said with a return of humor.

He smiled at her. "Do you need my help?" he asked, tilting his head and making the innocent question sound very personal.

"Again?" Dale teased.

He shrugged innocently. "I did try."

"Not very hard," Dale said caustically, taking a step back from him. Now she could fully examine the man in front of her.

His brown hair had a tendency to curl and grew long over his collar and his ears. It was hard for her to tell if it had a natural tendency to look ruffled or if it was styled that way. The face was square and handsome, with a firm, strong jaw set on a muscular neck column.

Dale suddenly felt an inexplicable wave of apprehension curl through her and, realizing that she was staring, made a pretense of straightening her coat and adjusting her shoulder bag. He was too masculine, too physical, and she felt immediately threatened. Bringing her head up once more, she found that he, too, was regarding her with a look of open curiosity.

"I suppose you're here for Mardi Gras," he stated rather than asked.

Dale raised her brows in amusement and grimaced with a smile. "That's what everyone keeps telling me."

"Don't you know?" he questioned with a dry laugh.

She lifted a shoulder slightly. "I didn't even remember it was Mardi Gras week."

He let out a low whistle. "Be careful who you say that to. Around here you can be hanged for an offense like that!"

Dale couldn't help laughing. Shaking her head, she looked at him. "I'm here for entirely different reasons."

"Such as?" he asked, and just as the words were out of his mouth, a bearded bear of a man clapped him soundly on the shoulder from behind, drawing his attention.

"I thought it was you! Spotted you from the door the minute I walked in!" The bearded man grinned broadly.

"Brad! How are you?"

Dale smiled at the exchange going on between the two men, and took another hesitant step backward.

"Ma'am?"

She swung around. "Yes..." Dale found herself facing her erstwhile helper of half an hour earlier. "Oh! I was just on my way to give you these cards." Dale held out the bent and mutilated registration forms with an apologetic smile.

"No problem. They had your confirmation." He held up an oval brass key ring and jangled a key. "And I've got your room!"

"Oh, great!" Dale let out with a sigh.

"Just follow me and I'll take you up to your room." The young man turned to snake his way expertly across the floor.

Dale turned back briefly just to politely wish the man of her encounter a nice stay. But his back was to her, and he was deeply involved in a rather cheerful exchange with his acquaintance. Dale hesitated a second, shrugged her shoulders and followed her bellhop to the elevators.

She categorized the man with the ruffled hairdo as probably a professional athlete. Not tall enough for basketball, but football was a distinct possibility. She recalled the hard, conditioned feel of his forearms under his jacket material, the biceps flexing and bunching. Dale stepped into the elevator and faced front.

And he had the broadest pair of shoulders she'd ever seen.

THE DOORS leading back into her room stood open behind her. On the balcony, Dale looked with delight over the scrolled rail to the square courtyard below, with its potted plants and trees, its flagged walkways and occasional wrought-iron bench. It was so quaint and old-fashioned. It was a place meant for relaxation, fun and romance. It was a place out of the past where you lost all sense of time and lived just for the moment. Dale sighed deeply and turned back to her room. She wished she hadn't come.

With the restless energy of someone used to constant activity, she paced the carpeted floor, ignoring the additional peaceful charm of her room. In her mind she ran through half a dozen things she could be doing now that needed attention, instead of waiting helplessly for her luggage to be delivered. Dale ranted inwardly at her colleague and partner, Dr. Lester Wallace, who had decided only a few days before that he couldn't make the trip and sent her in his place. He was also to have delivered her medical hypothesis on Thursday, during the week of conferences, seminars and panel discussions. Now she was here to give it herself.

Dale was very logical and methodical in her thinking, and professionally it had served her well. Yet it had never occurred to her that as long as she was there, she might as well enjoy herself. She'd missed too many years of having fun, years that would have given her social experience, and now it came awkwardly to her. She'd much rather be busy. When you're busy, there is no time for wishful thinking, remembering or regrets.

There was a knock on her door. Quickly moving to answer, she stood with her hand on the knob. "Who is it?"

"Front desk, ma'am. I have your luggage."

Dale pulled the door open. But the man carrying the suitcase had only just stepped inside the door when Dale put out a hand to stay him. "Wait a minute," she said, pointing to the case. "That's not mine!"

The man blinked at her and set the case down, reaching for the luggage label.

"Dr. Christensen, Room Five-eleven."

"Yes, I know, but that's not mine. My suitcase is soft-sided. And it's tan, not brown leather."

The man scratched his head. "I don't know, ma'am."

"Well, I do. You'll simply have to take it back and find mine." Dale looked at her watch. "And quickly! I have a dinner I'm supposed to attend in less than two hours!"

"Don't you worry. We'll get this straightened out right away."

Right away turned out to be nearly ten-thirty in the evening, at which point Dale only wanted a quiet meal and some sleep. She ordered through room service and went to take a shower. She'd just finished toweling her hair when dinner was delivered. But she was more tired than she realized and could only finish half the food. Giving up with a sigh, Dale crawled under the cool, fresh sheets of the absurdly large bed. She was asleep almost instantly.

The ringing phone sometime after midnight did not startle her but brought her instantly awake.

"Dr. Christensen," she answered throatily, her voice raspy from sleep.

"Good evening. This is Dr. Christensen," came a male voice somewhat drowned out by loud, boisterous activity in the background. Dale winced and moved the phone from her ear. She struggled up onto an elbow and with her free hand swept her thick hair back out of her eyes.

"Is this a joke?" she asked suspiciously, and was answered with a short, deep chuckle.

"In a way, but probably not a very funny one. I really am Dr. Christensen. I believe our luggage got confused this afternoon."

"Oh, yes." Dale nodded.

"I apologize for that. I was hoping to do so in person at the opening dinner this evening. But you didn't make it."

"No, I didn't. There was a small problem of having no clothes to wear," Dale said in amusement.

"Yes, that does make a difference," he agreed with a laugh. "But if it makes you feel any better, it's a dull affair."

"Yeah, it sounds like everyone's having a terrible time!" Dale said ruefully, and received another chuckle. She was trying to determine his approximate age, but there was too much noise overriding his voice and tone.

"You can still come down if you like. Dinner's over, I'm afraid, but there's still a lot of socializing going on."

"Are you serious? It must be almost one in the morning!"

"Almost two," he corrected.

Dale laughed now. "Well, I don't know about you, but I need my beauty sleep. And toward that end I'm already in bed."

"Oops. Did I wake you and your husband?"

Doctors are used to being awakened at strange hours. Dale wasn't the least concerned or put out about being awakened, but the assumption that she was married touched a chord, a long-ignored line of thoughts and feelings that even under other circumstances she didn't allow herself to indulge in.

"I'm not married," Dale informed him somewhat stiffly, and then bit down on her lip at her tone. "And besides, doctors are always called in the middle of the night. I think it's some sort of unwritten law."

He laughed. "In any case, I won't keep you. I just thought an apology was owed you."

"That was very nice of you but not necessary. After all, it wasn't your fault."

"But since you missed the dinner, I'd like to take you to breakfast tomorrow morning."

"Really, Dr. Christensen—"

"It's the least I can do."

"The thing is, I have appointments tomorrow morning and afternoon."

"You can't possibly! Tomorrow's Mardi Gras!"

Dale groaned and collapsed back on the pillows. "If I hear that one more time, I think I'm going to scream!"

"Don't waste the energy. No one is functioning tomorrow except to have a good time."

"But I do have appointments. And I *know* they'll be kept."

"If you say so. Then how about dinner?"

"I thought there were parades all day and all night?"

"True, but you still have to eat."

Dale sighed audibly. "Well..."

"I promise to get you back at a decent hour so you'll get enough rest for the meetings Wednesday morning."

"That sounds fair," Dale said, relenting.

"Good! Why don't I meet you in the lobby. Say, seven o'clock?"

"That's fine. And thank you."

"My pleasure. Good night, Doctor."

"Good night... Oh! Wait a minute, wait a minute!" Dale shouted.

"Yes..."

"How will I know you?"

There was a soft laugh on the other line. "Maybe you'd better tell me how I'll know you. Women tend to be much more distinctive in their dress."

Dale bit her lip and thought for a moment, running her four-day wardrobe through her mind. "I'll wear a light-blue shirtwaist dress."

"What's a shirtwaist dress?"

Dale shook her head, lamenting. "It's tailored like a man's shirt, but longer."

"What! No carnation?" He chuckled.

"Good night, Doctor." Dale laughed as she hung up the phone.

Chapter Two

The everyday sounds of the hospital were familiar and comforting. Not that a hospital by its very nature was a pleasant place to be; rather, it was a territory totally known to Dale, in which she functioned with expert knowledge.

She turned her head to examine the aging gentleman next to her who had been a source of inspiration to her in medical school. He had taught her that the only function of a hospital was to make people hopeful at least, well at best. Dr. Boris Teller was much older than Dale remembered. His hair was now completely white instead of just gray, and there was much less of it. His shoulders were a little stooped with the frailty of age, but as he talked of his work, his hospital, Dale had not the least doubt that his mind and ideas were as lucid as ever.

"We've had to fight for this facility. Most people don't want to give money to anything they can't see instant results from."

"Yes, I know," Dale agreed. "I think it's true everywhere. But I admit I'm not very good at soliciting for research money. I get too emotional," she added with a small smile.

Dr. Teller patted her arm affectionately. "That's because you believe so strongly in this work. And that's what we need every bit as much as the money. Believers!"

They turned a corner and walked the length of the hall. At the end, they went through a pair of doors into a room that was large and equipped just like a gymnasium. It was currently occupied by five young people, three boys and two girls, all between ten and thirteen years of age. It was a physical therapy room, and all the youngsters were being assisted through one kind of exercise or another by trained therapists.

"We have the usual kinds of structural damages here — nothing very special," Dr. Teller informed Dale as they walked through the room. "But there's one case that might particularly interest you. The young man has very weak tendons and muscles around his knee joints. Consequently, the joints separate, and his legs give out on him. Now we could operate and more or less tighten everything up. But you know as well as I do that there's still no guarantee."

They stopped at a bench where a young black boy lay on his back, his knees bent at the edge and dangling to the floor. There were braces around his knees and weights attached to his ankles. He struggled to bring the legs up and level with the rest of his body and then slowly let them down again.

"We've been working with Barry for three months now to see if a normal program of exercise will help. Operations are always the last resort."

Dale nodded and silently observed the young boy's efforts, watching the area around his exposed knees for the pull of sinew and muscles. They did not tauten the way fully healthy and elastic muscles should, and Dale felt for the boy's obvious struggle to make them work nonetheless.

Dr. Teller signaled to a nearby therapist and touched the youngster on the leg. "Why don't we rest a bit, Barry." The therapist came forward to help the boy into a sitting position and to release the weights from his ankles. "How are you doing?" Dr. Teller asked.

"It...it hurts," Barry mumbled from a pinched mouth, trying valiantly not to cry and embarrass himself.

"I know it does. But you're doing very well," Dr. Teller told him.

The youngster made a passing swipe with a hand over his teary eyes and peeked curiously at Dale, who stood to the side, smiling at him.

"I admire you for working so hard," Dale said softly. Barry didn't reply but looked openly at her. "You must get very tired."

"Sometimes..." He still mumbled. "You look a little like my teacher Mrs. Ross."

"Do I?" Dale asked, stepping closer.

Barry nodded. "Are you a teacher, too?"

"No, I'm a doctor, like Dr. Teller."

"Oh," Barry said, clearly disappointed and wary.

"I understand you want to be a baseball player?"

Barry shrugged. He understood better than anyone that he might not be able to. He didn't want anyone telling him everything was going to be okay. He'd heard that before. He couldn't play Little League the summer before because he couldn't stand too long, much less run bases.

"I don't know too much about baseball," Dale confessed guilelessly. "What position do you play?"

"Third base."

"What does a third baseman do?"

Barry sighed with the exasperation of the young having to put up with the idiocy of his elders. "You have to catch balls that come into your playing area. And you try to get out the runner at first or the one trying to get home."

"Is it hard?"

"You have to be fast!" Barry said knowledgeably.

"What other spot do you like?"

"I can pitch pretty good."

"And I suppose you have to be fast for that, as well." Dale continued to ask questions with such interest that Barry was soon caught up in talking about one of his favorite subjects and forgot his pain.

Dr. Teller moved discreetly to a chair and sat heavily, listening to the rapport between the young, attractive doctor and his even younger patient. One of the things he always found difficult was to deal with a child's pain. He had to be careful not to make too little of it just because he understood the principle behind it. Children only know that it hurts and that maybe it means they can't do what other children do. He realized that anyone who can get past the hurt and fear not only to heal but to empathize was rare indeed. Boris Teller had always been impressed with that capacity in Dale Christensen. He'd witnessed it first when she was an intern working a tour in pediatrics, and later in children's orthopedics. But then, she had come by her understanding at a young age, and firsthand.

There was suddenly laughter, and Dr. Teller came back

from his memories and found Dale and Barry giggling like conspirators. "What are you two up to?" the older man asked.

"I told Barry that what he needed was a pair of new knee sockets that he could screw his legs in and out of."

"That's dumb!" Barry scoffed and grimaced from his brown face, nevertheless laughing at the image.

"Well, if I can make new sockets so you can play ball, would you try it?"

"I guess," he responded skeptically.

"And if it works, will you invite me to the first game you play in?"

Barry watched her. "Would you really come to watch me play?" he asked.

"Sure. Besides, you'll have to explain to me what's going on!"

Barry rolled his eyes to the ceiling. Girls!

"Well, I know you still have a lot of work to do and you don't need me standing around." Dale turned abruptly toward the door, ending their chat. "Don't forget to invite me!" She turned back once.

"If I get those socket things you told me about, sure!"

Dale waved and pushed out the door into the hall, Dr. Teller behind her.

"You've got a special touch, Dale," he said, sighing.

She wrinkled her nose. "No, I don't. If I did, I'd know exactly how to help that child instead of hoping my idea will work."

"Well, we have to start somewhere. Hoping isn't such a bad way. And as you know, replacing joints is not a new technique."

"No, but I want him to have a synthetic that will allow him to run and jump like a little boy and play ball if he wants. I want him to have it all!" Dale said with conviction, unaware that her fervent feelings brought color to her cheeks and made her green eyes bright and sparkling. Her odd walking gait and gestures also made her hair swing about her face. "I want every child like Barry to have it all."

Dr. Teller laughed and took her elbow to steer her toward the elevator. "I see you haven't lost any of your steam!"

Dale relaxed and chuckled in a self-derisive way. "I guess I got carried away."

"Not a thing wrong with that." They entered the elevator, descended and continued on to the doctor's office. "I only hope that some of that boundless energy has been reserved for yourself."

Dale frowned and looked at the doctor. "What do you mean?" she asked as she sat facing him across a desk piled with papers, journals and plastic models.

"I mean, my dear, that you are young and attractive and might want to give some thoughts to your own personal life."

Dale didn't respond at once but meticulously lifted and folded her khaki jacket, which matched her slacks, and laid it across her lap. Her hair, held off her face with a red plastic band, fell forward to hide her cheeks and her expression.

"Haven't you ever considered that someday you might wish to marry and have children of your own?"

Yes, she had considered. But that was long before, and now she was much too busy. There was her practice, her research, her aging father. "I don't have time for a husband. And I have dozens of children!" she prevaricated with a charming smile. "Besides, doctors make the worst spouses. I...I've heard everyone say so." But her voice was not exactly steady or firm.

Dr. Teller easily detected the emotion behind her statement. He knew Dale too well not to realize that it was not said idly. "I want to see you happy," Dr. Teller said in a fatherly manner, and his gentleness and concern misted her eyes.

"I love what I do, Boris."

"I have no doubts whatsoever that you do. But it's not the same as being happy. Can you honestly say to me that you are?"

Dale bit her lip, a dead giveaway that there was a degree of doubt. Boris was one of the few people ever to enter her life and be able to read every nuance of her personality with a deadly accuracy. She didn't resent his familiarity with her now, for she recognized it was from true caring. But she didn't answer.

"Well, enough psychoanalysis for one day. How do you like New Orleans?" he asked, quickly switching topics.

"I haven't seen much of it yet." Dale breathed out, happy for the change. "But I understand this is the best time to be here."

"It's a crazy time to be here!" Boris laughed hoarsely. "Grown people dressed up in diapers and going to costume balls...." He shook his head, and Dale laughed with him. "But do try to see a parade or two. I promise you won't be disappointed. Maybe you can catch the Proteus affair this evening on Canal Street."

"I'm invited to go to dinner tonight."

"Oh? Anyone interesting?" He winked at her.

"I honestly don't know. We haven't met yet. That is, not officially. He's a Christensen, too. Our luggage got switched when I checked in yesterday."

Dr. Teller pursed his lips thoughtfully, scratching his almost-bald pate. "Dr. Christensen... Mmm... the only Dr. Christensen I know must be seventy-five if he's a day, and I believe his specialty is cardiology. West Coast man."

"If you say so." Dale shrugged. "He felt it necessary to make up for the fact that I missed the banquet dinner marking the start of the conferences."

"Good. Enjoy yourself. Now, Lester said you were giving a paper this week. Your old pet project?"

"Yes, I'm afraid so. I'm still trying to find a way for the idea of artificial bones to work. If we can do it for joints and organs—"

"Can bones be far behind?"

"Exactly! Anyway, I don't expect anyone to pay attention, but Lester insisted."

"You never can tell. There might be someone at the conference who's given it some thought, as well."

"Maybe..." Dale looked at her watch. "I really should be going now. I've taken up almost your whole day."

"It's been a real treat for an old man." Boris Teller chuckled, getting up from his chair. "If I were thirty years younger, I'd marry you myself!"

Dale laughed and leaned over the desk to kiss his wrinkled, dry cheek. "If you weren't already married, I'd accept."

"Oh, no. I have hope for you yet that you'll meet someone young and worthy."

"You're an optimist."

"Doctors have to be!" he responded sagely.

"Will you be at the assembly on Thursday?" Dale asked, gathering her things.

"Of course. I want to hear all this brilliant research you've done and ask a sharp question or two!"

Dale groaned playfully as they slowly walked to the main lobby.

"What do you think of Barry's case?"

Dale sobered. "I don't think there's any doubt you'll have to operate," she informed him without hesitation. Dr. Teller sighed, but Dale astutely assessed that he was not concerned that an operation was necessary but that he as the attending physician might not be steady enough to perform it. "How do his parents feel?"

"They're willing to try anything, of course. But when I knew you were coming, I wanted you to see him and then tell me what you thought."

It made Dale feel wonderful and very professional that Boris put such faith in her opinion.

"You read his case history. Do you think your way will work?"

"If we want to give him a chance to play ball, I think it's the only way! Eighteen months from now third basemen like Ron Cey and Graig Nettles will have nothing on that kid!"

Boris squinted at her. "I thought you said you didn't know anything about baseball?"

"Shhhh!" Dale gestured with a finger to her lips, causing Boris Teller's shoulders to shake with laughter. "Just don't tell Barry!"

"I wouldn't dream of it!" he said, holding the door open for her as she passed through to the street. "I'll let you know how things go with him. In the meantime, have fun, and I'll see you Thursday."

Dale left the hospital feeling a combination of professional excitement and frustration, and personal melancholia. She was excited by the prospects of her knee sockets for Barry and frustrated that her other idea for artificial parts was still received with such skepticism. She recognized the physiological problems involved, but that didn't mean she would give up. It only meant she must work harder. The melancholia was older. It seemed that it had been with her forever.

It was a fine day for a parade, and everywhere around her were the obvious preparations for it. But the anticipation was lost on Dale as she sank deeper and deeper into the images from the past and relived the agony of twenty years before and the events that decided the course of her life. Children like Barry were a constant reminder and only served to make her that much more determined to help them.

THE HUMIDITY of the hazy New Orleans day permeated everything, and Dale's skin was damp under her plaid blouse, down the valley of her breasts and down her spine. Yet she shivered, a chill suddenly cooling her body as she pictured Grandma Lacy's farmhouse settled in nearly two feet of snow....

IT WAS Christmas week, and preparations were well under way for the family celebration. There were wonderful smells from the large open kitchen and wood crackling in the fireplace. Her father was out getting a tree. There were snowball fights and hide-and-seek in the woods and a mountain of wood to climb in playing tag.

Dale saw herself at the bottom of the pile, two thick pigtails stuffed under a red knit hat, a scarf wound twice around her neck against the cold. Her brother David stood at the top, taunting her because she couldn't reach him. Each time she began the climb, the cut lengths of logs slipped and rolled away from beneath her feet. David's laughter only made her furious and determined.

"You kids get down from there before you get hurt!" Grandma Lacy's voice came from the open kitchen window. But the mountain began to move, rolling toward Dale as she stood frozen, watching in fascination. Grandma Lacy yelled her name, but already she was pitched backward falling blindly, her leg not following its natural bend. Something crashed into her arm. She heard a scream. Pain tore through her left leg.

A WHISTLE BLEW, and Dale jumped. She blinked rapidly to see a police officer in shirt-sleeves staying pedestrian traffic with a gloved hand so that a float could go by. Dale licked her dry lips and swallowed down the emotions evoked by her memories.

SHE HAD AWAKENED to find bandages on her forehead and a cast on her left arm. Her nine-year-old body had taken the full weight and force of the rolling cord of wood. The left leg was wrenched and separated at the knee. There was a tremendous loss of blood, and she went into shock. And then began what had seemed an endless round of corrective surgery. But still she was left with a slight limp. Until she was seventeen she remembered all the other Christmases as somber, David blaming himself for years after the fact, until she went away to school.

DALE TURNED onto Canal and headed toward the hotel. She thought of Barry and his desire to play pro ball. She knew that her joint replacements would give him the best chance. There was a lot of work ahead of him, but she knew that he would do it, because he wanted to be well. She smiled as she went through the revolving doors.

DAVID WAS GOING to make the grand gesture and become a doctor so that he could fix her knee. He'd been quite adamant about it until their last year at home together and his college entrance loomed on the fall horizon. Dale had asked him what else he planned to do after he fixed her knee, and he had no response. But she'd relieved him of his guilt. Dale became the doctor, and David went off to be an engineer in aeronautics. She fixed other people's broken bones and sometimes their spirits, as well. It was for David and Barry and herself. It was the least she could do for them all.

IT WAS SEVEN-TEN when the elevator reached the lobby and Dale stepped out into a confusion of people. She inched her way toward the center and stood looking around. She wasn't sure whom she was looking for and could only bring to mind the description Dr. Teller had given her that afternoon of the older Dr. Christensen he knew of. But it wasn't enough information to help her. Lots of men in the lobby seemed to be in their seventies, but no one was looking for a young woman in a blue shirtwaist dress. Dale looked down at her outfit as if to assure herself that she was dressed the way she said she would be. She had on a white jacket over the dress and hastily removed it so that the dress with its short sleeves was clearly visible.

This is ridiculous, she thought in a moment of pique. She felt very much like a teenager waiting for a blind date, even though the personal-relationship element was not a factor. Dale had never actually had a blind date, and the men she occasionally dated now were invariably connected to the medical field. Some formed a semiregular troup of escorts to professional and social functions—she didn't have time for an involvement.

Dale's watch now read seven-fifteen. When she looked up again, there was someone approaching her. Dale's stomach sank as she recognized the broad-shouldered man from the day before. Her earlier impressions were reinforced as his slow approach allowed her to view him again. He was dressed in charcoal-gray slacks worn with a V-neck pullover sweater in navy blue. The neckline exposed the powerful column of his neck, and again Dale had the thought that he was an athlete. But despite his build he had the quiet, lithe movements of a predatory animal, graceful and sure of himself. Dale felt herself responding to his magnetism, her breath drawing in and holding, her eyes unconsciously widening. He stopped in front of her, a lazy, surprised smile curving his wide mouth.

"We never had a chance to introduce ourselves yesterday," he opened.

She smiled nervously. "No, we didn't. Everything was happening so fast. Besides, you met a friend—"

"And *you* vanished! Am I correct in assuming you're, er, Dr. Christensen?" he asked, his voice holding a hint of hesitation as though he couldn't credit it.

"Yes," Dale responded, nodding.

His fawn-brown eyes looked her up and down. Not suggestively but certainly seeing and assessing every part of her. Some parts he was more familiar with than others, and he brought his eyes up from her gently heaving breasts to meet hers, his mouth quirked at the corners in memory. Dale flushed, remembering, also. She bit down on her bottom lip, momentarily nonplussed. If he saw her uncertainty, he gave no sign. But neither did he try to make it easier for her.

Obviously, they'd both been expecting someone totally different. He was not the least disappointed, but he could tell she'd thought she would meet an older man. His smile broadened. She would have been a lot safer with an older man.

Dale opened her mouth to speak again. "Are you the other Dr. Christensen?"

"In person!" He tilted his head at her. "I didn't expect to meet you again quite this way. Are you surprised?"

"Very," Dale admitted naively, drawing another smile from the man. "But I don't believe in coincidences."

"Neither do I. And it gets worse."

"How?"

"My first name is Damon."

A light dawned in Dale's eyes, and she grimaced. "Mine is Dale."

"You see! Now what are the odds of this happening again in a lifetime?"

"I still don't believe it's happening now!" Dale said caustically.

He laughed, a rich, deep, rumbling sound. "As it happens, my first name is really Michael."

"Then why don't you use it?"

"Because my father is Michael Christensen—Senior. It got to be a real headache working in the same city with him. To cut down on some confusion, I started using my middle name just after medical school."

"In this case, it hasn't helped. It's a wonder we know who we are!" Dale said with humor.

He grinned. "Now that I've met you, I'd say there was little chance of us getting mixed up. I'm always going to remember exactly who—and what—you are."

His eyes held a teasing sparkle and meaning. Dale found she couldn't respond. And seeing that she had no response, Damon was amused. It was going to be a very interesting evening, after all.

"Shall we go have dinner?" he suggested, waving his hand before him in a courtly manner.

Dale was not good at flirting, and she felt a little uncomfortable with his teasing of her, but she merely smiled and moved ahead of him toward the door. Out in the early-evening night, the pandemonium of the Mardi Gras celebration was taking place.

Chapter Three

They could not hope to travel very far. A cab was out of the question, and the crowds made progress by foot slow. They ended up off the parade route on Bourbon Street. Dale thought it was rather seedy and commercial-looking, but Damon walked on and stopped with familiarity at Galatoire's, and the attractive restaurant was a haven. They spent fifteen minutes performing the rituals of ordering drinks and their meal. Dale had deferred to Damon, letting him order for them both. Assured that she was fond of seafood, he ordered the shrimp remoulade for which the restaurant was famed. While he conversed with the waiter, Dale looked at her dinner partner again.

He was good-looking in a casual, offhanded kind of way, as though he didn't particularly care about his appearance or simply took it for granted. Tilting her head and speculating, Dale decided he could use a haircut or maybe just a more thoughtful attempt at some order. The present style gave him a rakish air. She had a desire in that instant to comb her fingers through his hair and set it to rights. The very idea sent color to her cheeks as she realized how personal her thoughts were becoming.

"Were you able to keep your appointments?" Damon asked as he handed their menus to the waiter.

"Yes, I was. A former professor of mine is on the hospital staff here. He's close to retiring, and this trip might be my last opportunity to see him for a while."

"What's his name?"

"Dr. Boris Teller."

"I know Dr. Teller," Damon said as their drinks were

placed before them. "I've studied some of his theories on orthopedic surgery."

"When I told him I was having dinner with a Dr. Christensen, he mentioned someone from the West Coast in cardiology."

"My father..." Damon supplied. "He died more than a year ago."

"Oh, I'm sorry. I'm sure Dr. Teller didn't know."

Damon easily went on, not making an issue of it. "Just what are you a doctor of?" he asked, his brown eyes intent on her face, examining the features one by one.

All at once, Dale became alert. Her green eyes probed his as she searched for any sign of patronization. She'd lost count of the number of times she'd been asked what her specialty was with amused skepticism, as though her being a woman meant she wasn't to be taken seriously as a doctor. She didn't know anything yet about Dr. Damon Christensen, but she'd hate to think he was no different from all the others.

"I'm in orthopedics, too," she responded, waiting for his reactions.

Damon raised his brows. "So am I" was his ready response. "Any particular area?" he asked with interest.

"Children's orthopedics," she answered.

"I suppose that explains why you're in New Orleans this week. There's a surgeons' convention—"

"Well, I'm here for the conference, but I'm not a full surgeon yet."

"I didn't think so." He smiled, the motion creating attractive grooves from the corner of his nose to the corner of his mouth.

Dale's brows came together. "Why didn't you think so?"

For a long moment Damon looked at her. "You're probably not going to like this, but... you don't look old enough to have completed the training."

Dale was intrigued. "You're right on both counts. But why did you say I wouldn't like it?"

He shrugged. "As a female medical student, I'm sure you've had your share of being slotted because of your age, sex, looks, abilities or lack of any of the above. I didn't want to ruin a perfectly good dinner by insulting you."

Dale digested his words and smiled a little ruefully to herself. "I didn't realize my defenses were so obvious."

"Actually, they're not," Damon said, crossing his arms and leaning a little closer across the table. "But talking about our professions is going to be unavoidable. I just thought we should get the defenses out of the way, obvious or otherwise."

Dale raised a brow and ran the point of her index finger around the rim of her glass as she looked at him thoughtfully. "And just what are your defenses, Doctor?" she asked.

Damon's eyes twinkled. "I don't like being thought of as a potential, insensitive male chauvinist."

His admission so surprised Dale that she stared at him openly for a moment. Then she laughed softly, seeing the humor in it. Damon joined in. A barrier came down between them. Damon raised his cocktail glass in a toast.

"To Mardi Gras!"

"Yes, to Mardi Gras," Dale agreed softly. She took a sip of her drink and stole another look at him across the table. "As long as we're slaying misconceptions, I have a confession to make," Dale said, wrinkling her nose pertly and missing the delighted sparkle in Damon's eyes. He merely cradled his square chin in the palm of his right hand and waited. Suddenly, Dale felt foolish, remembering the game she'd played with herself in the lobby the day before. "When...when I saw you in the lobby yesterday, I thought you were a...a professional athlete," she admitted.

Damon's mouth began to curve in amusement, and he quickly tried to keep a straight face. "I'm flattered," he responded. Dale frowned, not understanding. "I'm pleased to think that at least one person feels my body is in good enough shape to play pro!"

Dale blushed pink at the implication. "I...I didn't mean it that way. I...I just thought...well, you seemed so... so..." She stopped helplessly.

"I did play pro for a while," Damon quickly said, letting her off the hook. "May I ask what sport you assigned me to?"

"Football," Dale said weakly.

Damon nodded in appreciation. "You're psychic as well. I played two years with the Raiders."

Even though she had guessed correctly, Dale was still surprised. "Why did you give it up? You must have been very good to play pro."

He shrugged again. "I kept busting up my ankles, and I dislocated my shoulder three times. If I'd kept playing, there was a good chance I'd do serious, permanent damage. Then I wouldn't have been good for anything!" he concluded cheerfully.

"So you became a doctor? That's quite a changeover."

"Well, don't forget my father was a doctor. I came by the interest honestly, and I inherited the talent."

Dale smiled at his lack of modesty.

"Actually, it goes back further than that. I think I really became interested after I set my brother's broken leg. I was fifteen, I think."

"*You* set his leg?" Dale asked in great surprise.

Damon grinned wickedly at her. "It was only fair, since I broke it! We were on a camping trip with my father, and Peter—that's my brother—fell out of a tree. Well, I sort of pushed him."

Dale laughed, believing every word.

"Don't laugh! I did a great job. Even my father said so!"

"I don't suppose it will do any good to ask what you were both doing up a tree?"

Damon actually looked sheepish for a second. "He was flying a homemade kite of mine, and he'd gotten it all tangled. I was angry with him. So when he went after it, I went after him!"

Dale collapsed in a fresh round of laughter. "Do you miss not being able to play football?" she asked, wiping away laugh tears from her eyes.

A look of boyish excitement passed over Damon's face. "I keep in practice, so I don't miss it too much. I still work out sometimes with the team. They promise not to play too rough with an old man, and I fix all their broken bones!"

Dale laughed all over again.

"Now it's my turn." Damon grinned.

"What do you mean?"

"I had my concepts of what you'd look like this evening. I thought I was taking to dinner a quiet lady doctor with gray hair, a sense of humor and a throaty voice."

"Ouch!" Dale winced playfully. "Did I sound so bad over the phone?"

"Not at all. You sounded just like someone who'd been awakened in the middle of the night."

"Raspy and gray-haired?" Dale asked, laughter still brimming.

"Well, give me credit for being right about the sense of humor. And I'm delighted to find I'm wrong on the other two counts," he said, with a soft smile, in a low-toned voice.

She'd just been complimented, and Dale loved it, even if it was only playful gallantry on his part.

Dinner progressed in an easy, comfortable manner. It was to be expected that conversation for the most part centered around their careers and anecdotes about them. Dale began to suspect that the danger she'd felt from Damon earlier was all in her head, and she enjoyed the evening. At one point, as coffee was being served, Damon again looked at her with questions in his eyes. He took a thoughtful sip from the strong black brew laced with chicory.

"What demon possesses you?" he asked with shrewd curiosity. Dale could feel the hairs prickle on the back of her neck at the question with so many meanings, innuendos and answers. "What made you want to do something so hard and egotistical as being a doctor?"

With a frown, Dale laughed nervously at his choice of words. There was a certain truth in what he'd said but an unavoidable lack of understanding. For her it was so much more complicated than ego. "Why a demon?" Dale prevaricated. "Why not an angel of mercy?"

He raised his brows askance. "Do you have a Florence Nightingale complex?" he half joked.

"Do you?" she shot right back.

Damon's eyes narrowed and probed at her curt response. "I didn't exactly have a calling, but I'm very good at it," he said at once.

"So am I." Dale smiled.

Damon's eyes sparkled. The corners of his mouth lifted as his eyes deliberately roamed her feminine curves, settling on her chest for a long, provocative moment before coming back to her face. Imperceptibly Dale stiffened, relegating his examination of her body to a reason other than what he was actually thinking.

"If you're going to say what I think you're going to say, I'm going to be very disappointed in you," Dale warned him. Damon frowned at her in confusion. "You are thinking that I could have become a nurse instead of a doctor."

He was thinking no such thing. "Are you suggesting there's something demeaning about being a nurse?" Damon questioned pointedly.

"No, I'm not. But I wanted more than just a slice of the frosted cake. I wanted it all!" she declared.

Damon chuckled deep in his chest at her analogy.

"Besides," Dale added earnestly, "some of my best friends are nurses!"

Damon laughed outright at that, and their earlier light mood was restored. They declined dessert and finally left the restaurant, quickly being absorbed in the madness outside.

Damon placed a hand on the back of Dale's waist to steer her and to keep them from being separated. The touch was light and impersonal, but Dale was aware of the contact nonetheless. They approached Canal Street again, and for the first time Dale caught glimpses of the fantastic construction of the floats as they went rolling by. She must have caught her breath at the wonder of it, because Damon turned his head and looked down at her.

"You've never been to Mardi Gras before?"

"No, never!" Dale had to shout above the noise. There had never been much time in her life for just relaxing.

"If you're game, I think I can get us closer," he offered.

Dale looked at the colorful floats, the people, and felt the excitement. She nodded her head vigorously like a child. "Okay, let's!"

Damon smiled and took hold of her hand firmly. Dale felt the long, strong fingers close around her own and experienced an instantaneous but fleeting sense of possession and belonging, and her fingers tightened their hold, as well. It was pleasurable in the simplest of ways, making her feel thought of and cared for. The faint stirrings of apprehension returned with the touch, however, and she was sensitive to his very nearness and every move. Dale had had few enough physical encounters with the opposite sex, all of which had been at least pleasant and at best enlightening. But she'd never known, even in her most intimate circumstances, the kind of physical sensibility that came with just holding this man's hand. It was curious and also a little frightening.

Damon and Dale meshed with the crowd, but he never let go of her hand. He managed a spot behind a row of people somewhat shorter than himself and Dale, allowing them to just see over everyone's head. At once, Dale was caught up in the pageantry, indulging herself in the adventure just that once. She didn't notice Damon positioning himself protectively behind her so that she wouldn't be too badly jostled and shoved. Things only got rowdy when the individuals seated on the floats began throwing trinkets and favors into the crowd.

Elbows and arms came up fighting for souvenirs. Someone stepped painfully on her foot. Dale swayed backward and reached behind her blindly for balance. Her hand was grabbed by Damon's as his other settled around the curve of her side, fingers pressing in the soft flesh of her breast.

"Are you okay?" Damon chuckled, righting her once again.

"Y-yes," she whispered, hastily pulling away from the closer feel of him.

"People are generally prepared to kill for these keepsakes," he said into her ear, and his warm breath stirred her tendrils and tickled the skin of her cheek. Dale nodded and gave her attention to the floats again. More colorful items were thrown. Damon's arm raised over her shoulder and caught something out of the air. Something hit Dale in the chest, and her hand caught it against her. A laugh escaped her as she held a large shiny coin in her hand.

The festivities continued with no apparent end in sight. After a while, however, the noise and pushing became less and less fun. Jostled yet again, Dale fell forward suddenly and down onto her knees. She heard her name called, but it was so far above her. Then she was laughing, realizing the absurdity of the whole thing. When Damon pulled her up and turned her around, his concerned expression quickly turned to surprise, then relief, when he heard her laugh, even as she winced in pain.

"I think that's enough for one night," he said.

"Yes, I think I agree!" Dale nodded, smiling good-naturedly.

Damon put an arm around her waist and, holding her into his side, moved them away from the crowd. He placed her back against the side of a building and stood in front of her. They were awfully close. Dale could see a fine gleam of moisture at his throat, gently curling the silky wisps of chest hair visible at the V of his sweater. He smelled warm and heated and male. Dale lowered her eyes and gnawed on her lip, and he mistook the gesture for something else.

"Did you hurt your knee?" Damon asked.

"I—I'm fine," Dale stammered, but he had her by the arm and was pulling her into a nearby coffee shop that was virtually deserted. Damon sat her down and went to get a glass of water from the counter.

"Here," he said, passing it to her.

Dale obediently took a sip, her throat feeling very dry, but it seemed to have a basis in sudden breathlessness. She put the half-empty glass down.

"Had enough?"

She nodded, then watched as Damon took a napkin and dipped it into the water. He dropped to one knee and, carelessly lifting the hem of her dress, began to dab at the small abrasion on her knee, removing dirt and pebbles and a thin trickle of blood. He was gentle and easy, but Dale clenched her hands around her purse and jacket. She wanted him to stop.

Damon's left hand curved intimately around the flesh of her upper calf.

"That...that's enough," Dale said, trying to move her leg. But he only tightened his hold.

"I'm the doctor, and you're the patient," he murmured from bowed head. "So sit still!"

Dale did as she was told, although his hand on her leg, her dress above her knee, exposing a good deal of her thigh, made her very uncomfortable. His thumb began to rub lightly the skin on the inside of her knee. Dale drew her bottom lip in between her teeth. Damon looked up at her then, catching the action and seeing her mouth moist and shiny. They were enveloped for a long moment in a little pocket of silence during which discoveries were made and exchanged. A muscle jerked in Damon's jaw, and he abruptly stood up, shattering the tension that held them prisoner.

"So now you can say you've seen Mardi Gras," he said in a curiously thick voice.

"Yes," Dale answered, pulling down her dress. Her own voice sounded vacant.

"Are you ready to go back to the hotel?"

"Yes," she said, stronger this time. Picking up her things, she stood and preceded Damon out the restaurant door.

The silence between them now was different from a moment before and somehow laced with anticipation.

"I suppose that will go on all night," Dale said to fill the void.

"Very likely. Don't count on getting any sleep." He grinned, and Dale returned it, relieved that the awkwardness that had popped up between them was gone.

When they entered the hotel lobby, she turned to face him. "Well, this is where we started," she began.

"But not where we'll end," Damon interrupted, putting his hand to her waist again and turning her toward the elevators. "I'll see you to your room."

They rode up in silence, and she and Damon finally got off and walked the short distance to her door. Dale stopped and faced him again.

"Are you going to invite me in to see your room?" Damon quizzed.

"Of course not! Besides, you have your own room!" Dale retaliated.

Damon leaned a muscled shoulder against the doorframe and crossed his arms over his chest. "Is that a hint that I should leave and go find it?"

"You'll have to eventually."

His eyes grew warm and deep and swept slowly over her. "But not yet."

Dale jumped when his hand moved, but he only put it into a pocket and withdrew a pink necklace constructed of plastic beads and buttons. He held it out to her.

"A present from Mardi Gras," he said.

Dale hesitated and then, laughing, reached out to take it. "How exquisite!" she teased.

He shrugged. "It's the least I could offer for nearly getting you stomped to death."

"But I enjoyed it." Remembering, Dale reached into the pocket of her jacket and removed the pewter coin. She passed it to Damon. "And this is for your expert treatment of my wounds."

He whistled low. "These coins are highly coveted from Mardi Gras. You really should keep it."

"I'd rather you have it. I had a lovely evening. And it's only fair."

Damon turned the coin over and over between his fingers and looked at her with a funny uncertain expression. "And you believe in always being fair, don't you?"

Dale frowned at the question. "I . . . I try to be."

"The evening was my pleasure," he said, standing straight and putting the coin in his pocket. "But still . . . you're not going to let me in?" he tried again.

"Nope!" She smiled, shaking her head.

"Then you leave me no choice." As he spoke, Damon took a slow step forward. Alerted too late, Dale's smile faded, and her eyes widened to his face.

Damon's eyes, however, were focused on her mouth, and his hand came up to grab her chin, his thumb finding the shallow cleft and holding her head still.

Dale saw his head descending but could only close her eyes as he came closer and his features blurred. His mouth, firm and wide, the lips slightly parted, settled on hers. He applied the smallest pressure, enough both to part her lips and roll his across the open surface. He pressed again, and Dale felt the tip of his tongue, rough and warm, insinuate itself in a most provocative and suggestive way past her parted lips. Immediately, she realized an answering response that was instinctive and apparently against her will and better judgment. But the kiss ended, and Damon's head moved back. Dale's eyes fluttered open. Her apprehension, first experienced just twenty-four hours before and fully recognized that evening, was back again in full force. Her heart began to pound in her chest, and her breathing became shallow.

"You lied to me," Damon suddenly growled against her quivering mouth.

"What?" she managed in confusion.

His eyes once again swept over her face. "I've never met anyone less in need of beauty sleep," he said softly.

Dale blinked at him, only understanding his meaning when he was halfway down the hall and once again entering the elevator.

It was a few seconds before Dale remembered she was standing numbly in the hallway, staring into space. She got the room door opened and went inside. Not bothering to put on the light, Dale dropped her things on the bed and headed out onto the private balcony.

Dale paced for several minutes up and down the confined space, trying not to make too much of a good-night kiss. She hadn't seen their evening together as a date with possible intimate overtones. Damon Christensen had been fun, straightforward and reasonably easy to be with. But he had also been decidedly overwhelming in his presence, and she couldn't play the hypocrite and pretend she hadn't been affected. She'd been attracted to men in the past and had explored the attraction in the obvious ways. So she knew that with Damon there was a difference. And therein lay the threat. She was very susceptible to his presence and physical aura, which was sensual and potently virile. She was made aware of his complete masculinity, and it made her feel vulnerably female. Dale couldn't afford that right now, because it would divide her time and attention away from a purpose that fairly consumed her—her career. She had voluntarily given up one for the other. Not that she had ever been in love or even close to it—therefore, the decision had been easy. But it had been made clear enough to her in the past that no man wanted to take second place to a woman's career. She knew that at the outset of most relationships, so she chose her career.

Dale slowly removed the blue dress, slightly soiled from where she'd fallen to her knees. At once, an image was summoned of Damon washing the cut as his hand held her leg.

Damon hadn't questioned her about the other injury to her knee. He couldn't have missed either her limp or the scar tissue from her childhood operations. Yet he'd said nothing. Dale didn't like people to pretend it wasn't there. She just didn't want people to treat her as if that made her different from themselves.

Dale turned on the light in the main room and hung up the now-wrinkled jacket. She caught a glimpse of the pink necklace hanging halfway out of a pocket. She removed it and put the necklace over her head and let the extra length of it settle against her breasts. It was a cheap party favor, but the color was becoming to her skin. Dale smiled softly, feeling absurdly pleased. No man had ever given her a gift before in her life, cheap or otherwise. She carefully took it off and put it away in a drawer.

The rest of her clothes came off, and she slipped between the sheets of the bed, once again getting lost in its size. She'd half expected the phone to ring again as it had the night before. But it stayed depressingly silent until the evening lost some of its magic and sense of fantasy, and she drifted off to sleep.

Chapter Four

"Well, I must say, it all sounds rather fantastic!" Dr. Emil Kessling lisped through a distinctive German accent.

Dale sighed inwardly and looked at the ancient good doctor. "Theories are always fantastic until someone puts them to practice. Then they become something else."

"Yeah, progress!" Frances McCann said dryly from her seat next to Dale. "And it's always so slow in coming." She and Dale exchanged long-suffering looks, in perfect communication with each other. Generation gaps were not limited to parent-child relationships.

Dr. Kessling was an East Coast authority on current physical therapy methods and postoperative rehabilitation of orthopedic patients. But he didn't know fiddlesticks about developments in surgery. And by his comments all that morning in the seminar, he wasn't all that interested.

Dale knew from experience, however, that professional people of Dr. Kessling's caliber could not be sidestepped and ignored.

"Now, what do you propose these things be made of?" Dr. Kessling questioned with a skeptical little laugh.

"I propose that these *replacements*," Dale emphasized, "be made of a fairly hard and flexible material not unlike regular rubber. It would allow for give-and-take in the joint, unlike harder materials such as metals, which can scrape and rub against sensitive nerves and muscles."

Dr. Kessling nodded thoughtfully, poking out his bottom lip. He peered at her through rather thick optic lenses, making him look so much like an owl that Dale had to force back her amusement at the image.

"Well, Dr. Christensen, I'm not convinced it would

work. There are still so many problems to face. But I would not object to seeing prototypes and reading any test results you may have gathered."

"Thank you, Doctor," Dale said gracefully, and sat back in her chair. She let out another sigh and momentarily let the conversation drift around her. She stretched out her left leg, easing the ache in the knee joint. Absently, she rubbed at the pain and turned her head to Frances on her right.

Frances McCann was from New Jersey. Dale didn't know her very well but knew of her work with geriatric patients, whose recovery from broken bones was so much slower and more uncertain than in younger patients. Frances was a solidly built woman in her late forties who'd spent twenty years in the air force as a nurse before she officially retired and turned her talents to physical therapy. Her presence and manner bespoke someone who commanded obedience, or else. But she was one of the most sensitive and caring therapists Dale had ever met.

"The old dragon!" Frances said out of the corner of her mouth. Dale smiled and rolled her eyes heavenward. "If I didn't have so much respect for his work, I'd tell him to go fry an egg!"

Dale wrinkled her nose. "Oh, I guess he's not so bad. No worse than some of the others with the same opinion on this," she said, disheartened as she flipped carelessly a corner of her report.

"Well"—Frances shrugged—"I admit it all sounds radical, but as long as someone has come up with the idea, why not try it?"

"Can I quote you on that?" Dale grinned.

"Of course. And if anyone wants to argue about it, tell them to see me!" Frances growled in fun.

They gave all their attention now to the same tall, robust, bearded man that Damon had greeted in the hotel lobby two days earlier. His name was Dr. Bradford Coombs, and his specialty was psychiatry. He counseled quadraplegics and amputees, an area that was discovered to need much attention since the Vietnamese war. Dr. Coombs had a caustic sense of humor that produced in the small group as many smiles as he did information.

Thinking now of Damon, Dale casually looked around the large meeting room. She had not seen him that morning when she came down for breakfast, nor could she spot him in the auditorium of nearly three hundred people who'd already sat through an hour and a half of opening statements, greetings and instructions. Afterward, everyone had gone to predetermined groups, and her thoughts of him had vanished for the moment. Dr. Coombs finished his presentation with a small joke, and Dale's group joined in pleasant laughter. Someone else then began to speak.

"I never realized you were married," Frances whispered.

Dale's head swung around sharply to face the other woman in total surprise. "W-what did you say?"

"How long have you been married?"

Dale frowned in bewilderment as she stared at Frances. "I'm not married!"

Now it was Frances's turn to frown. "I could have sworn I saw another Christensen listed in the program."

Dale laughed softly. "You probably did. But that doesn't mean I'm married to him."

"Oh..." Frances reacted in such a deflated manner that Dale laughed again.

"Having two Christensens created quite a mess the day I checked in."

"I can imagine," Frances said ruefully. "But still, that's too bad," she added regrettably.

"I'd just as soon not complicate matters by having everyone think what you're thinking."

Frances gave a short, loud snort. "I bet it could prove to be a lot of fun!"

"It depends on one's idea of fun," Dale said dryly, her mind already thinking of a number of ways it could at least be embarrassing. What if his wife or girl friend called to reach him and she got the message? Dale sobered rather quickly. She'd given no thought at all as to whether he was married. He had taken her out to dinner, but he hadn't mentioned wife, girl friend, children, pets or anything. She didn't even know where he was from. California? And do men give women whom they've only known a few hours good-night kisses?

Dale was still fussing over the question when the last

speaker finished. People began to stretch and unfold themselves in preparation for shifting to the next group.

"Are we in the next group together?" Frances asked, standing, haphazardly stuffing conference papers under her arm.

"I don't know," Dale murmured, searching for the program among her own pile of materials. "I think I'm supposed to watch a demonstration and slide presentation."

"Ugh!" Frances grimaced with a mock shiver. "Slide shows are guaranteed to put me to sleep!"

Dale chuckled, gathering her things and smoothing the fabric of her forest-green gabardine skirt, which made her eyes look a deeper green that day. "We're paying too much money to sleep through any of these sessions. Where do you go next?" she asked.

"We're going on a field trip to one of the local hospitals to see some new therapy equipment."

"Well, have fun. Maybe I'll see you later."

"Yeah, maybe." Frances smiled and waved, leaving the room with everyone else.

Dale slowly left the room, trying to figure out where the Governor's Lounge, in which her next session was to be conducted, could be located.

"Hello," a deep voice said directly in front of her. She looked up into the smiling face of Damon.

All inside, Dale's body responded. But her surprised expression changed at once to a friendly smile. "Hello, yourself," she answered.

"I didn't see you this morning," he ventured, looking her slowly up and down. It was pleasing for Dale to know he might have looked for her, although she didn't volunteer that she'd done the same for him.

"I'm not surprised. There were a lot of people in the auditorium this morning."

With a rather pleased expression on his face, Damon looked her over more carefully, making Dale feel funny and exposed. "And you seem none the worse for last night."

Dale laughed softly. "I enjoyed last night."

She also examined him again with his casual air. He wore a light-blue shirt that made his skin look tan and healthy, and a pair of navy slacks.

"I'm glad that you did. Oh, by the way. I think this is for you." Damon reached into his shirt pocket and withdrew a folded piece of paper and handed it to her with an apologetic grin. "I'm afraid I had no choice but to read it. But I know it's not for me. I'm not likely to get urgent phone messages from someone named Allen."

"Oh!" Dale exclaimed as she accepted the note and quickly read its contents. She missed Damon watching her face carefully for any change of expression, but she gave nothing away. She simply read the message and stuck it between the pages of her notebook. But when she looked up at him, there was a frowning, thoughtful expression on his handsome face. He thrust his hands into his pockets.

"How were your morning sessions? Are you holding up okay?" he asked blandly.

Dale grimaced, making her look mischievous. "It's been...interesting," she answered carefully.

Damon chuckled at her. "It's okay to confess that you find some of it a dead bore. Some of it *is*!"

"No, really," Dale countered with a shake of her head, sending her wavy hair into motion about her face. "It's been okay so far."

"You're not convincing me, Doctor, but that's okay. This is obviously your first conference. By your next one you'll feel less guilty," he said with insight.

Dale's brows drew together. "Then why do you come?" she asked.

Damon shrugged offhandedly. "It's therapeutic—no pun intended. Sometimes you need to get away from your hospital, your patients. Sometimes your colleagues really have been working on interesting new developments worth hearing about." His eyes warmed and twinkled seductively at her. "Sometimes you meet interesting new people that make the whole trip worthwhile," he said in a lower voice.

Blood rushed to Dale's cheeks, and she dropped her eyes, laughing nervously. "May-maybe you're right." Then she hastily added to hide her confusion, "Next time I'll be better prepared."

Damon glanced at his watch. "Where are you off to now?"

"Oh, a lounge somewhere," she said, once more trying to locate the program. She spotted the note. "But first I'd better return this call." She grinned.

Damon's expression grew closed and indifferent. "Yes, I suppose you'll have to. I'll see you later," he said abruptly and moved past her, not even waiting for her to answer his question.

Dale stood looking after him, her mouth parted in surprise. She frowned all the way to the telephones, trying to understand if she'd said something wrong. Giving up and feeling oddly let down, she had the hotel switchboard place a long-distance call to Nassau County on Long Island in New York.

To DALE'S SECRET SURPRISE and excitement, Dr. Michael Christensen, Jr., was conducting her next session. He was turned three-quarters from her and talking to a number of conference participants when she saw him. A large number of people were in the room, but not knowing anyone at the session, Dale sat quietly near the back.

She indulged in an open perusal of Damon as he interacted with the people around him. He was smiling, easy and full of charm. Dale suddenly wondered how old he was. Thirty-eight—nine, maybe. Her head tilted thoughtfully. He took very good care of himself—mostly. Although he didn't seem to pay much attention to fashion or clothes, she concluded that his casual way of dress suited him. A rather attractive brunette came up to the group. She stood on tiptoe and put her arms around Damon's neck, giving him a smiling, joyous kiss as everyone else looked on. Damon's arm encircled the woman's slender waist, and he gave her an affectionate squeeze in return.

The warm, complacent state dissolved. Feeling as though she were intruding on his privacy, although it was hardly a private occasion, she quickly averted her eyes to her notebook. Turning to a blank page, she began to scribble arbitrary notes. Curiosity consumed her, but she didn't look up again in Damon's direction.

Someone moved to sit next to her, apologizing for stepping over her legs. He settled himself.

"Th-this is quite a turnout," he offered in a soft, shy

voice. It was a long second before Dale realized that he was talking to her.

"Y-yes, it is," she stammered, coming to attention. She smiled briefly at him, noticing he was short, thin, balding and with eyes so close together they appeared crossed. He was such an odd little figure of a man that Dale wondered what he did that was connected to orthopedics.

"This is my first conference," he added, again shyly.

"Mine, too," Dale admitted.

A thin, sweaty hand was pushed under her nose. "My name is Melvin Sutter."

Feeling for the man's obvious sense of displacement, Dale accepted the damp limb and shook it. "I'm Dale Christensen. How do you do?"

"Oh! Are you Dr. Christensen's wife?" he asked, excited.

"No, I'm not," she said firmly. "What do you do, Mr. Sutter?" Dale asked, really wanting to know.

"I'm . . . I'm a salesman," he stammered, brightening, ignorant of Dale's thoughts that she'd never met anyone less like a salesman.

"Of what?" she encouraged.

"Orthopedic equipment and supplies."

"I . . . I don't suppose you have need of anything?" he asked softly, already shaking his head to his own question.

"I'm sorry, but I don't. I have a rather good supplier I've worked with before at home in New York."

"I understand," he replied, nodding vigorously. "My equipment is generally used in athletics, anyway."

"Then you really should talk to Dr. Michael Christensen. I believe athletics is his specialty."

"Do you think I should?" he questioned with rounded eyes.

Dale bit her lip to hide her smile. "Yes, I'm sure of it. I'll introduce you later if you like."

"Why, that's very kind of you!"

"No problem," she answered as the lights dimmed and the program began.

Dale was fascinated. First of all, Damon was an excellent speaker, and he fielded questions from the audience concisely. His slides were well chosen, followed a logical order, and clearly showed equipment, use, treatment and results so that the audience could understand. He performed a demonstration on the stage floor using himself, which explained his choice of casual clothing. Later, he used a number of volunteers from the audience to try and demonstrate how an athlete might feel under certain conditions using some equipment or exercise. He answered questions for another half hour after his presentation, and only when someone complained good-naturedly of the need for food did the assembly break up around one o'clock for lunch.

True to her word, Dale made her way to the stage, Mr. Sutter in tow. Damon turned from speaking to another man and raised his brows in surprise when he saw her standing next to him.

"A question, Doctor?" he asked evenly.

"No," Dale said, smiling, "you explained everything very clearly. It was a good presentation."

"Thank you."

"I wanted to introduce you to Mr. Melvin Sutter. He especially wanted to meet you." Dale pulled the little man forward. Damon raised his brow further, and a questioning amusement darted in her direction. He put out a hand to the shy man.

"Mr. Sutter," Damon said, shaking his hand.

"If you'll excuse me," Dale said, backing away, "I'll leave you to talk business."

Damon opened his mouth to say something, but Dale waved cheerfully and turned to walk out the open doors. She made a trip to her room to comb her hair and freshen her lipstick. Leaving her morning's paraphernalia on the room desk, she went out to have lunch.

She'd just exited the hotel onto an overcast New Orleans day when Damon caught up to her, grabbing her arm and swinging her to face him.

"That's one I owe you, Doctor!"

Dale smiled innocently, her eyes widening. "I don't know what you mean!"

"Mr. Sutter," Damon informed her sternly.

"I thought he was a very nice man."

"He's a better salesman," Damon said caustically. Dale's eyes rounded even more.

"You mean—"

"About five hundred dollars' worth," Damon said, nodding.

Dale laughed merrily, and reluctantly Damon joined in. "I didn't think he could do it!"

"I didn't, either. And he says he owes it all to you."

"Did he?" Dale asked, surprised.

"Yes, he did. And the very least you could do for helping to separate me from my hospital's money is to have lunch with me."

"A bribe, Doctor?" Dale asked with a mock look of scandal.

"Penitence!" Damon growled.

"I'd love to!" she said, laughing. Together they started off across Canal Street.

Their choice of restaurant was decided by a sudden deluge of steamy rain. They entered a quaint little place called the Gumbo Shop to avoid getting soaked. They sat and ordered and through the windows watched the downpour until it gradually turned into a steady drizzle. Dale insisted, however, that lunch was her treat. There was a small, cheerful argument over it before Damon gracefully gave in, and Dale beamed at him triumphantly. For a while they ate in comfortable silence and covertly watched each other. Damon was appreciating the novelty of having a woman treat him to lunch. It was a pleasant switch.

Damon made note of the full, wavy sweep of her hair against her shoulders. It was made thicker by the damp air frizzing it. Her eyes were as bright as ever but darker now because of her green outfit and the gray lighting of the day. Damon laughed silently to himself when he recalled not particularly wanting to come to New Orleans for the conference. He was a little too cynical to recognize it as such, but he was actually having a good time.

Dale was having similar thoughts, although to be more exact, she was thinking that she couldn't believe she was sitting casually in a cramped little restaurant in the French Quarter, having lunch with a good-looking man whom she rather liked.

"So what do you really think of the conference?" Damon asked as their plates were taken away.

"It's not at all what I'd thought it would be," Dale confessed.

"Just what were you expecting?"

She shrugged. "I guess something dry and boring — thoroughly academic. And I didn't like being away from my work and patients."

"You shouldn't take your work so seriously all the time."

"I don't know how else to take it," Dale answered, frowning.

"There's a real danger in that," Damon said, shaking his head in disagreement. "You end up belonging too much to your work and patients and never spend enough time on yourself. You have to let go and get away from it sometimes. There is such a thing as overkill and burnout."

"My patients wouldn't think so," she said, knowing the fears and doubts of every one of her kids.

"I don't expect them to. But *you* should," he said firmly, and Dale smiled vaguely at his odd, solicitous air.

"Now that you're a participant, do you still feel the same way?" he asked, referring once more to the conference. He watched the lovely dimple in her chin and the expressive curving of her mouth.

"Well, as you said this morning, it has its purposes."

"And if you hadn't come, we obviously wouldn't be sitting together having lunch. That would have been a shame," he said softly, holding her eyes locked to his.

Dale was going to respond flippantly, but when she saw the deep, probing look of his eyes, she stopped. He was serious. "Yes, yes," she stammered, completely flustered and unsure of herself again. The danger began to close itself around her as Damon continued to stare openly at her.

"Did you make your phone call?" he asked suddenly, and Dale blinked at his stiffly polite inquiry. Again, his sudden switch in moods confused her.

"Yes, I did. It was a very important message."

"Was it?" he asked, drawing circles on the tablecloth with the point of his table knife.

"Yes. At least Allen thought so, and you know how important everything is to a teenager."

Damon's head came up sharply to look at her.

"It seems his friends were all going on an overnight

camping trip and he didn't want to go with a cast on his leg. So of course his mother—"

"His mother?" Damon mouthed blankly.

Dale looked at him quizzically. "Yes, his mother told him he'd better check with me first. I called his clinic and told them to go ahead, and—"

Damon was suddenly smiling at her.

"Wh-what's so funny?" she asked in bewilderment.

"Just me," Damon answered mysteriously, while Dale wondered if she'd missed something in the conversation.

He stood up now and held out his hand to her. "Come on. Let's go for a walk in the rain." But the rain had finally stopped.

They wandered over to Louis Armstrong Park and idly followed a wet, leaf-strewn path. The silence began as comfortable, but the farther they walked into the park, the more that silence was filled, at least for Dale, with an anticlimactic aura.

Damon used his pocket handkerchief to wipe rainwater from a bench. Then he turned and, clasping her firmly about the waist, lifted and swung her so that she could sit on the back of the bench, her feet resting on the seat. The motion had been swift and unexpected, and she watched Damon, round-eyed and puzzled.

"What are you doing?" she asked, stunned.

"I want to see how the patient is recovering," he murmured, and, with a nonchalant gesture, moved her skirt a few inches above her left knee.

"Doctor!" Dale said apprehensively. "I can do this myself. It was only a small scratch, you know."

"Which you wouldn't want to get infected," he said, ignoring her protests. Holding her leg, he examined the bruise through the meshing of her nylons.

Dale sat stiffly holding her breath. She resented his high-handed manner with her, as if she were a child. But she was equally disturbed by the personal contact he had instigated between them. She had no idea, really, how to deal with him when, seemingly with innocence, he touched her, which evoked such intimate feelings and responses from her. And again, that ever-present sense of apprehension grabbed at her as she watched his bowed head and its ruffled hair.

"Is it stiff?" he asked.

"No, I don't think so. Well, I—I don't know. I mean, that knee is always stiff, I guess," she whispered. His fingers slid over the silken leg. Dale bit her lip.

"It's healing all right," he concluded professionally, and a welling of amusement suddenly filled her as she thought how wasted his concern was on a silly abrasion. "And it's scabbing over."

Dale giggled then, as much in tension as anything else. "I haven't had scabby knees in years!" she said.

"At least not since you were nine, maybe ten."

The smile faded from her face, and her head jerked up to look at him. "How do you know that?"

Damon stood straight and tall, forcing her head to tilt so that she could see his face fully. He stepped closer, his hand still comfortably on her knee.

"I'm a doctor, *Doctor*," he responded flippantly. His fingers glided, feather light, over the slightly puckered scar tissue inside her left knee.

"This tissue is old," Damon said. "Fifteen to twenty years. You have a slight limp, which suggests your operations were done before medical science in joint surgery could ensure otherwise."

"That's very good, Doctor," she said stiffly. She didn't think he'd been ignoring her gait, but now that he'd actually mentioned it, perversely, all her defenses were raised.

"Damon," he corrected automatically, wanting her to use his name.

Dale couldn't look at him. She sat proudly; some of the natural color of her complexion drained from her face.

He frowned at her. "Your injury hasn't kept you from doing anything in life you want, has it?"

Maybe one or two things, Dale thought sadly. Dancing, and biking and softball with friends. "No, it hasn't."

Damon's voice dropped to a low soft timbre. "Then there's no reason to be offended now that I've let you know I've noticed."

"No, there isn't, Doctor." Her voice shook for no good reason, and she was angry with herself.

A muscle tensed suddenly in Damon's strong jaw. With his hair all windswept, he looked dangerous to her, towering over her as he did. "Damon," he instructed again. Dale did not respond.

Then, slowly, Damon bent toward her, and every nerve in Dale's body was alert, threatened, bunched together for protection. Damon braced his hands on either side of her on the bench top, bringing his handsome, strongly male face within inches of her own.

"And your injury certainly hasn't stopped you from having a terrific pair of legs," he crooned hoarsely. Dale stubbornly kept her eyes down. "Say it," Damon commanded.

"Say what?" came the whispered question.

"Say my name."

Dale's eyes came up slowly to focus on his wide mouth, to notice peripherally the tensing in his jaw. "Damon," she said, somewhat mesmerized. The square mouth slowly smiled.

"That's better." And then he gently kissed her. His firm mouth covered hers, possessing it, staking an immediate and undeniable claim.

Dale tried to tuck her chin, to pull away, but his lips held her captive, moving slowly over her. There was a tiny moan of protest from her throat that went unnoticed. She felt his tongue flick across the surface of her lips, wanting her to respond and give him access. She did.

Damon deepened the kiss, instantly sending waves of quivering sensations all through her. There was an unconscious urge to place her arms around his neck. But she couldn't, and they lay in her lap, her hands clenched tightly. Then he drew back, their mouths separating with a moist little sound.

Neither spoke right away as they searched each other's face. Dale watched him in growing awareness and fascination. It finally occurred to her that she was being gently seduced. Her amazement lasted for several moments, making her cheeks rosy again, her eyes bright, her lips soft and moistly parted, all of which made her more appealing to Damon as he, in turn, studied her.

Dale felt a kind of hysteria rise within her, and she bit her lip in a characteristic way. She had never before in her life been the object of a seduction. She had known from the first that Damon was dangerous, because she was attracted to him. But she had no expectations that it meant anything, because she also had no expectations of doing anything about it. But Damon had taken matters into his own hands, and now she wasn't sure what to do.

She'd hate it if his feelings for her were nothing more than pity. However, Damon chose that precise moment to place a large hand on her waist and, with the other, to settle and stroke her damp hair. She had to admit from the look in his brown eyes that she didn't feel as if she were being pitied. Then what was it he wanted from her?

The question was, in part, answered when the hand stroking her hair then cupped the back of her head as his mouth descended once more. Dale now allowed herself to hold to his strong shoulders and parted her mouth to receive his kiss.

Damon tightened his hold, bringing her against him closely, and took a step back until she came away from the bench and was totally supported against his hard, broad chest. He slowly lowered her so that her feet could touch the ground again. Damon's kiss was deliberate and controlled, and Dale felt as if she were being slowly drugged. The repetitive stroking of his tongue against hers was seductive and so blatantly a reminder of another embrace that her knees inadvertently pressed tightly together as if to protect herself from further invasion.

When he released her mouth a second time, Dale dropped her eyes and pushed away from him. He let her go. The silence surrounding them now was rather awesome and eerie, as if they were the only two people in the world.

"I...I think we'd better go back," Dale managed in a funny voice not at all her own.

"Yes, that's a good idea." He sounded so far away behind her.

Dale flipped a shaky hand under her hair to fluff it out. She ran a tongue over her dry lips and straightened her skirt and tucked in her blouse.

"Dale..." She jumped at the sound of her name. With his hands on her shoulders, Damon turned her to face him and lifted her chin so he could see her eyes. His were warm and mellow and smiling. "Look, I'm not going to apologize for kissing you. Quite honestly, I've been thinking about it all day. And I enjoyed it."

Color immediately infused her cheeks. She didn't know a single thing to say. It was so out of her league.

Damon searched her face, not really understanding her lack of response now. Then he grinned and raised his brows beguilingly. "And besides, Spanish moss does that to me."

Dale's mouth quivered, and then she was laughing.

"If I ever get married," he suddenly added, "it will have to be under hanging moss!"

Now Dale really laughed, easing the tension she felt earlier.

"Now, are you ready for an afternoon of medical jargon, classroom demonstrations, textbook hypothesis and films?"

"Yes!" she said. That was exactly what she needed to reestablish her sense of order and her equilibrium.

Damon casually took her hand, and she let him hold it until they were within a block of the hotel. Just as if they were lovers, Dale thought wistfully as they entered the lobby.

Chapter Five

"I think I may have overeaten!" Dr. Boris Teller chuckled as he patted his middle and sat back in his chair with a sigh of repletion.

Dale nodded. "It was a very good dinner." She took a final sip of water. Casually setting the glass down again, she lifted her eyes to find and lock momentarily with those of Damon, who winked at her. Dale smiled back almost imperceptibly and lowered her eyes to the table.

It was hard to know what he was trying to communicate right now to her. And although she had the feeling that she and Damon were sharing a secret, she had to admit she knew not what the secret was. Dale did know that he had appeared disappointed but had deferred at once to Dr. Boris Teller's taking her to the banquet dinner on the last evening of the conference. She had been pleased by that.

The day before, when they'd returned to the hotel, she found her concentration was gone. And at times during her afternoon sessions her hands seemed to develop a tremor whenever her thoughts turned to Damon. She'd let out a sigh of pure relief when, upon entering the lobby, she was accosted by Frances McCann, who was going to be in her afternoon group. Dale had introduced Damon and Frances, only to have Frances blurt out something totally outrageous.

"Did Dale tell you I thought you two were married?"

Dale's stomach curled over and sank in embarrassment. She laughed nervously, avoiding Damon's eye. "I—I didn't think it was necessary to tell him that." Then, taking a quick glance at Damon, she found his light eyes twinkling and amusement playing around the corners of his mouth.

"No, she didn't tell me," Damon confirmed, watching a becoming flush tinge Dale's cheeks.

Frances, realizing that she'd put her foot in her mouth, laughed heartily at her own blunder. "Well, it was just playful speculation on my part!"

"Perfectly understandable. It's a natural mistake," Damon remarked evenly, his smile charming and taking in both women.

"Listen," Frances began again, changing subjects, "there's a terrific restaurant near here I was told to try. I don't suppose you two would care to join me for dinner this evening?" she said, moving her eyes back and forth between the other two adults.

"I'd love to!" Dale responded at once, looking for an excuse not to be alone with Damon should he ask her out himself. And then, to cover herself, she looked hopefully at Damon. "Will you join us, Doctor?"

Damon raised a mocking brow at her; an emotion blazed briefly in his eyes and then was gone. Damon shook his head. "I think not."

"That's too bad," Frances said. "I hope I wasn't intruding on any plans you may have had," she added innocently, and won a full smile of appreciation from Damon.

"Nothing that couldn't be done some other time," he replied with a cryptic glance at Dale. "Besides, I was going to ask Dr. Christensen if she'd sit with me at the banquet tomorrow night."

Damon tilted his head, waiting for her answer, and because the request was so unexpected, Dale had no time to think of an excuse not to.

"All right, if—if you like," she said.

"Fine! Well, then, I'll leave you ladies." He glanced at his watch. "I have another demonstration to prepare for. Ms. McCann, Doctor." He nodded and walked away.

Dale knew a moment of regret at watching his tall, athletic person retreat. She realized her ambivalence at wanting to know a little more about Dr. Damon Christensen but being also somewhat afraid to be alone with him. Now she was not to know how they would have dealt with each other the rest of the afternoon.

Dale felt a large warm hand on her arm. She turned back to the woman standing beside her.

"I hope I didn't interrupt anything," Frances said contritely. Dale smiled reassuringly at her.

"Don't be silly. I hardly know the man."

"Well, I certainly robbed you of a chance to change that."

Dale gave Frances a wry look. "And what makes you think I'd want to?"

Frances looked incredulous. "Are you kidding me?" she scoffed, as if Dale would have to be out of her mind not to want to. Dale laughed softly in self-derision. Maybe she was crazy.

In any case, she'd not seen Damon the rest of the afternoon or evening, and she couldn't help but wonder where he'd had dinner, and with whom. Later that night, there was that unconscious hope that he'd call. But again, when the phone failed to ring, she chastised herself for acting like a giddy adolescent. However, she'd tossed in the bed for a full half hour before falling asleep.

DALE BLINKED as someone's sudden boisterous laughter rang through her reverie. The conference participants were obviously enjoying the formal banquet prepared to mark the end of the meetings. Dale was now glad she'd worn a dress rather than the more severe black pants with a high-buttoned white ruffled blouse that she'd originally planned to wear.

The dress was a pale-gray georgette covered in salmon-pink polka dots and belted with a wide pink silk belt. The bodice was wrapped modestly, revealing the valley between her breasts. The sleeves were sheer and elasticized, stopping just above her elbow, and the skirt fell in a soft A-line to her knees. Her full light-brown hair was combed in Gibson fashion, with feathering tendrils sweeping her nape and forehead.

Detecting Damon's eyes upon her, Dale nervously tucked a loose strand here and there into the top bunching of hair.

"Am I keeping you from anything, my dear?" Dr. Teller murmured as he watched his dinner companion's constant fidgeting.

Dale smiled at the older man and absently reached over to straighten his black bow tie. "Of course not. What gave you that idea?"

"You seem to have something else on your mind. If it's a problem, perhaps I can help. If it's pleasant, perhaps you'd like to share it?"

Dale was caught off guard. Actually, she supposed it was both. The problem was that it was the last night of the conference. The next morning would be closing statements and an exchange of last-minute information. Then everyone would leave New Orleans for parts unknown. Where would Michael Damon Christensen be leaving for? She'd been wondering all afternoon.

The pleasant part of it was that she'd enjoyed herself. Even when she'd felt unsure or threatened, there had been that heady sense of adventure. There hadn't been many moments in her life when she'd allowed herself pure frivolous pleasure. Her adolescence was spent in and out of hospitals; later, medical school had precluded it. But her time that week with Damon had been one of them.

Dale thought the world of Boris Teller, but she couldn't explain all those feelings to him.

"Actually," Dale finally answered, "I was wondering if I could have handled this afternoon a little differently."

Boris shook his head and laughed softly. "Well, my opinion is that you did very well. People get set in their ways and after a time begin to believe they're right in everything. Old doctors are no less vulnerable to that. I don't think anyone's the worse for having you put them in their place this afternoon. After all, they were rude, and you did know what you were talking about!"

"Yes, but will they forgive me my temper and take my work seriously?"

Boris laughed again, grabbing her hand in an affectionate scold. "Ah, child! We're old, but we haven't forgotten the energy or enthusiasm of the young."

Dale wrinkled her nose. "I'm not *that* young!" she reminded him.

"My dear, to us you are!"

Dale squeezed his hand. "And what do you think of my hypothesis? Am I really just spouting hot air?"

Boris's brows came together, and he stroked his jaw thoughtfully. "I rather thought it was original and not at all unreasonable. And I agree with that young man who suggested to me that you should contact some of the biomedical people at NASA, who are doing wonders with synthetics."

Dale looked puzzled. "What young man?"

"The one I sat next to in the auditorium this afternoon. The one who showed some impatience at the audience's lack of attention to you. And the one who was bested out of taking you to dinner but did so in good humor." Boris leaned into the center of the table and looked past a stunned Dale to another table. "And the one who, I suspect, would still like to spend some time with you!"

Dale's cheeks burned with the sudden rush of blood. "But—but I—I—"

Boris interrupted Dale's attempt at a disclaimer. "Of course I'm very flattered that you chose me over him, but I bet he would have been more fun!"

"Oh, but Boris, you don't understand!"

"All right"—Boris soothed her with a pat—"I won't tease you anymore about him."

Dale sat in silent frustration and anger next to him. She could handle the teasing. But she was not a femme fatale; in fact, she felt inadequately equipped to act the role. She'd hate to think that she was so transparent in her acquaintance with Damon or that he was gallantly portraying an interest that wasn't really there. She didn't want to appear foolish. But now she suspected that perhaps that was the case. She was assailed by thoughts that Damon's attraction to her had simply been because she seemed inexperienced. Some of Dale's enjoyment in the evening—indeed, the whole four days—wilted and died under her own insecurities.

Dale covertly sought out Damon again, but he was deep in conversation with his friend Brad. She wished she was better able to read a man's interest. Boris had said something about Damon's response to her presentation earlier in the day. Perhaps that was just polite interest. It didn't necessarily mean anything.

DALE HAD NOT BEEN in the least nervous when she was announced and it was explained that she would actually be presenting her own paper. But very shortly after she'd started talking, little murmurs of individual conversation had broken into her reading. Dale had spoken up a bit, thinking that her voice was too soft or too low for the large room. But the talking had continued. And then she got angry. She just stopped talking, and few people actually noticed. Using the rounded end of a fingernail, she'd tapped against the microphone, finally drawing everyone's attention. Chairs scraped the floor; several people coughed. She waited until there was dead silence in the room.

"I realize that some of you were looking forward to Dr. Wallace being here. He always speaks so highly of the association's membership. However, I'm sure he would expect the same courtesies to be extended to me that you would have given to him." Dale let a deliberate pause settle on the gathering.

"And I can assure you that the information and intent of this paper will not be lessened just because I'm reading it to you."

Someone coughed again, and there were snickers of amusement throughout the silent group.

"I also realize that after nearly three days of hearing technical papers, your attention span is not what it was. But think of it this way—in fifteen minutes, I'll be finished!"

There were one or two mild hands of applause while Dale located her train of thought, and continued with her presentation without further interruption. When the group burst into a round of applause at the end, however, it was hard for her to tell if it was genuine or just sarcasm. And when she was about to step down from the podium, someone in the audience asked if she would answer questions.

There had been a series of astute questions from Boris, who asked about the theory's application to children. Damon asked a question about replacing the replacements. Finally, she came down from the lectern and found both Damon and Boris Teller approaching her.

"You were excellent, my dear! Allow me to say I'm very proud of you!" Boris gave her arm a gentle squeeze.

"I think you're more than a bit biased." Dale smiled warmly at the older doctor before turning equally warm eyes to Damon. His eyes roamed with familiarity over the slender curves of her body before raising a brow.

"I'm impressed, Doctor. That's a formidable body of information you've gathered. This was obviously not idle speculation."

Dale stiffened defensively even as she realized that Damon's comments were only honest observation and a compliment.

"I hope you'll tell me more about the experiment part of all this at dinner," Boris said, drawing her attention.

Dale swung around to him, her eyes wide. They flickered briefly in Damon's direction. "Well, I—I—"

"Did you have other plans?" Boris asked, and it reminded Dale of Frances's intervention of the day before. That day she'd needed a reprieve from Damon's potent presence. Now she neither needed nor wanted it. She looked at Damon in helplessness.

"Dr. Christensen and I were going to share a banquet table," Damon began to explain. "But I know you two are friends, so I'll relinquish my seat to you, Dr. Teller."

"Oh, come now, that's not necessary. If you've already planned, couldn't we three sit together?"

"I'm afraid that would mean finding a third person to switch with. Too complicated." Brad Coombs gained Damon's attention at that moment, effectively ending the discussion.

IT HAD BEEN MADDENING, Dale thought, letting out a sigh. As always, Boris had been comfortable, amusing company, and she didn't begrudge him one minute of her time. But all evening she'd been more aware of Damon, devastatingly rugged and handsome in his formal dinner suit, the crisp white shirt startling against his tanned skin.

"My dear, I think I shall leave you now and head home."

"Oh, must you?" Dale asked at once.

"I'm afraid so. I've left my wife alone all evening. If she didn't know you, I'd never be able to explain being away so long!"

Dale laughed, and he smiled at her affectionately from his wrinkled face.

"And I'm rather tired. These affairs are for much younger minds and bodies."

Dale linked her arm comfortably in his, and slowly they walked together to the elevator. Once in the lobby, she had the front desk phone for a cab, and while they waited, they sat together on a plush lounge chair.

"So how did you enjoy Mardi Gras? Did you see the parade?"

Dale nodded. She had a memory of a slightly scraped knee, a pink plastic necklace and a pair of light-brown eyes from a strong, handsome face. "I enjoyed it very much. Noisy—but fun."

"And your first professional conference?"

"I'm glad Lester made me come," she admitted honestly. "It was a good experience talking to other people in the field."

"Such as that young doctor from California?"

"Is that where he's from?" Dale asked guilelessly, causing Boris to grin at her.

"I believe so, but why don't you ask him yourself?" he asked, looking over her shoulder at someone approaching.

Dale turned around to find Damon parting company with Brad and several others from his dinner table. Then he caught her eye and was walking toward where she and Boris sat.

"I'm glad you're here, Doctor. This young lady has been bending my ear all evening!" Boris said, joking. "Now that you're here to rescue me, I will say good night and farewell!" He and Dale stood up then. But suddenly she realized that she might not see him again for a long time. She gave him a warm hug.

"Now none of that." Boris stroked at her shoulder. "I can't very well go home to my wife with lipstick on my collar."

Dale laughed at his dispelling the sudden sad mood. "Take care of yourself, Boris."

"I will, my dear. And you, too. And think about some of those things I told you the other day," he admonished. "Doctor," Boris said, turning to Damon and shaking his hand, "I thank you for the great sacrifice this evening. Perhaps you can still salvage some of the night."

"I'm going to try," Damon said as they walked Boris out to his waiting cab. Dale kissed him once more and waved silently as the cab pulled away into the night.

"You think a great deal of him, don't you?"

She nodded. "A *great* deal. He bullied me into finishing med school. Every time I wanted to quit or my leg hurt or the instructors were crude and insensitive or the hours and work too long and hard, he pushed me. He'd tell me I was just looking for an excuse—an easy way out. He was very hard sometimes, too."

"But effective. I'd say it all paid off, Doctor," Damon said, looking down at her in the dark. She looked at him in return, seeing the way his hair curled over the collar of his formal shirt, and it seemed oddly, distinctly masculine. She liked the soft layered look of it. Dale smiled shyly at him now that she was alone with him again.

Dale was a good doctor. Competent and caring. But all her self-assurance as a woman seemed to desert her in his presence, especially when he looked at her so intently, the way he did now.

Dale looked to the lobby of the hotel. Damon followed her eyes. Neither said so, but both were thinking the same thing. If they went back now, they were bound to get caught up in conversation with other people. Damon looked at her again.

"Would you like to go for a walk?"

Dale merely nodded and smiled, falling into step beside him. Slowly, they made their way down to the wharf, walking toward the French Market. They talked about dinner and the various people at their individual tables. Damon admitted he'd much rather have had her sitting next to him. And he told her how beautiful she looked that evening.

Without really thinking about it, they stopped at a café and ordered beignets—doughnuts covered in powdered sugar—and had café au lait to go with them. Damon grinned at her in amusement when she asked openly for another beignet.

Looking thoughtfully at his now-empty cup, Damon spoke. "I'm intrigued with your ideas for replacements."

Dale laughed shortly. "You make the third person who doesn't think I'm crazy. The odds are getting better!"

"I think it has possibilities. I know some people you should talk to."

"Yes, Boris said you had suggestions to offer."

Damon raised a wicked brow at her and smiled suggestively. "You realize there is a price to pay for this inside information."

Dale froze, looking at him suspiciously as he began to write down names on a paper napkin from the dispenser on the table. "What?" she asked weakly.

He looked into her bright eyes, widened by her expecting the worst from him. Damon didn't know whether to laugh or be annoyed with her. "I expect to share the Nobel Prize in medicine with you when you win it!" he said softly.

Dale began to smile ruefully at herself. "Thank you," she said, accepting the information. She found now that his sudden support meant a lot to her. "I'm sorry about dinner. It was kind of you to have asked me, but—"

"I didn't ask you to be kind," he said evenly. "I asked because I very much wanted your company. And if it was anyone else but Boris Teller, who obviously means a lot to you, I never would have given in." Damon's eyes bored into hers, making her believe him.

"You—you're being gallant," she murmured, nonetheless unsure.

Damon shook his head, taking another napkin out of the dispenser. "I'm not being that, either." He leaned across the table and surprised Dale by gently touching the napkin to her chin and wiping. She put her hand up toward her face, but with his free hand Damon caught and held it. He moved the napkin to the corner of her mouth, his eyes following the movement and then slowly coming up to meet her gaze.

"What is it?" she asked.

A smile lifted a corner of his mouth. "Powdered sugar."

"Oh!" Dale colored over, freeing her hand and wiping again the areas he'd touched. Damon watched her with open enjoyment.

"You're presentable again," he confirmed.

Dale chuckled. "I'm sorry. You can't take some people anywhere!"

Damon reached for her hand and stood up. "Some people you wouldn't want to," he said dryly, helping her to her feet.

They'd walked a long way, and he looked at her for a fast second, seeing the hesitant first step. "We'll take a cab back."

"Okay," she agreed gratefully.

There was a breeze off the Mississippi that lifted the fine waves of Damon's hair. The wind swept around her legs and the fabric of her dress, swaying it and touching a chill to her exposed neck and throat. She shivered, and at once Damon shrugged out of his jacket and put it around her shoulders. Dale was immediately enveloped in a cocoon of heat, hugging to her and smelling the very essence that was Damon. It was almost like being held by him, and her heart raced at the image of his having done so the day before.

In the dark of the cab, Dale's green eyes sought his for a hint of what was to happen next. She could put no words to it but could feel it stealing up on her. The air of tension between them had been building up for more than three days.

Nothing was said between them all the way back to the hotel, and the hotel lobby was deserted and quiet. They headed toward the elevator.

"Would you like to stop for a drink?" Damon asked. Dale shook her head, her throat too closed and constricted for speech.

They boarded the elevator, and the silence continued until Dale thought she'd scream just to relieve the tension. She finally turned to Damon with the intention of saying something witty but stopped cold when she found his eyes watching her with such intensity.

Dale unlocked her door with shaky fingers, nearly dropping the key once. She turned to face Damon and found him not even a foot away from her. He began to bend toward her as she opened her mouth to speak, but there was a scream from inside her room. Dale jumped violently at the sound, and Damon pushed past her to get to the balcony and the direction of the noise. Dale slowly followed, closing the door.

Over the balcony rail, Damon was watching the drunken antics of several hotel guests who were staggering around the courtyard. Dale came to stand next to him and watched as an irate manager came out to shoo the rowdies quickly back into the main building before sleeping guests could complain.

"I wonder if they're still celebrating from Tuesday?" Damon asked in his deep voice.

Dale turned with an audible sigh back to the room. "Someone should tell them it's over," she replied sadly, with a double meaning to her words.

Damon followed her into the dark room. "Maybe for them it's not over." He stood directly behind her. She didn't move as his hands settled on her shoulders. One came up to allow a finger to gently trace the outline of her ear. The other pulled her back until she rested against his chest and then circled her waist to keep her there.

Dale's eyes slowly closed, as his exploring finger sent warm sensations down the cords of her neck. "Damon..." She whispered his name, becoming languid and soft against him.

"Are you still cold?" Damon crooned in a low tone, his lips against her hair.

"N-no," she whispered.

"Then why are you trembling?"

Dale turned in the circle of his arm to face him, trying to see his face. "I—I'm not. It's just that...I—I—"

Damon's hand stroked her cheek. "I know," he whispered back as his mouth came slowly down to meet hers.

Damon's tongue lightly explored her mouth with a familiarity that was erotic. He removed his jacket from her shoulders and dropped it onto a nearby chair, continuing to kiss her. He curved a hand and let his knuckles massage under her jaw and slowly down her neck. Dale came forward into his embrace. Her hands rested on his chest, feeling the firmness under his shirt. His mouth rocked back and forth over hers, coaxing further response, his tongue stroking and kindling an internal flame that threatened to suffocate her with its heat. Damon's hands caressed her with an assurance and expertise that confirmed all of Dale's first impressions of him as a man used to having his own way and that underlined her own sense of inexperience and naïveté.

She'd never clearly understood the rules of the game of love. It was a pursuit that she'd found herself the object of too infrequently. It had been confusing. With Damon it was no less so, even though she felt herself physically drawn to him.

Dale became aware of the bed behind him, its top cover discreetly turned back, inviting and suggestive. The space of the room seemed smaller with the lights out, and it was harder to breathe in the electrified air. With a moan of both pleasure and uncertainty, however, Dale twisted her mouth free. She took a few unsteady steps away from Damon and felt her mouth alive from the pressure of his. She touched her lips.

Damon came up behind her once more. One of his hands slid across her stomach; the other, over her shoulder and down her bare throat, with just the tips of his fingers. They slipped beneath the thin layer of dress material to rest over her pounding heart. Her skin seemed to burn.

"Damon," she pleaded weakly. He nibbled at her ear, his hand further cupping her breast. Dale grew dizzy. "Damon, don't."

"Why not?" he murmured into her skin, tickling the surface.

She brushed his hand away and stepped out of his embrace. "Be-because I'm going h-home tomorrow."

"So am I," he returned, "but that should have nothing to do with right now."

Dale shook her head. "Oh, yes! Yes, it has everything to do with right now! Four days is too short, and California is too far away from New York for this to happen now."

Damon stood still. "Don't you realize we've been building up to this? Haven't you noticed what's been happening between us?"

"Yes," Dale admitted in a small voice. "But I didn't think it would go so far. There...there didn't seem to be enough time."

"It doesn't take very much, you know," Damon said, his amusement sounding somewhat inappropriate in the dark.

Perhaps if she could have seen his eyes and his tenderness for her, she would have felt less raw, less as if he were laughing at her. But Dale turned stiffly and faced him.

"Well, it hasn't been enough time for me. I—I'm sorry. But I—I can't do this lightly."

Damon came close to her and put his hands gently around her waist. Dale's hands rested on his chest to keep them apart. "I didn't suppose for one moment you could. But this hasn't happened lightly. There certainly have been enough interruptions," he said wryly. "But something very real was taking place."

"Perhaps," Dale said shakily. "But by tomorrow it will be over. And the next day it'll be a mere memory. And next week totally forgotten."

Damon said nothing for a time. His fingers tightened their hold as though reluctant to let her go. "Of course I'm not going to force you."

"I—I'm sorry." She laughed nervously. "I didn't mean to let you think . . . make you believe—"

"Stop it," he said softly. "You didn't make me believe anything." And with a sigh Damon released her and picked up his jacket, slinging it over his shoulder.

"I thoroughly enjoyed meeting you, Dale Christensen. You made the week more than tolerable. And if we had more than a week, I'd prove it to you."

Damon bent to kiss her lightly on her warm mouth.

"And California is a lot closer than you think. Good night."

Dale stood in a daze as she watched him walk to the door and out. She remained in the dark for a long time before she realized that her eyes were filling with tears. Impatiently, she blinked them away. What was there to cry about? She had not let Damon Christensen have his way with her, and surely that had been his intention.

The flirtation was over, and she was going home. The following week, she'd be back at her normal schedule and her normal life. And memories were short. But she cried, anyway.

Chapter Six

Dale paid even less attention to the plane ride home than she did coming. She sat silently by her window seat and wondered with a vague air of unsettlement why she felt— different. She'd come to New Orleans almost a week before, reluctantly. She felt as though she were going home the same way.

So much had happened during that week's time. So much had *almost* happened. Her brows drew together when she recalled how she'd cried after Damon had left her room the night before. The tears had been spontaneous and over quickly. But she didn't understand why. And although she'd fallen asleep almost at once and slept deeply, she had gotten up that morning feeling exhausted. Everything inside her felt on edge and open, like a raw wound.

Dale had skipped breakfast and had spent the time packing for her trip back to New York. The bright-pink Mardi Gras necklace had slipped out of its protective covering to the floor at her feet. She'd picked it up and turned it over in her hands. Then she'd moved toward the trash bin and poised with the necklace over the opening for a second. But she'd changed her mind, rewrapping it in a kerchief and placing it in a corner of her suitcase. Then she'd called the front desk to pick up the case for her and proceded to the assembly room for the closing statements of the conference.

With her stomach muscles tensing alarmingly, Dale walked into the room and found most people already seated. She concentrated on just finding a seat and not looking around. Not allowing her eyes to seek out a tall, broad-shouldered man with unruly hair, not feeling particularly in the mood to talk to anyone else, she sat alone and heard almost nothing that was said. She was busy wondering what it would have been like to have such a man as Damon Christensen make love to her. Her skin grew warm as she tried to imagine the feel of his hands all over her, as she remembered the sure way his hand had sought out and caressed her breast.

Dale took a shallow breath, more uneasy than ever but also disappointed. She was not the kind of woman for brief interludes and romantic trysts of no consequence. There was no such thing as "no consequence" in her life. She'd made the right decision for herself the night before, but the knowledge carried no satisfaction at all in the light of day.

Taking a deep breath, Dale stood gathering her bag and tote and black winter coat. She turned to leave the assembly room and jumped with a gasp at the bulky body confronting her.

"Did I frighten you? I'm sorry!" Frances McCann said with concern.

Dale chuckled weakly.

"That must have been some daydream you were having," Frances said slyly. "I called your name twice."

"No daydream," Dale responded quickly, gathering her wits. "I was just trying to remember if I packed everything."

The two women left the room and walked slowly toward the bank of elevators.

"I know," Frances was saying ruefully. "I'm taking back at least fifty pounds more than I came with. Some of it from all the paper materials that were handed out. And the rest in rich New Orleans food!"

Dale smiled, but her eyes were unconsciously darting around the corridors and the movement of people, searching for one in particular.

"What time are you leaving?" Frances asked as they boarded the elevator.

Dale looked at her watch. "Almost at once. I have a twelve-thirty flight into Kennedy."

"You're lucky. The earliest I could get a flight was three o'clock this afternoon into Newark." Frances looked at the younger woman for a quick moment in speculation. "I'd ask you to have an early lunch with me, but I had a big breakfast this morning. We didn't see you in the dining room."

"We?" Dale asked.

"Yes, Dr. Christensen and myself."

Dale came immediately alert. Her head lifted, and her jade-green eyes grew wide and curious. "Oh?"

Frances nodded. They left the elevator and headed toward the check-out counter. "I came in and found him sitting alone and asked if I could join him. He was very nice...."

Dale lowered her eyes to the carpet. Yes, she knew he could be.

"Then he asked if I'd seen you yet this morning, and I said no. Were you supposed to meet him for breakfast but stood him up instead?" Frances teased, frowning slightly at her.

"No! Not at all. I...I really didn't feel much like having breakfast. Besides, there was all that packing to do."

"Yes..." Frances murmured, sounding unconvinced. "That's what I told him. Still..."

"Still what?" Dale asked.

Frances was still frowning at her, watching as Dale chewed nervously on the inside of her bottom lip. The older woman let out a sigh.

"Look, I'm going to put my foot in it again. I think he was hoping to see you. He spent an awful lot of preoccupied time watching the dining-room entrance and asking me questions about you. Nothing personal," Frances hastened to assure Dale. "And he was only half listening to my chatter. Are you— Did you and he, I mean, get together, so to speak?"

Dale stared at Frances and suddenly started laughing, first at the blunt question and then at the almost indelicate way in which it was asked.

"No, Frances, nothing happened between Dr. Christensen and myself. We had some meals together and took a couple of walks. And basically that was it." Dale faltered at the end.

"Well, then," Frances started, "maybe something should have! You two looked so cute together!"

Dale's mouth quirked wryly as she lifted a brow at Frances. "I think we're both a bit too old to be cute!"

"Well, you know what I mean!"

"Yes, I think so," Dale replied, sobering.

"You liked him, didn't you?"

Dale nodded, suddenly not trusting herself to speak. Frances touched her arm lightly.

"You're looking exactly the way he did at breakfast," she said softly. "Maybe if you said good-bye to each other you wouldn't go home feeling as if it was all unreal."

Dale looked long and hard at Frances. "You amaze me," she said seriously, no longer embarrassed that someone else may have seen her doubts and her desires.

Frances shrugged, equally serious now. "Being observant is part of my training and job. And sometimes the direct approach is the best approach to problems."

They finished checking out, and Frances turned once more to face her. "Well, I've got time to kill, so I think I'm going to explore some of the stores." She took Dale's hand and squeezed it. "Have a good trip back, and if I can ever be of service to you—"

"I'm going to take you up on that someday!" Dale laughed. Frances waved and walked across the lobby toward the revolving doors.

Still, Dale had seen no sign of Damon. She now believed that Frances was right. If they met once more and simply said good-bye, that would end it all. She could go back to New York feeling she'd had an interesting and lovely time. Nothing more or less. But Damon was nowhere around. It was possible that he'd already left, and glancing quickly at a wall clock, Dale knew that she'd have to head for the airport within the next half hour herself. She continued to look around the lobby as she wandered over to the newsstand and absently picked out a magazine to read on the return flight.

"Excuse me, Dr. Christensen..." She turned to find the shy salesman, Mr. Sutter, standing hesitantly.

"Yes, Mr. Sutter." Dale smiled. "I hope you enjoyed your first conference."

"Oh, yes, indeed! It was very profitable!" he said with a surprising show of humor that made Dale laugh. "I just wanted to thank you for your kindness in introducing me to...to the other Dr. Christensen. I got some very valuable leads from him that led to more orders!''

"That's wonderful! I'm very pleased for you, Mr. Sutter.''

"Yes, thank you. I'm leaving now, and when I saw you standing here, I thought to say good-bye.''

"That was nice of you.''

"And I believe Dr. Christensen was looking for you.''

"He was? When?''

"Well, I saw him just moments ago with his luggage. He was ordering a cab to the airport, and—''

"Thank you, thank you. It was nice meeting you. And good luck!''

A bewildered Mr. Sutter stood alone, watching Dale hurry away across the lobby.

Because it was check-out time, the lobby was once again crowded with people generally getting in her way. Suddenly, it became the most urgent thing to find him and say good-bye so that he could go his way and she hers. She wanted to show him she'd survived the night and that they should both be glad that things were left uncomplicated. Bodies moved across her path, slowing her down. Then, suddenly, there was a gap, and in front of the revolving doors stood Damon, a trench coat thrown over a shoulder. He was holding his brown leather suitcase while the other hand combed absently through his hair. He was looking intently around the lobby, looking for her, Dale was sure. She opened her mouth to call his name, but her line of vision was suddenly blocked again.

In frustration, Dale walked wide, around a pillar and toward the door. Damon was no longer there. Dale rushed to the door and waited her turn to swing through. On the other side, she watched a cab pull slowly away from the curb, Damon settling down in the back seat.

"LADIES AND GENTLEMEN, the no-smoking sign has been turned on. Please return to your seats as we prepare for landing at New York's Kennedy Airport...''

The plane landed, and there was the whole process of deplaning, retrieving luggage, getting to the long-term lot for her parked car and an hour's additional drive home. Dale was tired, and her knee ached a little.

She was thankful for the weekend ahead. She'd rest, catch up on correspondence and mail. On Monday she'd go back to the clinic and her daily routines. She'd have no time to think about a handsome man with golden eyes and hair in need of discipline, of a deep laugh and firm mouth capable of gentle, seductive kisses. The memories would become part of the occasion: just a four-day period out of her life. And soon everything would be back to normal, as it had been before.

DAMON CLOSED the door of the silver-gray Mercedes and adjusted his long legs in front of him. He turned his head to look at the beautiful and stylishly groomed woman next to him.

"I appreciate your meeting me, Jessica, but it wasn't necessary. I'd already made arrangements with a car service to pick me up." It was said evenly, but there was an edge of annoyance that caused the woman to turn appealing large brown eyes to Damon. She pouted prettily and shrugged a feminine shoulder.

"I know, Day, but this is so much more comfortable and cozy." Her brows raised, and she tilted her head with a soft smile. "You're not really annoyed with me, are you?"

Damon's eyes swept over the pretty face. He quirked a corner of his mouth and squeezed her soft hand on the seat between them.

"No, I'm not angry. I'm sorry if I seemed waspish."

She wrinkled her nose and started the car. "I guess I'd sound put out, too, if I'd just wasted five days in New Orleans going to meetings."

Damon looked absently out the windshield. "It wasn't all meetings. And it wasn't as dry as you make it sound."

"I bet you even missed Mardi Gras! I knew you should have let me come with you. I would have seen to it that you had a good time!"

Damon turned his head to her. "What makes you think I didn't have a good time?" he asked curiously.

There had been a moment of doubt reflected in her eyes before she smiled charmingly. "Because I wasn't there, silly. And you look tired," Jessica said with a toss of her curly blond head.

Damon frowned and didn't respond, turning once more to watch the traffic. He was tired. He'd spent an irritating night trying to deal with surprise, frustration and a slightly wounded ego. At first came the frustration, just after having left Dale's room the night before. He had enjoyed the subtle courting of her, somehow guessing that to her the overtures would be important. The touching and kissing in his experience usually led to his making love to the woman. He hadn't anticipated Dale's refusal in the end. The surprise, of course, was that she had.

Damon did not think of himself as a conceited man, just one who was reasonably sure of his attraction to women. He'd never had an experience that would lead him to think otherwise. And in the realm of someone who was confident, he was used to having his own way.

The moment he'd literally gotten tangled with the slender young woman with thick wavy hair in the lobby of the hotel, he'd known that he wanted to have her. She wasn't beautiful like Jessica, but then few women he'd ever met were—and Jessica worked very hard at it. But she was rather pretty, and he'd been caught by a pair of light-green eyes in a face that was curiously young—and innocent.

It had not been his idea to seduce her. He believed, in any case, that it wasn't much of a turn-on for a man to have to seduce a woman into joining him in bed. Seduction smacked too much of one person pulling the wool over someone else's eyes.

Damon's jaw tensed. He just couldn't seem to let go of the thought of her. She had filled his mind the entire plane ride back to Oakland. It would probably have been easy to phone her and try to reassure her that he didn't mean to upset her or make her do something that was uncomfortable. But it sounded so foolish when put into words. Some things are better left unexplained. Either they happen or they don't, when the time is right. But then it amazed him that he'd spent the whole morning hoping to see her once more. He had no idea what he would have said to her, and even now that the chance was gone completely, he wondered what would have happened had he found her.

Damon didn't think she'd deliberately avoided him, but he really wasn't sure. That was the confounded thing about her. There was an air of naïveté, of vulnerability, and he'd spent four days trying to decide if it was real or not. She had a habit of biting her bottom lip when she was unsure or confused. He'd found it rather appealing.

Damon let out a sigh and swept a hand through his hair. Perhaps the frustration of not being with her when he'd wanted to had blown the whole situation out of proportion. Maybe if he hadn't been thwarted at almost every turn by meetings, other people and circumstances, he'd have no thoughts other than just reasonably pleasant ones of her right now.

"Were there many young doctors there?" Jessica asked, interrupting his thoughts.

Damon blinked reluctantly from his daydream. "*I* was there!" he responded flippantly, but absently.

Jessica laughed, flashing him her lovely smile. "I mean, young and attractive, as in *female*!" she clarified with an arched brow.

Damon's jaw tensed again, and he shrugged. "There were a few," he admitted, turning his eyes to gaze out the car window. "But not enough time for pursuit."

Jessica laughed nervously, not sure if he was joking or not. Tactfully, she let the subject drop. She'd learned that Damon did not like probing questions of that kind. It was just a shade too possessive.

"I don't suppose I could persuade you to come to the house tonight. I thought you might enjoy a good home-cooked meal and a relaxing evening."

Damon smiled lazily at her, knowing full well that the "home-cooked meal" was being prepared by Jessica's Oriental chef and served by a host of well-trained servants. He wasn't sure he was up to being hovered over like that tonight.

"Jessica, I'm sorry. I'm going to sound like a real drag, but I'd rather just go home. I could use some sleep," he said, feeling very tired.

Jessica attempted another small laugh. "Of course! I understand."

Damon was relieved that she wasn't going to try to coax

him into changing his mind. He normally would not have minded dinner with Jessica and her kids. As if on cue, Jessica spoke offhandedly.

"The kids missed you."

Damon allowed himself a rueful half smile without answering right away. He liked Jessica's children. Two years earlier he'd treated her son, Bobby, then eight, for a broken arm. And there was Tiffany, who was nearly seven now and a physical miniature of her mother. When he spent time with them, he enjoyed their company. But he thought no more of them than that. And he seriously doubted if they'd really given thoughts enough to him in four days' absence to miss him. What Jessica was no doubt trying to say in a roundabout way was that *she* missed Damon. With only a small movement of his mouth, Damon realized that he'd not thought of Jessica Hilton once the whole time he was away in New Orleans.

"How are they?" Damon asked politely.

Jessica sighed. "Tiffany is fine. Last week she wanted to be an airline stewardess. That's because you were making that plane trip. This week it's a truck driver."

Damon's brows came up in amusement. "A truck driver? Where on earth did she come up with that one?"

"Oh, at the service station one morning this week while I was having the car filled. Tiffany got into one of her friendly questioning conversations with a perfect stranger. He was a long-distance trucker, and she wanted to see what the world looked like from the cab of his truck. So he let her. She decided it was great, and someday she wants to drive a truck just like his!"

Damon had to laugh. Tiffany knew no fear, only unending curiosity about everything around her. "And Bobby?"

Jessica growled, taking an alternate route that would bring them shortly to Damon's apartment. "I just don't know what to do with him. He wants to play football. He already has a whole team organized with the kids in the neighborhood!"

Damon shrugged. "So...."

"Day, it's all your fault. You know I don't like Bobby getting involved in those rough sports. He thinks it's fantastic that you played pro for two years. He's bound to hurt himself."

"When children play, they usually do," Damon said reasonably. "You can't treat them like hothouse flowers, Jessica. Children are very resilient."

"Tiffany wasn't when they decided to play totem pole last year. Do you realize she knocked a front tooth clear out?" Jessica said incredulously.

Damon gave her a patient smile laced with laughter. "She didn't need that one, anyway. As I recall, another has taken its place."

"Oh, you!" Jessica shook her head, laughing. "You're worse than they are!"

"I might point out that, if it wasn't for Bobby's broken arm, you never would have met me."

Immediately, Jessica softened. She pulled the car into a driveway of an apartment complex and turned off the motor. "That's very true," she said.

Damon dug into his pocket to search for apartment keys, and his fingers closed over a flat, round object somewhat larger than a coin. He withdrew his hand and opened it to find the pewter coin denoting Proteus from the Mardi Gras parade he'd taken Dale to on Tuesday night. A corner of his mouth curved in memory as he examined the raised surface of the medallion.

"What's that?" Jessica's voice broke into his reverie. At once, Damon's hand closed protectively over the coin.

"It's nothing."

"Let me see," Jessica said, prying open his fingers and lifting the coin. She looked at him quizzically.

"It was thrown from one of the parade floats at Mardi Gras," Damon found himself saying after a moment's hesitation.

"It's cute," Jessica said doubtfully, and then frowned at Damon. "I thought you said the conference was all business?"

"I never said that," Damon reminded her with raised brows. "You did."

She shrugged indifferently and dropped the coin back into his hand. "What are you going to do with it?"

Damon's brows furrowed together as he gestured impatiently. "I don't know. Maybe it will become my lucky piece," he answered, putting it back into his pocket.

Jessica slid closer to him on the plush velour seat. "Sure I can't persuade you to come to dinner?"

Damon nodded his head.

"Would you like me to come later, after the kids are in bed?" Her voice was a seductive whisper. But Damon was not moved.

He looked into her rich sable eyes; his nostrils flared with the subtle hint of her expensive perfume, with her nearness and its promise. He bent to touch his lips briefly to hers. "Not tonight, Jess. I'm beat."

She smiled forgivingly and patted his cheek. "I'll let you go this time. But you know I don't like to be called Jess!"

"You know I don't like to be called Day," he said easily, tweaking a blond curl. "Look, why don't I come by Sunday. We'll do something with the kids."

"Terrific!" she agreed, smiling again.

Damon opened the car door and swung his legs out. He removed his trench coat and leather case, walked around to the driver's side and quickly kissed Jessica's upturned face. "Thanks again for the lift. I'll see you on Sunday."

"Fine. Get lots of rest, now!" she shouted with a laugh, backing her car out of its space.

Damon entered his large four-room apartment and at once began opening windows to let in fresh air. Then he absently leafed through the mail his twice-a-week house-keeper had piled on a side table. Looking with disinterest through half of it, he dropped the rest back on the table. Thrusting his hands into his pants pockets, Damon walked idly over to the terrace doors just off the dining room and glanced out onto the marina below. He was glad he'd decided to come on home, and although he had already forgotten most of his conversation with Jessica, he still thought briefly of her.

Damon's relationship with Jessica Hilton had been intimate but limited by mutual agreement. She was good company and, until recently, noninhibiting. He wandered into the kitchen and looked in his refrigerator. He grabbed a beer and went back to the terrace, half sitting, half leaning on the railing.

He wasn't in love with Jessica. Their physical relationship was satisfying, undemanding and uncluttered with expectations. She had already survived one bad marriage, which had left her very wealthy, with no immediate desire to marry again, as far as he knew. And because he was not in love with her, or anyone else for that matter, he'd given marriage no serious thought himself. Just lately he'd begun to think it was time they both considered loosening the ties and moving onward. In some ways he had filled a gap for Jessica, giving her attention and time after her divorce when she needed it. But Damon suspected that Jessica was developing a kind of exclusiveness that he never wanted, and given time and opportunity to examine the case carefully, she wouldn't, either.

Damon knew his existence had proceeded evenly for a number of years without undue pressures or responsibility. He did have a widowed mother, but Madge was strong and more than capable of taking care of herself. He was a doctor because it had been easy for him. He lived in a style that few people would reject; it was also decidedly singular.

Damon came back into the apartment and with a weary sigh lowered his frame to the sofa, slouching and putting his legs on top of the glass coffee table. He stared thoughtfully at a print on his wall of a lion with a thick, luxurious mane.

He'd never lacked for companionship, male or female, and the thought of forming a relationship with more depth, promise or permanence had just not occurred to him. And it was only a vivacious green-eyed lady with a cheery smile and very soft, responding lips that made Damon wonder why he'd never met anyone like her before.

Chapter Seven

It was the Ides of March. She'd remembered the line as some dire proclamation made by a character in Shakespeare's *Julius Caesar*. With a deep sigh she gave up any speculation as to what it meant to the ancient Romans. For herself it marked a month since the conference and a month since she'd met Dr. Michael Damon Christensen. And, Dale thought ruefully as she finished notations on a patient's chart, it marked a solid month of thinking about him every day.

At first, Dale had not been surprised. Some rather elemental feelings had been sparked between them. It was rather lovely to be sought after by someone as sure, handsome and accomplished as Damon. It had stroked her ego.

But the other startling discovery had been that she couldn't stop thinking of him, seeing him with his engaging smile and strong jaw, his fawn-colored eyes and his haphazard hair. Dale sorely wished she had let him make love to her.

After two weeks, Dale was concerned about how much longer the memory and speculation would persist. How much longer would she imagine him kissing her until she was senseless and limp. After another two weeks, the images remained, reinforced now with the dawning realization that something more than just physical attraction had been started between them.

Dale hated her obsession with Damon. And she was impatient that she didn't seem to have enough strength to overcome it and put it aside. If it hadn't been for her work and normally busy routine, she had no idea what she would have done to combat it.

She worked overtime at the clinic, performing all the simple surgery that no one else wanted to do, just to keep busy. She drove home at night to her small Cape Cod house on the south shore of Long Island, exhausted. She contacted two of the NASA people whose names Damon had given her, and they were interested enough to ask her to send copies of her research notes, test results and hypothesis for further consideration.

She turned over the soil in her minute garden, working until her back and knees ached and the pain precluded any other thought. Dr. Lester Wallace, her office partner at the Nassau Health Center, wondered about the sudden surge of energy and purpose but didn't question his attractive colleague about it. It was hard enough getting dedicated, selfless doctors without complaining of the ones who were. But it seemed to the portly middle-aged man that Dr. Dale Christensen was like a woman possessed. It all seemed to have started upon her return from the conference in New Orleans. She pushed herself so hard that by the beginning of April he was beginning to be concerned.

Dale accepted only the most innocent invitations to go out. She'd decided on that after realizing that she was comparing every man she met with Damon. Not wanting to find out if her physical response to those men was in any way the same or different, she stayed away from finding out the answer. But if she'd had any idea that Damon was experiencing a similar disorientation, it would have frightened her even more.

During the first week of April, Dale received a call from Dr. Boris Teller informing her that the parents of the youngster Barry had decided to risk the operation for their son. Dale was delighted because she was so sure she could help him. She grabbed on to the opportunity gratefully, knowing she'd have to put one hundred and ten percent of herself into the procedure if she was to be of help to Barry. There'd be no time to think of Damon Christensen.

Dale spent one evening on the phone talking to Barry's mother and father long distance. At the end of the conversation it was agreed that they'd fly to New York to have the surgery done at the hospital where Dale practiced, with Barry under her care. A week before the scheduled surgery,

Barry arrived, and it took an hour of Dale's talking to him to reestablish the easy rapport they'd shared in New Orleans in February. Dale put him in a ward with three other boys about his age, and he finally settled in.

On the afternoon of his surgery, Dale went quietly to his bedside and talked to him. His small brown face was stiff and closed. The eyes, like black buttons, were enormous and frightened. Dale sensed the need in him and opened her arms just about the same time he threw himself against her. Waves of empathic emotion quivered through Dale as she hugged Barry and rested her cheek against his tightly curled head. There was no need for words. There wouldn't have been any appropriate to the occasion in any case. She knew exactly how he was feeling.

In a grown-up way that was touching, Barry finally pulled away and rubbed away tears with the heel of his hand. "Okay, I'm ready," he said.

"Good for you!" Dale said, accompanying him up to surgery, but he was asleep long before he was wheeled into the sterile room.

As far as she was concerned, it was a success. The right knee joint was completely replaced, and the tendons and cartilage tightened and adjusted on the left. He'd be in casts for two months, and then the physical therapy would begin. If nothing else, Barry would at least be able to walk normally again one day. Dale was aglow with the results. It had been long, tiring and delicate, but the work was good.

Orthopedic surgeons were often referred to indelicately as "body mechanics." *So be it,* Dale often thought with spirit. She was a damned good one, and one of only a handful of women in the field. And unlike in other medical disciplines, she at least saw results.

While Barry recovered from the initial surgery, Dale got in touch with Frances McCann to see if she'd be willing to be the therapist on Barry's case.

"Why, I'd be delighted! Thank you for thinking of me. What's Barry like?" Frances asked professionally after her surprise at hearing from Dale had passed.

"He's mature for twelve. But then, what he's been through has contributed to that."

"I'm sure," Frances agreed.

"He's determined to be able to walk. He doesn't kid himself that he'll ever play professional ball, but he'll work hard toward that."

"Good! I like a fighter. He's going to need it for all the pain!"

"Believe me, Frances, this kid *knows* pain!"

"When will he be ready?"

"Well, he'll be in casts for another eight to ten weeks, but I wanted to make sure we could get you."

Frances laughed heartily. "I'm honored! What did I do to deserve such faith?"

"I know you're good at what you do. And I...I've had a glimpse of how sensitive you can be."

Frances, not one to beat around the bush, pursed her lips and let out a significant "Mmm" across the phone line. "What happened after I left you in the lobby of the Fairmont?"

"Nothing," Dale said easily. "I didn't see Damon, after all. He, presumably, went back to California, and I came home to New York. The end."

"Gee, that's too bad," Frances murmured.

Dale laughed softly. "Why? I'm fine! I was fine before I went to that convention, and now I'm back to my work, and my life is back to normal."

"Look, Dale, you're not a traitor to the cause of independent womanhood just because you got turned on by a handsome and charming man!"

"Come on, Frances."

"What's wrong with wanting to fall in love and maybe even getting married? Some of us still do, you know."

Dale laughed in real amusement. "Aren't you jumping the gun a bit? I was never talking about love, but mere physical attraction!"

Frances scoffed on her end. "Honey, that's a start! Who knows where it can go from there?"

"Frances," Dale began patiently, "it's not going anywhere. I knew him less than a week, and I'll never see him again."

"*Never* say never," Frances said sagely. "Wasn't a few days enough time to know if any fires had been lit?"

"Not for me it wasn't."

"Then you're crazy!" Frances said unequivocally. "What do you want, a neon sign flashing? Instead, you come home and torture yourself with speculation! Dumb!"

Dale shook her head at Frances's vehemence and her insight. "How do you know I've been speculating?"

"Haven't you? What's the matter? Did you have to fight him off?"

Dale was aghast. "Of course not!" she admitted in a thin voice.

"But he was after you. Why condemn what he was after when you're really mad at yourself?"

"Why should I be mad at myself?" Dale asked, incredulous.

"Because he made you curious. Because he probably scared the hell out of you by wanting you."

Dale went pale, a cool wave of sensations washing over her and a recognition of truth in what Frances was saying.

"Look, honey, my advice to you is to stop being so professional. Don't forget how to just be a woman. Believe me, there are a lot of lonely people out there unnecessarily."

Dale thought about that. She'd never considered herself lonely, but—

"Now *me*," Frances went on, "I knew a long time ago that I was much happier alone. I bully a man. Probably my service training! That's no good, either."

Dale could only chuckle, because she could well believe it. "How do you know that I wouldn't be happier alone, as well?" she asked Frances. There was another loud burst of laughter.

"Because we're having this conversation, that's why, and you're asking yourself a lot of questions!"

Dale didn't want to put much credence in Frances's words. She was already schooled in a certain way of life, and she was happy with it. There was interesting, hard work and gratification from it. There were colleagues with mutual interests and companionship. There was her father, who still lived in West Virginia, and her brother and his family. Should there be anything more?

The fact of the matter was that she no longer knew for sure. But there was a restlessness now that hadn't existed before. There were now sleepless nights wondering about a tall, dark stranger and many nights of dreaming about him.

It was only after the stimulation of a hectic day at the hospital, where the reality of fighting for lives far surpassed any dream, that Dale could laugh at herself and her occasional giddiness. It was ludicrous to think that she was behaving like a woman in love.

"For heaven's sake, Damon, sit down! You're making me nervous with all that fidgeting and pacing!" Madge Christensen admonished her youngest son in a soft voice of exasperation. Obeying, Damon lowered his frame into a canvas garden chair and stared moodily at the toe of his sneaker.

Madge Christensen, a small, very attractive woman of sixty-four with peppered brunette hair worn in a youthful, becoming wedge cut, recognized the familiar restlessness in her son. First of all, he'd inherited that from his father. Second of all, it was his unconscious way of reacting to any occasion he wasn't in total control of. It used to happen when he disagreed with his father, when he was taking his certification board exams, and for a two-year period when he was preparing for a game. However, none of these was a likely reason, since all of them, in one way or another, had been eliminated from his life.

Madge smiled wistfully as she stared at Damon. He was a lot like his father. Full of energy and good at anything he decided he wanted to do. Personable and proud. Sometimes she'd see so much of her late husband in Damon that it was almost like having him still with her.

Madge tilted her head and rested her cheek against her hand, watching him. It could be work, but she'd never known Damon to complain about that or to have difficulties with it. He was a good doctor and very much enjoyed working with athletes, identifying very closely with them. He didn't have a private practice but was affiliated with two different hospital services in the city of Oakland. Perhaps there were administrative problems. He'd sometimes talk of relocating to another city but really seemed too comfortable where he was. Then Madge remembered that it was the third night in two weeks her son had graced her with his presence for dinner. Certainly a record in the last four or five years and worthy of questioning.

"What did you and Jessica fight about?"

Damon blinked in confusion at his mother. "We haven't fought about anything. What made you think that we had?"

Madge's dark eyes widened innocently, and she lifted her shoulders in supposition. "Well, I haven't seen her in a number of weeks, and I just thought—"

"Well, we didn't fight," Damon said with a shade of impatience. If the truth were known, he realized with a belated sense of guilt, he hadn't been in touch with Jessica. And now that he thought of it, he hadn't returned any of her phone messages left at his office or on his answering machine. "I haven't seen Jessica recently," he finally admitted offhandedly.

"Then what is the trouble?" Madge asked.

Damon jumped up and riffled his hair carelessly. He caught his mother's eye at that moment, and she smiled ruefully, communicating with him silently the way she used to when he was younger. Damon smoothed his hair boyishly and started pacing once more.

"There's no trouble between us, either." He misinterpreted the question.

Madge let out a small sigh. "If you say so, dear."

She believed him. At least Jessica wasn't directly the problem. Madge liked Jessica. She thought the young woman attractive and outgoing, even if she did live a life that sometimes didn't touch on the real world. Jessica was spoiled, uninvolved and unmotivated but harmless. Madge was pretty sure, also, that Damon wasn't in love with Jessica and therefore looked on their relationship as two adults amiably passing time together. Certainly not the stuff of which lasting love and devotion are made. Then what was it that had him tied up in knots?

"Is it something I can help you with?" Madge volunteered.

Damon stopped his pacing long enough to direct a look at his mother. But his thoughts were clearly elsewhere as he looked at her with unfocused eyes. "No, Mom," he finally answered. "But thanks for the offer." He smiled fondly at her.

At the same time that Dale was making arrangements to bring Barry to New York for surgery, Damon was the admitting physician on the case of a fifteen-year-old Oriental girl severely injured in an auto accident. She had suffered a crushed tibia and patella, causing the knee to separate. At first, it wasn't clear whether the leg could be saved. She was comatose for nearly four days, and when she regained consciousness, she was withdrawn and wouldn't talk to anyone. But Damon had performed the initial surgery to save her leg, and it was to him the young girl responded.

Damon found out from her parents that she was on the U.S. skating team and had been scheduled to compete later in the year. Damon could treat her leg, which needed some time to see if the surgical procedure would take, but he couldn't treat the other hurt, which held her heart and mind captive, not allowing her even to cry. Her withholding of real emotion slowed down her progress. After two weeks, the staff was concerned. Tai Chin wasn't responding, except occasionally to the sound of Damon's voice and his presence. The hospital staff began to talk of calling in another specialist, someone who worked exclusively in children's orthopedics and perhaps understood better the workings of a child's mind.

The idea took hold of Damon, and he thrashed it around in his head. There were legal problems involved in bringing in an outside consultant. There were administrative and logistic problems, too. But he swept all of them aside. He had plans to help Tai Chin, but they became curiously interwoven around images of Dr. Dale Christensen. He wanted to see her again. He had to see her again or forever find himself trapped in a pool of murky ifs and maybes that had kept him unsettled for more than a month.

As Damon stood in his mother's garden rejecting her offer of help, he knew who could help him. And he knew how he could help Tai Chin. He kissed his mother a brief good-bye and left her as bewildered as when he'd arrived. But Madge smiled after him indulgently as she heard the motor of his car start. He'd obviously just come to an important decision. She hoped it was the one he'd been looking for.

Damon drove back to the hospital and from his office

placed a long-distance phone call to New Orleans and Dr. Boris Teller. After several moments of recalling who Damon was, Dr. Teller listened as Damon outlined the problem with his young patient and what he felt was the solution.

Dr. Teller listened carefully, only occasionally grunting or uttering a long "Mmm." He was hearing two things in Damon Christensen's questions.

"Doctor," Boris began when Damon was finished, "I've seen Dale Christensen at work. I trained her. In my opinion, she's always been a valuable asset when it came to working with children and adolescents. They trust her instinctively. But I find it very hard to believe that California is such a wasteland that you don't have someone on staff or nearby capable of the same relationship to your patient."

Damon chuckled softly, appreciating Dr. Teller's observation. "I've worked in this field close to fifteen years, Dr. Teller. California is not overwhelmed with good orthopedic people. I know the people out here. I admit I've never seen Dale work, but I'm willing to bet she's exactly what's needed in this case."

Boris was curious. "Just what makes you say so?"

"Well, a lot of enthusiasm comes through when she talks about her work," Damon improvised uneasily. He had not actually given it a lot of thought, but he sensed it to be true.

Dr. Teller pursed his lips and rubbed his bald pate. "Yes, Dale could help your patient. I have that much faith in her talents."

"Good!" Damon said, relieved.

"Now, I want you to tell me something else, Doctor. What do you *personally* want from her?"

The question was unexpected, but Damon was not fool enough to deny it. There was no hesitation in his answer, and it came quite honestly. "I'd like to see her again. I want to see her work and get to know her better. She'd never come to California for that. But she might come to help a child—at your suggestion."

"Are you admitting to using me, Doctor?" Boris smiled wryly.

"Yes, I suppose I am," Damon admitted, a note of defeat already in his tone.

"Mmm... Well, assuming you can even get this past your board, I'll talk to Dale. I think if I explain the unusual circumstances of your patient, she'll be willing to make the trip."

"Thank you, Dr. Teller."

"Don't thank me yet, young man. This isn't to be a one-sided deal. I have a request to make of you in turn. I don't want you to do anything that could hurt her," Boris stated baldly. "I suppose I'm assuming an awful lot, but when you reach my age, you're allowed to. And I may be old, but I'm not blind. I believe I detected a certain, er, interest in her...." Boris let the rest hang.

"I'd call it curiosity," Damon corrected evenly. But Boris laughed softly.

"Mere semantics, Doctor. I've never seen myself in the role of matchmaker before, and I don't much relish the idea now, but I care deeply what happens to Dale. I want to see her happy."

"Dr. Teller, I assure you I'd never do anything—"

"Maybe not intentionally," Boris interrupted.

"My main concern is her medical talents with children," Damon said somewhat defensively, and Boris smiled to himself again and wondered about the secondary concerns.

"I'm sure," Boris confirmed dryly. "Nevertheless, you will be working closely together, and things have a way of happening. And I guess I'm a bit concerned myself about the ethics of all this."

"There can't be anything unethical about helping a patient any way we can," Damon offered formally.

Boris chuckled. "Let's just hope that Dale agrees with you" was his skeptical reply.

Chapter Eight

Anyone looking at Dale as she got off the plane from New York would hardly have considered her a doctor. She was dressed in a toast-colored spring linen suit with a cream silk blouse and a tie at the neck. Her wavy hair, looking lighter because of the darkness of her suit, was loose and full, bouncing rhythmically against her neck and shoulders with the movement of her unusual walk.

Dale scanned the crowd looking for someone who might be there to meet her. She felt a sense of being out of place, however, and knew the fluttery apprehension of the unseasoned traveler making connections on her own.

Dale had been informed by letter a week earlier that someone from the Oakland Central Hospital would meet her upon arrival. But even the information Boris Teller had given her over the phone had been sketchy beyond the facts and details that he knew of the case. And Dale had asked the same question of Boris that Boris had asked of Damon Christensen. Why me?

Boris had given the professional reasons, not liking it very much now that he had to prevaricate with someone he was so fond of. Dr. Wallace had told her she needed the time away; the trip would give her some hospital experience elsewhere. He did not add that perhaps time away would reduce her hyperactivity a little. So there she was, three thousand miles from home, again making a reluctant trip to a place she'd never been before.

Damon saw her first. She had the same wide-eyed look that had so caught his attention in New Orleans. He'd spent twenty minutes pacing, not really conscious of his state of anticipation. His face was tight and watchful, concerned now for the first time what her reaction was going to be seeing him there.

Damon could see that her soft caramel hair was a bit mussed and wispy around her cheeks and forehead. His mouth began to curve into a half smile as he imagined her looking that way after sleep or after having been made love to. The smile slowly faded, and his eyes glistened in disturbed speculation. A sudden possessiveness made him unreasonable; he didn't like to think that anyone had made love to her since they'd met. Then his eyes narrowed, trying to judge from her walk if her knee was bothering her from the long plane ride.

For Dale's part, Damon Christensen was the last person she'd expected to see. And when her eyes located and locked with his, she momentarily faltered in her steps and felt her heart thud painfully against her chest wall in anxiety. For a crazy second Dale felt herself to be somewhere else. The two of them were in New Orleans again, facing each other in surprise across a hotel lobby. And right on cue, the tension she'd felt then twisting at her insides tightened again protectively against his unique male potency.

Dale took in his handsome face, suntanned, making his eyes lighter, almost topaz in color. He looked like a true Californian, kind of larger than life and filled with fresh air and the vitality of outdoors. He looked sure and in control, in possession of everything good life had to offer. Damon didn't look as if he'd ever known a moment's unease, painful doubts, confusing loneliness or crushing disappointments. He belonged more there than in New Orleans, and she began to have doubts about her first impressions of him from the conference.

A sudden questioning smile broke the straight line of his mouth, and the one that Dale answered with was surprised and questioning, too, even as her heart continued to race at his presence.

"Dr. Christensen," Dale acknowledged.

"Dr. Christensen," Damon answered with equal formality, his eyes nonetheless bright and amused.

"What are you doing here?" Dale asked, wrinkling her forehead.

"I'm here to pick you up for Oakland Central. You *were* expecting to be met?"

"Yes, but not by you."

"Aren't you glad to see me?" He smiled softly at her and was rewarded by seeing two bright spots of color high on her cheekbones.

"Don't tell me this is another coincidence," Dale said lightly, ignoring his question.

Damon lifted a shoulder and raised a brow. "It's a small world."

"Not that small, Doctor!" Dale quickly took in his casual pullover yellow knit shirt. A pair of well-cut brown slacks fit closely to the muscular lengths of his long legs. The thought occurred to Dale that he still didn't look much like a doctor, but rather like someone just off to play a round of golf. But she did also spot the medical beeper attached to his belt.

Damon's large hand settled partially on her waist and hip, steering her in the direction of baggage claims. There was an instant shock of memory for both of them, and they looked sharply at each other. For long moments both re-lived that last evening of the conference in New Orleans when they'd embraced with awakening passion. Damon turned his head and watched her draw her bottom lip delicately between her teeth for an instant. His eyes dropped in fascination to the motion before lifting to see a flush cover her face, effectively betraying her thoughts. He smiled complacently to himself. But her look also held a fear that he didn't understand. Damon didn't want her to be afraid of him.

They continued to walk, and Dale was aware of the casual contact of his hand, marking her as having already been selected and claimed. The sensation was eerie and tena-cious. Damon was cognizant of the feel of her in his arms. Her soft breasts pressed against him—the sweet tenderness of her answering mouth, the fluttering hands, not sure where to rest or what to hold on to. He knew an immediate urge to take up just where they'd stopped two months ear-lier, in a dark room learning about each other. But there would be time to discover each other again. And he had every intention this time of making the knowledge com-plete.

Damon suddenly spoke. "Speaking of small worlds, there are really only about a thousand people in the whole world, and you keep running into them over and over again."

Dale laughed gratefully at the opportunity to change the mood. "If that's true, are you telling me it's possible that we'll keep seeing each other again and again?"

Damon looked down at her, his smile enigmatic and thoughtful. "It's very possible. The fact that we met somewhere else halfway across country months ago proves it. Who knows where we'll meet next."

Dale puzzled uncomfortably over that as Damon turned his attention to getting her luggage. Dale remembered with irony Frances McCann's advice to "never say never." She was with Damon again, and she had no idea what was going to happen, or even if anything should. She was in California for professional reasons. She didn't know what part, if any, Damon played in that.

Her response to him was as strong as ever. But she had never been one to be guided by the emotions of the moment. And perhaps when she really thought about it, everything had changed, after all. New Orleans had been a neutral ground. The feelings and emotions that had sprung up between them belonged to that time, as well. They were on his home territory now; he had the upper hand. And in more ways than not, she really didn't know him at all.

Dale bit her lip and took a look behind her in the direction she'd just walked. Damon swung her case to the floor and followed the direction of her eyes.

"Are you sorry you came?" he asked, watching her carefully.

"I...I guess I don't understand exactly what I'm doing here," she responded hesitantly.

Damon knew the answer he wanted to give her but held to his caution. "Your reputation precedes you," he said lightly, but she didn't respond to the humor. Damon sobered and looked directly at her. "I'll tell you all about it as soon as I get you settled. You must be tired and hungry."

"Yes, I am." Dale smiled wanly.

"Then let's get out of here," he suggested.

Damon got her settled into his car, a white sports car sev-

eral years old that had seen better days. It was functional, not
sleek and shiny for show, and had been used well.

Dale let her travel exhaustion envelop her for a while in
silence as Damon maneuvered the little car out of Oakland
International Airport and headed toward the bridge that
would take them into Oakland.

Even though Damon's open window sent in a breeze that
lifted his hair and cooled the interior of the car, Dale felt
stifled. Every time Damon shifted gears, the back of his
hand somehow managed to brush against her thigh or knee.
She could see the muscle movement in his hand and arm.
His profile was powerful and arresting. For an odd moment,
Dale had an image of the kind of woman someone like Damon should be with, and it was all the more amazing that
she was there next to him.

Dale shook her head impatiently. Of course, it wasn't a
pleasure trip. Damon was simply there because of the dic-
tates of the situation. A sigh escaped her, and she looked
absently at the scene outside her window.

Damon heard the sigh and turned his head briefly to
watch her pensive profile. "Have you ever been to California before?" he asked.

Dale started out of her reverie. "No, I haven't. I—I've
never done much traveling. Actually, New Orleans and
here are the farthest trips I've ever made from New York."

"You don't like to travel?"

Dale shrugged. "It's not that, really. Mostly I've always
been too busy to travel." She swept her eyes over the landscape beyond her window. San Francisco was west of the
Oakland airport across the Bay. To her right was Oakland.
"This is very pretty. And it's so sunny in California."

Damon chuckled. "You're just seeing the larger cities.
There are parts that are lots prettier. And the sunshine is a
fluke. I arranged it just for your arrival."

Dale smiled in amusement at him.

"We get a lot of fog and gray days. This spring has been
very rainy."

Damon drove them over Nantucket Way from the airport into Alameda County. They made their way across the
narrow stretch of land and eventually crossed into Oakland.
Damon cheerfully continued his narration.

"Some people here, who obviously prefer to be in San Francisco, call this section the 'East Bay.' It's not. It's Oakland. Period!"

Dale laughed softly. "I hope they're paying you extra for this tour!"

Damon pursed his lips, and his eyes darted a bright look at her. "I don't do this tour for everyone. This is Dr. Christensen's VIP Special."

Dale stared at him for a confused second and then looked away. "Then I suppose I should consider myself privileged," she said lightly.

"Yes," Damon said evenly, without a moment's hesitation.

Dale was feeling as if Damon were sitting closer to her than he actually was.

"You can't see the Golden Gate or Alcatraz from here. Maybe some other day."

Once they were in Oakland, Damon drove the car through the downtown sector, with its scattering of skyscrapers, which could in no way compete with those of New York.

"Oakland has a lot going for it," Damon said, driving more slowly. "We have Lake Merritt practically in the middle, so there are some terrific marinas and harbors. We have our own ball team and some great parks."

"You like it here," Dale observed.

"It's an interesting city, with lots of diversity and nice people—yours truly included," he said archly, and grinned when Dale grimaced playfully.

Damon made a series of turns, taking them off the main thoroughfare on Fruitvale Avenue. The car swung past a white building of contemporary design and a modest size.

"That's Oakland Central," Damon informed her. "You'll see it tomorrow."

After another block, the car turned into a lot adjacent to an apartment complex. Damon stopped and parked the car near the building's entrance. When they were both out of the car, Dale absently flexed her stiff left knee and looked around her.

"This used to be an old nursing residence. Ten years ago it was converted into regular efficiency apartment units for visiting staff, guests, conference and seminar attendees."

Damon led her into the building, and they took the elevator to the fifth floor. It was getting late in the afternoon now, and the inside of the apartment seemed dim. It had two fair-sized rooms, plus a bath and kitchenette. Dale was sure it was a charming and comfortable setting but was at the moment too weary to pay much attention.

Damon left her suitcase by the bedroom door. He briefly explained everything and turned over the keys to her. Dale offered to take them, but Damon didn't release them into her hands completely. She raised puzzled eyes to his face.

"Would you like to go out for dinner, or would you rather stay here?"

"I really don't feel up to going out again."

"Fine. Then we'll eat here. Go unpack. I'll see about dinner."

The small bedroom, with its double bed, also provided a bureau of drawers, a floral upholstered armchair and ample closet space. Dale heard Damon on the phone and thought that he was checking in with the hospital. Twenty minutes later, everything was put away. She recombed her hair and came back slowly into the living room just as the doorbell rang.

"I'll get it," Damon said with a presumptive authority that made Dale smile. When he turned from the door, he held a small flat pizza box in his hand. "Dinner!" he informed her grandly, setting the steaming box on the kitchenette counter.

"Oh, wonderful!" Dale responded cheerfully, removing her linen jacket and heading for the kitchen cabinets to find plates.

Damon followed behind her and opened the small refrigerator to take out a chilled split of wine, then shut the refrigerator door as Dale turned from the cabinet. They collided gently.

"This is getting to be a habit," he murmured in amusement, his bright eyes sweeping over her face.

Dale laughed nervously and moved past him into the larger, safer area of the living room. "The...the kitchen is awfully small. It's not made for two people."

Damon opened the wine and poured. "It depends on the two people," he answered significantly, and looked at her. "Making meals together could be interesting."

Dale took a hasty sip of wine. "I—I'm not a very good cook."

"Busy doing other things again?" Damon asked as he placed the hot slices of pizza on white porcelain plates. Dale didn't answer. "What do you do to relax?"

Dale blinked. "I'm not very good at relaxing, either. I like to keep busy with my work."

Damon frowned at her. "All the time?"

"Just about, I guess."

Damon was thoughtful for a moment before finally lifting his slice to bite the triangular end off. "That must not please your boyfriends too much."

"Oh, I don't have a—" Dale stopped suddenly in confusion. She picked up her slice. "They...they would just have to understand, that's all. Doctors don't have regular, predictable hours like everyone else."

Damon watched her silently for a moment before he spoke again. "That's true, of course. But you could make the time for other things in your life that are important to you."

"I do, when I have to," Dale responded quietly. There was a moment's silence while Dale avoided Damon's gaze, which was pointedly directed toward her.

"I'm a very good cook myself," he suddenly said.

Dale raised her brows in surprise.

"It comes from mixing all those funny things in chemistry and pathology lab."

That made her laugh.

"It was also a matter of survival."

"I know," Dale teased. "You're not into starving to death! Was it from bachelor living?"

"No, my mother," Damon said around a mouthful of pizza.

"Your mother?" she asked skeptically.

He nodded. "When my older brother and I were teenagers, my mother went back to work. She said we were old enough to fix meals for ourselves, which was not unreasonable. But I wasn't keen on peanut butter and jelly sandwiches, so I learned the one hundred and one things to do with hamburger, eggs and a can of mushroom soup!''

Dale was chuckling in joy and amusement. He so easily made her laugh. She was sitting on an overstuffed sofa, her legs tucked comfortably under her, and Damon sat cross-legged on the floor. They attacked the pizza, shamelessly licking fingers and lips from the messy food. Dale began to relax and enjoy herself, but she soon began to ask questions in detail about the case she was to consult on. Damon told her about Tai Chin and what had been done medically so far to treat her damaged leg and knee. They talked serious technicalities all through the meal, with Dale so intent that Damon began to laugh.

"Whoa, Doctor! You'll find out everything tomorrow. In the morning you'll meet the chief of staff, Dr. Anders, and others who will be working with you. And you'll get to meet Tai.''

Dale hesitated, absently shredding her paper napkin. "Will I be working with you as well?" she asked casually.

Damon was suddenly remembering Dr. Boris Teller's predictions, and a corner of his wide mouth lifted in a rueful smile. "We will, on occasion, be working very closely; particularly where Tai is concerned." He tilted his head at her. "Do you have any objections to that?"

She colored deeply. "N-no, of course not!"

Dale sat back in her seat and watched Damon finish the last of the pie. She was fascinated by the strong workings of his jaw as he chewed, seeing the tension of cords in his thick neck and feeling a languid, comfortable warmth assail her as they sat quietly. She was suddenly also wondering what he was like with his patients. Did he have the same sense of humor with them that he showed so readily to her? Was he gentle and concerned and involved? Did he always have attractive young females with interesting injuries?

Damon looked up and caught her staring rather dreamily and curiously at him. A slow, questioning smile curved his mouth, and Dale blinked in embarrassment.

"Do I have tomato sauce on my chin?" he asked, chuckling.

"No." Dale smiled wanly. "I . . . I guess I'm just catatonic from the long plane ride." She began to gather the crust remains nervously and close the empty box. "Since you were so kind as to provide me with a gourmet meal my first night, the very least I can do is the dishes," she teased, and unfolded her legs from the seat. But she stood up too quickly on limbs in which the circulation had been temporarily cut off, and her left knee began to buckle.

Dale had no time even to utter a gasp of surprise, but Damon responded quickly, grabbing her by the midriff tightly, and eased her back into her chair. He remained bent over her until Dale lifted her head with an expression of mild exasperation.

"That was foolish of me," she said, and then realized that Damon still held her. Their eyes met. Dale could detect the amber flecks in his brown eyes, he was so close.

Slowly, he released her, his jaw tensing. "I'll do the dishes," he said, taking the box from her and carrying it to the trash bin in the kitchen. "It's all part of the Christensen Special." Damon turned his head to smile at her, concern in his eyes.

In a minute he was back and sitting easily next to her on the sofa. Dale clasped her hands together and kept her eyes averted from his. She already knew what she would find there. The same kind of male interest she'd seen since first meeting him, which continually threw her off guard and into an emotional tailspin.

"Did you twist your knee?" he asked evenly, laying his hand along the sofa behind her head.

"No," Dale whispered.

"Shall I check it for you?"

She shook her head. "No need to. My knee is as fine as it's ever going to be. I'm used to its quirks. I just leave it alone."

Damon smiled to himself. Idly, his fingers played with the wavy strands of hair brushing her neck. "Has anyone suggested otherwise?"

Dale sat perfectly still, afraid to move lest he move, also, and bring all those earlier-felt emotions flooding into her again. "Occasionally. You know, one more operation, and this one will be it. The last one I had at fifteen was the last 'one more'!"

Damon sensed her tenseness. Slowly, a finger found its

way under the heavy mass of hair to gently stroke the skin of her neck.

"Do...do you think I should have another?" she asked, her voice sounding slightly high-pitched and a little anxious.

The finger made gentle caressing circles. "I like your legs just the way they are."

Oddly, the response perversely pleased and annoyed Dale, but she didn't have time to consider why as a shiver, along with a pleasant tickling sensation, coursed through her. The kind that, if allowed to continue, would make her very bones soft. She turned her head and finally looked at him. Her eyes were sparkling but were also an intense darker green just now. They were questioning, innocent, appealing.

Damon had a sudden flashing image of Jessica with her brighter than bright smile, her upturned face with its skillfully arched brows and careful makeup. Jessica never knew a moment of uncertainty. With her, Damon always knew exactly where he stood. With this attractive young woman, who was probably no older than Jessica, Damon felt less sure of himself.

Dale was like a welcome summer breeze, ruffling through his life suddenly, upsetting the patterns and routines. Effervescent and unpredictable. Pleasant, comfortable—and something else. Just what, he couldn't say yet. But it had become very important, all at once, to find out.

Women had never been a mystery to Damon. He'd understood them well enough all his adult life. That the depth of his knowledge could be questioned had never occurred to him, and it had never mattered before, since it also hadn't previously affected his life-style. But Dale had. In some way, that was new to him.

"Dale..." He spoke her name softly. It was distinctly his own way of saying it that made her alert. "I still feel the same way," he dared to inform her honestly. And it wasn't until it was said that Damon realized it was true.

"Oh? And what way is that?" she asked, hoping her voice didn't betray any of her insecurities or sudden sense of his maleness.

"Good to be with you. Glad that you're here," he supplied in a seductive voice that rasped over the words. She shivered again.

Dale flushed and dropped her head a little, losing contact from the disturbing exploration of his finger.

"Probably just an overactive thyroid," she whispered flippantly.

A smile lifted a corner of Damon's mouth. "You're not giving yourself nearly enough credit. Do you really believe that what happened in New Orleans was all glands?"

"Are you saying it was something else?" she countered, looking briefly at him.

Damon wasn't sure. Before that night he hadn't explored it too deeply. And that was part of the malady that had attacked him for weeks.

"I'd like to find out."

"I . . . I'm going to be very busy with Tai."

Damon thought of arguing that point, but caution dictated otherwise. Being overly aggressive was not the way to get through to Dale.

"And so you shall," he said briskly, startling Dale. He stood up and, grabbing her hands, pulled her to her feet. He only released one as he headed toward the door. "But only during the day."

"I really won't have time for much else."

Damon stopped near the door and turned to face her. His fingers closed possessively over hers, and with a straight arm he brought his hand down to his side, forcing Dale closer to him. "We'll make time," he responded firmly, offering no compromise.

Dale looked openly at him. Would there be time to really know each other before she went home? Dale's eyes grew somber and thoughtful. She had only just arrived, and already leaving was a fact to be faced and accepted.

"I'm going to leave now," he announced in a drawl. "I suggest you try and get some rest."

Dale nodded. Damon put both his hands on her waist. Instinctively, Dale brought her hands up and spread them flat on his chest as she was maneuvered against him. She could feel his chest, stomach and thighs.

Damon purposefully lifted her chin, searched her eyes for a long second, and then gently plied a kiss from her mouth.

"You can get to the hospital by yourself tomorrow morning. It's just across the square in front of this building. Dr. Anders wants to see you at ten o'clock. I have surgery in the morning, so I won't be there."

"I can manage," she said firmly. But Damon only smiled at her. There was something else she meant to protest about on her behalf, but the look in his eyes stopped her. There was a dizzying moment of déjà vu.

Damon's head lowered again as Dale waited, as she'd been waiting all day, perhaps for the last two months. There was a gap that had to be bridged, an unended episode. Dale made no protest as his hands slid the rest of the way to her back, holding her. It was like slow motion, his gestures and intentions lasting forever. His eyes spoke volumes and were making her afraid again.

Damon's mouth opened, settling completely over hers, this time in a kiss that was much more eloquent and much less polite. It took from her, manipulated, then gave back with his probing tongue and warm, moist breath. In this one sweet meeting he had managed to revive all that had been between them before.

Suddenly, she found it hard to breathe, and was about to move her head when Damon ended the kiss. He reached beyond her to open the door and faced her again.

"Welcome to California. And I really am glad you're here." It was so simple and so direct that at first Dale wasn't sure she'd really heard him. It didn't seem like the kind of thing a man like Damon Christensen would say.

And it held so much promise.

Chapter Nine

"This isn't a very large center. You'll probably know the complete workings of it in a day or so," Gloria Mendez said.

Dale nodded as she walked beside the middle-aged woman who was the head nurse at Oakland Central. Dale had encountered her at the information desk when entering the hospital a half hour earlier. Mrs. Mendez had offered to take her to meet Dr. Anders.

Dale felt immediately at home. The butterflies flapping around in her stomach on the short walk over from her temporary apartment were put to rest when she walked through the front doors of the center. She was a professional. She was very good at what she did. And she was there at their request. There was no need to feel apprehensive.

Mrs. Mendez stopped at a nursing station for a moment to answer a question. Dale noticed her efficient and quick handling of the details and her friendly way with the staff. Her plumpish form was neat in an immaculate uniform, and her black hair, streaked with gray in places, was twisted in a fat bun at the back of her head. She turned back to Dale with a smile.

"Orthopedics takes up most of the fourth floor. But the whirlpool baths for physical therapy are on the lower level."

They were on the eighth floor at the moment and headed into a wing of the hospital that seemed to hold more administrative offices than services and treatment centers.

"All meetings and conferences are held on this floor. All major decisions, orders and changes are decreed from here." Gloria Mendez gave Dale a rueful side glance. "The staff calls it the Cloisters."

Dale smiled in appreciation. From her own experience she knew that those in the upper echelon had a tendency at times to "cloister" themselves away from the rest of the hospital, making them seem more special and elite than anyone else. They had always been men of stature, with imposing professional profiles and egos to match. They often wore the air of benevolence and goodwill like a shield to hide smug superiority and aloofness. She'd had to prove herself to men like that ever since college and medical school. She was prepared for Dr. Anders.

Dale and Gloria stopped at a teakwood door, and Gloria knocked quietly, pushing the door open without waiting for a response. She explained to the secretary her mission, and then Gloria turned once more to Dale.

"You're going to need an ID and a badge and an office somewhere. I'll be happy to help in any way I can when you're finished here."

"That's thoughtful of you."

"Just come back down to the first floor when you're ready," Gloria said, heading back out of the door, and then she was gone.

The secretary was smiling at Dale. "What a coincidence! We have another Dr. Christensen on staff!"

"Yes, I know," Dale said smoothly, feeling the color steal up her neck.

"You're not related, are you?"

"No." Dale shook her head.

"Well, nonetheless, I can see how it's going to get very confusing around here!" She picked up her phone and pushed a button. "Yes, Dr. Anders. Dr. Dale Christensen is out here to see you. Shall I send her in? Fine...thank you." She put down the phone.

"Just go on in right through there." She indicated a door to the side. "Oh, and good luck!"

Dale took a deep breath and pursed her mouth, wondering if she was going to need it. Luck had never had anything to do with what had transpired in her life thus far. Just a lot of hard work and determination.

A gentleman behind a long desk stood up the moment the door opened. He was reed thin and very tall, with a face that reminded Dale of Norman Rockwell. Dale found herself being stared at openly, and with an uncharacteristic show of haughtiness, she raised her chin and guessed at the trend of his thoughts—that she looked entirely too young to be a doctor or to handle the delicate case assigned to her.

Dr. Anders reached across the span of his desk to put out a bony hand to her.

"Welcome to Oakland Central, Dr. Christensen. Please have a seat," he directed pleasantly, and sat once more.

Dale made herself comfortable, straightening her long lab coat. Dr. Anders sat back heavily in his spring-action chair and picked up an unlit pipe to clamp between his teeth.

"I had to give up smoking three years ago. This is really just a pacifier," he said conversationally, and grinned suddenly at Dale.

She relaxed completely in her chair and smiled in return. "I understand."

"Now, I know Dr. Christensen, er, Damon picked you up yesterday. I hope he made you welcome."

Dale squirmed in her chair and by sheer force of will didn't blush. "Yes, he did," she said with admirable calm.

"Good, good." Dr. Anders looked at her thoughtfully for a second, leaning in his chair in such a way that it bounced gently on its springs.

"I haven't forgotten anything from my youth. I fully appreciate the feelings and attitudes about, er, administrative heads. I promise this is not to be an inquisition, Doctor." He said it with a perfectly straight face; she couldn't help smiling.

"However, I don't mind telling you that I for one didn't think it was necessary to bring you all this distance. We have some very fine doctors here, although California is by no means overwhelmed with people in orthopedics. I'm sure in time we would have made progress with our young patient."

"I agree with you, Dr. Anders. I myself don't offer any unusual treatment. But I do especially well with children."

Dr. Anders drew an imaginary puff through his cold, dry pipe. "You seem so young yourself, Dr. Christensen, and very sure of yourself."

"I am," Dale responded at once. "And if you weren't at least a little bit curious yourself, I wouldn't be here."

"I concede the point." Dr. Anders chuckled. "After all, the most important factor is the patient." He narrowed his eyes at her another long moment. "Tell me about your own injury, if you don't mind."

Two pink spots heated her cheeks and neck. "I...I don't mind at all," Dale said, and gave a brief chronological history of her accident and subsequent operations.

Dr. Anders listened intently, nodding occasionally. "Mmm" was his first response, which told Dale nothing of what he was thinking.

"I suppose you felt the doctors blew their chance with you?" he asked pensively.

Dale shook her head. "I was never angry with the doctors. Just childishly disappointed, I guess. I thought that because they were doctors they could fix anything."

Dr. Anders raised a pale, rueful brow. "Magic, or a miracle," he murmured under his breath.

Reluctantly, Dale nodded. "Children believe in them, I suppose, when all else fails."

"It's understandable. So you became a doctor to try and do better?"

"Not necessarily better. But having already been there, as they say, I thought I had something very personal to offer. My own experience."

Dr. Anders inclined his head a little. "Are you somewhat of a crusader, Doctor?"

"Aren't we all to some extent?"

He just watched her, his eyes twinkling rather mischievously. Dale chuckled dryly and lifted her shoulders.

"Well, to be honest, I sometimes think I became a doctor as a result of my accident. I spent so much time in hospitals and around doctors it just somehow became the obvious thing to do."

He nodded in understanding. "Exactly what is it that you will do for our patient?"

"Mostly spend a lot of time with her. I want to find out what her injury means to her. How it's going to change her life right now. I'd also like to meet her parents and her coach. I understand that Tai is a champion skater. Then, of course, I want to examine her and go over the medical records with Dr. Christensen. It may be that more surgery is needed."

"Well, I'll talk to Damon and see to it that all of that is made available to you. We just don't have the time or personnel to get so involved normally. So we'll leave it to you."

"I don't expect it will take more than four or five weeks. Children need a lot of time, in this area particularly."

"Why treat children so differently?" he asked.

Dale smiled knowingly. "Because they are different. Children are *not* little people. They are uncertain, inexperienced, unformed, unknowledgeable, and they feel things differently because of it. They should have that consideration."

There was a little silence while Dr. Anders thought over her words. "Mmm, it doesn't sound particularly revolutionary in terms of ideas."

"It's not," Dale said simply, "and the simplest ideas are the ones that work best."

"In any case, Doctor, you may need a lot of time. Her parents have given consent to your coming in on the case. After all, they want their daughter to skate and compete again."

"It's more important that she walk first," Dale interrupted.

"Yes, well, you know the old saying about the 'inscrutable Chinese.'"

"Don't laugh," Dale advised in gentle reproof. "That might actually be a helpful hint in dealing with Tai. It might help me to understand her motivation and where it comes from."

Dr. Anders lifted his hands in supposition. "It's in your hands now. And Dr. Christensen—*Damon*," he added to make himself clear. "You know, it's going to be damned difficult with two Dr. Christensens around!"

She laughed. "Please call me Dale."

He gave an acquiescent little tilt of his head. "I just wanted to say that Damon is a good doctor to work with." Dr. Anders pushed away from the desk and stood up, Dale following suit. "You have competent people to help you if you need it. And please feel free to come to me if there's any problem."

They said their good-byes, and feeling rather pleased with the way that she'd handled herself, Dale made her way back to the first floor. She located Gloria Mendez and was taken to have a photo ID shot. They were still laughing over how awful the picture was when they got off the elevator on four so that Dale could be shown the facilities for orthopedics. The rooms were bright and large and well equipped.

"And this," Gloria said dramatically, reaching for a doorknob, "is the office you'll be using. It belongs to a senior staff member who's on a visiting professorship at Stanford. Oops!" Gloria exclaimed as the door was suddenly pulled open and Damon stood in the doorframe.

Dale's heart lurched alarmingly when she saw him and knew a quickening and excitement within herself. All day she'd harbored hopes of seeing him, building up her expectations repeatedly. She'd tried so hard since meeting Damon to deny her feelings, but this desire to see him and be with him had so gained in strength and feeling that she now welcomed it.

"Oh, sorry, Gloria," he apologized, turning his gaze very briefly to Dale. But it was enough time for remembrance, and for electrifying sensations grabbing at them both.

"Dr. Christensen," Gloria said, "I was just showing Dr. Christensen her, er, office." Gloria's voice faded, and she looked, confused, from one of them to the other and at the grin on each of their faces. "Well, you know what I mean!" she said, laughing.

"Yes, we do," Damon answered. Turning a purely professional face to Dale, he inquired, "Did everything go all right this morning?" He winked at her secretly.

Dale's mouth quivered. "Yes, thank you. Very well. I met with Dr. Anders, and Mrs. Mendez has been very nice in showing me around." Dale smiled calmly and politely, while her eyes took in Damon's blue shirt and dark blue trousers visible under his opened lab coat. His stethoscope was looped around his neck, and his hair was as windy-looking as ever. His conservative red-striped tie was askew, and Dale wondered if he ever wore it knotted.

"Have you had lunch yet?" he asked casually, but Dale read the expectancy in his gaze.

Her brows lifted helplessly, and she looked at Gloria Mendez. "I was just on my way to lunch with Mrs. Mendez. I ... I thought I would talk to you this afternoon about the case," she finished, trying to squelch her own disappointment.

Damon good-naturedly raised a rueful brow. "The story of my life," he murmured with significance, and Dale was also remembering the times he'd been thwarted in New Orleans. "But if you could just spare me a few minutes, I'll give you the patient's records," he suggested smoothly.

Gloria touched her arm. "The cafeteria is on two. I'll meet you there in twenty minutes."

"Okay," Dale agreed gratefully as Gloria left them. Then she was able to give her full attention to Damon. Her smile was a little hesitant now that they were completely alone, but it was all for him.

Damon's eyes quickly swept over her, noting her hair clipped off her face, as was her habit, to keep it out of her way. There was a becoming high color to her face. Not really shy or embarrassed, as he'd seen, but sort of rosy and bright—as if she was happy. Damon gave her a slow smile filled with an intense kind of light Dale was coming to know in him. He stepped a little to the side.

"May I show you your office, Doctor?" he asked evenly as two staff members passed them.

Dale moved into the office. She looked around quickly and suddenly started laughing. She turned around to face Damon just as he was closing the door.

"This is cheerfully and correctly referred to as 'the hole in the wall' by the absentee doctor whose office it normally is. I hope you like it!" Damon said grandly, sweeping a long arm around the eight-by-eight-foot space.

"It will do fine," Dale declared. Then they stared at each other; the smiles slowly faded, and the room closed in around them.

Damon took a step toward her, and Dale's head tilted back so she wouldn't lose eye contact. Damon leaned a little past her and reached for a thick folder and two oversized envelopes. He bent so close that the end of his stethoscope swung out and tapped against her shoulder.

"I brought you Tai Chin's medical record and all the X rays. I'll take you to meet her this afternoon after visiting hours when it's quiet." He showed her the thick pile and laid them down again. Then he stood in front of her. "I've been looking all over for you," he stated unexpectedly in a low timbre.

Dale blinked. A multitude of emotions sent a slithering chill down her spine. She didn't have to read anything into his words. He'd made himself perfectly clear. Dale just looked at him as if he were some wonderful apparition, or a dream come true.

Damon took her by the arms and turned her so that her back was pressed against the closed door. Their eyes locked. There was a familiar warm, heated smell of his body. It was now mixed with the distinctive smells of the hospital. His large hands tunneled inside her open lab coat and encircled her waist, pulling her toward him. Her back was forced to arch when her hips were met by his.

Dale's lips parted with the physical wonder of him as Damon bent forward in the quiet room to kiss her with a controlled urgency that was a total surprise to her. Her hands went to the back of his neck for support and balance, weaving into the locks of his fine hair. His mouth moved and gently roamed against her own until her knees began to tremble, and she was afraid the left one was going to give out on her again.

A mechanical voice intoned hollowly through the corridor outside the door. "Dr. Christensen to admitting. Dr. Damon Christensen to admitting, please...."

Dale came to her senses first, twisting her head away. "You...you're being paged, Doctor." Barely able to breathe, she slid her hands down from his neck and pushed him away.

"Dammit," Damon exploded softly. He straightened and pulled her from the door. His eyes devoured Dale once more, and he let out a deep sigh of frustration. "Read whatever you can of those records."

Dale nodded, staring at the hollow of his throat.

"Meet me here at four, and we'll go see Tai together."

"That sounds good," she agreed. Dale twisted around in front of him and hastily opened the door. Damon gave her one more quick look, touched her mouth with a finger and was striding off down the hall.

Dale took a deep breath and left, also, to meet Gloria Mendez for lunch. Her euphoria, shared just moments before with Damon, was quickly replaced by a cold, frightening realization. It didn't change the way she was feeling about him. But it made the feelings all perfectly clear.

DALE HAD the door to her office swung open all the way. Her sense of caution and propriety told her it would not be a good idea for Damon to be encouraged to embrace her again, as he had earlier. While she had enjoyed it, it was also disturbing and disruptive.

Dale was bent over the folders when there was a soft tap on the door. She looked up to find Damon leaning in the doorway, watching her with probing intensity. Slowly, he began to smile. Dale crossed her arms on top of the folders and returned the smile. The very air around them was swept through with the exchange of feelings between them.

Damon opened the conversation, nodding toward her desk and its litter of reports. "So what do you think?"

Silently, Dale let out a breath of relief that he wasn't immediately personal with her. Damon correctly interpreted the wide-eyed look on her face and smiled to himself at her need for control. It was enough for now that her eyes told him that she was pleased to see him.

"I think there's a lot of work to be done," Dale said.

Damon moved into the small office and perched on the edge of the desk, looking down at her.

"Did you perform the surgery when she was admitted?"

Damon shook his head. "Not all of it. I worked with a microsurgery team to first save the leg. We didn't want to do much more without first consulting and carefully deciding what to do next."

Dale frowned and gnawed at her lip in concentration. Damon couldn't help a private smile as he watched her.

"Well, the X rays indicate the first work was well done. If we let it go at that, she'll probably only need surgery to repair and replace ligaments and muscles around the knee."

Damon tilted his head. "But?" Dale looked up at him.

"I want to talk to Tai first. It depends on what she wants. I would go for replacing the whole joint. But it's up to her."

"Do you really think that's wise, or necessary?" he asked curiously.

"I do." She nodded. "It's her leg!"

Dale didn't add that she wished someone had thought to ask her when she was a child. Having her participate might have changed the whole direction of her life.

Damon sighed and stood up. He swept back the open lab coat and rammed his hands into his pockets. "I don't know. She hasn't been overly responsive. She's still understandably depressed and no doubt disappointed about the fall competition."

"Wouldn't you be, too?" Dale asked softly, also standing up.

"Yes!" Damon agreed at once. "As an athlete myself, I'd be damned upset! Except that Tai hasn't been angry. Just withdrawn. She will respond to me at times."

Dale smiled as she preceded Damon out of her office. She didn't reply that it was very likely because he was a young attractive male and the attention, even to a fifteen-year-old, was flattering.

"Is there anything else I should know before we go in?" Dale asked.

Damon frowned and shrugged. "She hasn't had many visitors beyond family and her coach. Not even other members of her team. It's very odd and spooky, as if they're all afraid they'll be similarly cursed if they have anything to do with Tai."

"I can imagine," Dale commented wryly.

Damon stopped in front of an open ward door through which the muted sounds of a television set could be heard. For the first time, Dale experienced a little nervousness. She always did when she first met a new young patient. It was rare that she had a totally disagreeable youngster, and she was usually able to make some allowances for surliness or ill temper. It was sometimes justifiable. Dale hesitated outside the door. She wanted to like Tai Chin.

She absently brushed down her hair, and Damon lifted the corner of his mouth at the unconscious gesture. Giving him one small, wan smile, Dale walked past him into the room. Two little girls of about twelve were seated in wheel-chairs in front of the TV. But Dale only had eyes for the pale, thin person in the far bed near the window, listlessly leafing through a teen magazine.

She looked up at their approach from intense black eyes. Her smooth cap of glossy black hair was cut in a short, cute bob with a silky layer of bangs over her forehead. Her mouth, small and bow-shaped, was closed, unsmiling and somber. Damon and Dale stopped at the foot of her bed.

"Hello, Tai," Damon said in a light voice.

Tai stared at Dale for a moment longer before turning her solemn oval face. "Hello, Damon," she whispered in a very young, very sweet voice.

"Tai, this is Dr. Dale Christensen. She's heard a lot about you. Dale, this is Tai Chin."

Dale smiled, and slowly Tai responded. Dale thought she looked much younger than fifteen. "It's a privilege to meet you. May I call you Tai?"

"Yes." Tai looked from one to the other. "Is she your wife?" she asked Damon.

The question was, as usual, unexpected. Damon shifted almost in embarrassment. Dale grinned at the young girl, amused once the surprise had worn off.

"No, we're not married," Dale answered. "It's just a co-incidence that we have the same name." She heard Damon groan next to her and swallowed back a laugh.

"You could be married," Tai observed further.

"What makes you say so?" Damon asked.

"She's very pretty next to you," Tai said simply. Dale and Damon exchanged embarrassed glances. Tai turned back to Dale, and her voice dropped and became a thin whisper. "Are you going to do something to my leg?" There was no surprise, no fear, no anger—just plain curios-ity.

"Perhaps. I think we should talk about it first. But even before we do that, we should get to know each other."

"If you like," Tai said softly.

Dale looked down at the girl's elevated leg, swathed in an unbelievable amount of plaster, gauze, tape and towels. The size of it all was almost as big as Tai herself.

"That's awful-looking," Dale said bluntly. Damon looked

sharply at her, surprised to hear her say something that he perceived as cold and insensitive. But Dale was ignoring him. She turned to Tai in time to see a fleeting smile of humor on her face. Damon caught the smile, too. "How do you sleep with that?" Dale asked with a humorous smile.

"It's not easy—mostly on my back!" Tai suddenly giggled. But then the smile faded again.

"Are you missing a lot of practice?" Dale then asked.

Tai nodded. "I used to skate six or seven hours a day."

"Then you don't mind hard work and long hours?"

Tai looked at her. "I don't mind at all."

"That's good. We have hard work for you to do. And it's going to hurt a lot—and take time."

"I know...."

Dale patted her frail arm. "Tomorrow I'll come by again. We can talk some more. Would that be okay?"

Tai shrugged. "Sure."

Dale made to turn away. "Oh, by the way. I do have one other thing to ask you." Dale put her bag on the side of Tai's bed and extracted a cloth-covered notebook from the bottom.

She opened the book to a clean page and passed it to Tai with a pen. "I love watching champion skaters perform. Would you mind giving me your autograph?"

Tai stared and blinked for a long moment. And then her face positively lit up.

Chapter Ten

Damon stood discreetly outside the ward room without being seen. He was watching Dale and Tai with a combination of amazement and exasperation. Since being introduced two days before, they had been together almost constantly.

The morning before, Damon had stopped by her apartment, only to find that Dale had already left for the hospital; in fact, she was found having a glass of orange juice as she kept Tai company over the young patient's breakfast. Damon had been taken aback by Dale's enthusiasm and excitement over working with Tai. He'd also been moved and impressed by the way Dale had finally won Tai over by asking for her autograph. Nothing short of a perfectly healthy leg and knee could have served better to make the girl feel worthwhile again. But it had also been clear to Damon that it had not been a simple ploy on Dale's part. She'd really wanted that autograph. Tai had written her name in Chinese characters, delighting Dale even more, and the previous morning, when he'd peeked into Dale's office, he found the autograph matted and pinned to the bulletin board.

Damon had never felt more superfluous in his life than he had standing there while Tai and Dale became friends. So much for being indispensable, he'd thought with a wry grin, his ego suffering a little.

He'd wanted to be with Dale. Spend some time with her alone getting to know her. Hold her again. But in her efforts to be available to help Tai, she was inadvertently not cooperating with him.

Damon's hand closed around a pewter coin in his pocket, and he continued to watch the two females together. Tai was talking and gesturing with her thin hands as Dale sat in rapt attention, listening and nodding occasionally in understanding. Once, Dale laughed outright, and at the musical sound, Damon's mouth began to curve in a smile. And then Dale was talking, and Tai was listening. It had gone on all morning and would probably continue in the days to come.

That first night, when he and Dale had finally left Tai, he found himself apologizing for not being able to take her for dinner.

"I'm committed to a board meeting in San Francisco tonight," he told her.

"You don't have to explain, Damon," Dale said. "I don't expect you to lead me around or always to be with me. That's not even reasonable."

Damon lifted a corner of his wide mouth. "You're not very flattering."

Dale blushed. "That's not what I meant. I . . . I mean, I'd love to have dinner with you, but I understand if you can't."

"Well, at least one of us does," he said with humor. "It's going to be dull."

Dale laughed merrily. "You seem to spend a lot of time going to dull affairs!"

Damon liked the way her eyes changed color with her moods. "My punishment for being so conscientious." Then he sobered, searching her face. "Still, your first night here should be a celebration."

Dale smiled warmly at him. "I believe I had a lovely celebration last night."

"And I don't like the thought of you going out alone. You don't know the city well enough yet."

Dale grimaced. "I'm a big girl, Doctor. I can take care of myself. Besides, I won't go out alone."

"You won't?" he asked suspiciously.

"No. I'm going to go back to the apartment and make my own dinner."

Damon relaxed and smiled. "I thought you said you couldn't cook very well."

"I can't. But there's not much I can do to ruin a sandwich and salad."

That morning, Damon had again hoped to catch her at
the apartment. But he was not early enough. He caught her
as she was walking through the small green square park that
separated the hospital and her building. They'd had breakfast together in the second-floor cafeteria. Hardly private,
but at least they were together for an hour.

Damon shifted his position in the doorframe. He had
taken it for granted that they'd have dinner that night. But
he hadn't really asked her, and when he did, it was to find
she'd already committed herself to dinner with Gloria and
two other nurses. In all good conscience, she couldn't suddenly back out. It recalled to mind his having asked her at
the conference in New Orleans if she was always fair. He
could see now that she was. It was endearing, and maddening.

Damon pushed away from the door and turned to walk
down the hall. After all, she'd been sent for to be of help to
Tai Chin. He himself had convinced everyone of that. He
had no doubts as to her ability as a doctor. But he was interested in the woman. Damon wanted to get at the heart of
her and find the essential woman within. He had a feeling
that no one else had tried before, or if they had, had failed.
She was beginning to respond openly with him, and he
wanted to be the first man to watch Dale Christensen blos-
som into the full flower of womanhood. If he could ever get
her to himself. Damon grimaced ruefully.

Dale had said what she needed was time with her patient
to do any good. Well, she had it, and she was certainly making good use of it. Dr. Anders, at least, would be pleased.

ONE OF THE LAST THINGS Dale had done before leaving the
hospital to have dinner with Gloria Mendez and the others
was to say good night to Tai. Dale told the young girl that
she could always be reached by having one of the nurses
page her. The second thing Dale did was to secure a beeper
from Gloria to use as long as she was in Oakland.

Dinner had been fun and filled with laughter. She had to
bear the predictable speculation about her and Damon because of their common last name.

There had already been the unavoidable mix-ups at the
hospital between her and Damon whenever a Dr. Christen-

sen was being paged. Dale was remembering the most recent mix-up and the one that had been the least amusing.

It had been the previous afternoon. She'd been in the
X-ray lab. The doctor on duty there was helping her read
and interpret several of Tai's charts. There had been a page
in the corridor for Dr. Christensen to please report to first-
floor information. Dale had responded at once, not even
thinking right away if the call was for her or Damon. When
she got to the desk, the receptionist informed her there was
someone asking to see her.

Dale couldn't imagine who it could be.

"She's sitting right over there. She said her name was
Jessica Hilton." The receptionist pointed in the direction of
a waiting area.

Dale turned her head to scan the few people sitting in the
lounge area. There was an elderly Hispanic couple who
were talking to a nursing aide by way of an interpreter. And
there was a lovely blond woman sitting rather haughtily,
examining her red lacquered nails for imperfections. She
wore a lovely yellow sundress, which showed off her slim,
rounded figure gracefully. She was the epitome of feminin-
ity. Dale thought with some amusement that the myth of
the California blonde was alive and well.

The woman's attention was caught by Dale's lilting walk
and her swaying wheat-colored hair. Dale was smiling pleasantly at her, but a look of confusion settled on the young
woman's face.

"I'm Dr. Christensen. May I help you?"

The woman's brows shot up, rounding her lovely sable
eyes, and her lips parted in surprise. Then a disbelieving
chuckle escaped her.

"*You're* Dr. Christensen?" she asked.

Dale began to feel uncertain, and her smile began to
waver. "Yes, I am. Didn't you ask for me?"

Slowly, the woman came to her feet, and then she began
a slow, deliberate scrutiny of Dale. Dale began to stiffen
defensively and to feel very uncomfortable. The woman
shook her head slowly, and a smile of skeptical amusement
made her beautiful mouth look full and red.

"I did ask for Dr. Christensen. But you are *not* what I had
in mind exactly. I was hoping to see someone a bit taller and

decidedly more masculine!" she said with some humor. Dale tried smiling again.

"I think you wanted to see Dr. Damon Christensen."

"Yes, I think so" was the caustic reply.

"I'm sorry. He's not here this afternoon. I believe he had commitments at another clinic."

"Oh, pooh!" the young woman said charmingly.

"He might return later," Dale offered. But suddenly she found it hard to keep up an indifferent, professional front. The woman was gorgeous and obviously knew Damon. Dale suddenly quelled a desire to know how well. She felt awkward, gawky and unattractive standing next to the blonde. Somewhat like a brown moth next to a fully opened butterfly.

The woman shook her curly blond head and let out a sigh. "How horrid of him not to be here."

Dale clasped her hands together demurely over her functional but not particularly fashionable dark skirt. "Would you like me to take a message?" she inquired politely.

The woman once more gave her a considering up-and-down look. "No, I think not. I'll try calling him later." She laughed softly. "The message is personal."

Dale hoped the color draining from her face wasn't evident.

The woman wasn't petite but certainly shorter than Dale, making Dale feel all the more odd. The lovely blonde tilted her head to stare openly at Dale.

"Tell me, how long have you worked here?"

"I don't really work here. I was brought in as a consultant on a special case."

"Oh! Then you won't be staying?"

Dale swallowed. "No, I won't be staying."

The woman frowned. "If you're a consultant, then you're not *really* a doctor, are you?" she asked in amused skepticism.

Dale's mouth tightened, and a lot of very old defenses were resurrected. "I can assure you I am an M.D. I have all the framed degrees to prove it. Unfortunately, I don't usually carry them around with me."

The sarcasm went over the woman's head. "You seem awfully young to be a real doctor!"

A sweet, hard smile spread Dale's mouth, and her eyes were questioning. "Just how old do I have to be?" she asked. The woman was momentarily thrown. She blinked at Dale and shrugged indifferently.

"Well, I'm sure I don't know. Anyway, it's not important." She looked at her watch. "I've got to go."

"I'll leave a message with Dr. Christensen that you were here."

"I'm sure he'll be amused by the mix-up, miss," she said cheerfully, waving a hand eloquently and walking through the lobby door.

"Doctor," Dale corrected too late under her breath.

"I'LL GIVE YOU a ride back to the apartment," Gloria was saying, causing Dale to start.

"Oh, that's not necessary. We're not that far away. I can walk."

Gloria laughed. "You're from New York. You must know that's not a good idea to do alone at night. Especially in a strange city. I have to go by there to get home, anyway. So no arguments."

They said good night to the other two women outside the restaurant. In Gloria's ancient car, they drove back toward the hospital.

"Thanks for inviting me out," Dale said.

"I think we all enjoyed it," Gloria said, and then laughed. "Of course my husband is probably very hungry!"

"What do you mean?"

"Latin men don't really understand that if the wife is out for the evening, they should fix their own dinner. I'll have to go home now and cook something, anyway, for him!" And she laughed softly. "You know, you must be something really special." Gloria chuckled as she slowly drove through Oakland.

"What makes you say that?" Dale asked, puzzled.

"Well, it's more or less known that Damon Christensen is not overly fond of women doctors. Maybe you two having the same last name has made you an exception."

For a split second, something awful dropped like a lead weight in the pit of Dale's stomach. She digested the information as a cold wave washed over her, chilling her flesh.

She couldn't have heard Gloria correctly. If she had, then the implications were terrible. Had she so misjudged Damon Christensen, and been blinded by subtly developing feelings that were new to her? How could she have missed something so basic as how he would think of her professionally? Or was he so clever and deceitful that she hadn't thought to question.

"Is there any particular reason he might feel that way?" Dale asked in a low voice, trying to keep it steady.

"Well, he once said he'd only ever seen two kinds; the hard, overzealous ones who have to prove they're just as good as everyone else and the ones who are overemotional and have to prove they're just as good as everyone else! You must fall somewhere in between. He worked damned hard to convince the board to let you come."

"*He* did? You mean, Dr.... Dr. Christensen was responsible?" Dale asked in a bleak voice.

Gloria glanced, confused, at the other woman. "Why, yes. Didn't he tell you?"

From the tight look on Dale's face, the compressed lips and wide eyes, the nurse knew he had not. In fact, Dale didn't seem at all pleased by the information. Gloria was not normally a gossip, and seeing Dale's stricken face she now knew why.

"*Ay Dios*!" Gloria murmured. "I'm sure it was an oversight."

Dale remained silent.

"Besides, you must be very good, or he wouldn't have troubled himself. Three thousand miles is a long way."

"Yes," Dale responded dully, thinking that Damon had no idea of her worth. None whatsoever, she thought in dismal, bitter disappointment.

DALE HAD WASHED her face so often in cold water to remedy her puffy, tear-ravished face that the skin felt tight and drawn. It was an absolutely gorgeous day, and she wondered bleakly how her spirits were going to survive it. But survive it she would. She'd done so before for far more painful reasons than someone's mere deceit. But Damon was no longer just anyone. The hurt wasn't going to kill her. It only felt that way.

Dale had cried so much that she got cramps in the middle of the night. Damon Christensen was actually making her sick! But oddly, even in her anguish, her traitorous body knew an aching desire to be held, comforted and reassured by him. She wanted her worst suspicions proved false. There was more she expected of him, too; respect, of course, but also something abstract that her now-hurt pride wouldn't identify and admit to.

Dale checked her hair and face once more before leaving the apartment. To her own eyes, her hair looked dull and wild. She wished she knew the art of makeup to hide the telltale blue shadows under her eyes, the sallow cheeks and drooping mouth. She settled for a dab of blusher, which succeeded in making her eyes look rounder and larger and empty.

Thankfully, Dale avoided seeing Damon the entire morning. But her luck ran out just after lunch when she found him standing outside her office door. Her heart suddenly thudded in her chest when she saw him, but she tightened her mouth and resolve and, lifting her chin stubbornly, walked toward the door.

Damon smiled immediately upon seeing her, but the cold expression on her face stopped him instantly, and the smile quickly faded.

"Hello, Doctor," she said distantly, and walked right past him into her office.

Damon, momentarily stunned, followed her with puzzled eyes. Then it occurred to him that maybe something had happened to her. Coming out of his shock, he quickly stepped behind her. He took hold of an arm and pulled her around to face him. He scanned every square inch of a face that was closed and looked at him as though he were a stranger, or an enemy.

"What happened?" he shot at her sharply. "Are you all right?"

Dale twisted her forearm up against his wrist and broke the hold he had. "I'm fine," she said evenly, bracing herself against the concern in his voice and eyes. Dale limped that morning, not walked, around her desk and sat down to open a folder, consciously ignoring the man standing opposite her.

"What happened?" Damon asked again, changing his voice from concern to low, quiet inquiry.

Dale didn't look up. She turned a page in the folder. "Nothing. I'm just a little tired, and very busy, if you want to know."

Dale's heart pounded and raced, and her body felt overheated being in the same room with him.

Damon's jaw tightened, and his speculation grew. He reached over and closed the door. Dale looked up finally to catch the action. Then Damon slowly leaned over her desk, closed the folder in front of her sharply and braced both hands flat so she couldn't open it again.

"I want to know what happened, Dale," he stated rather than asked this time.

Dale looked directly at him, and Damon's probing eyes grew puzzled all over again at her expression. She was like a woman he'd never seen before. There was something tightly controlled and aloof about her.

"I had a very interesting conversation with Gloria Mendez last night."

Damon stood up again and put his hands into the pockets of his lab coat. "About what?"

"You," she said quietly, dangerously.

"Oh?"

"Why didn't you tell me that it was you who wanted to have me come to California?"

Damon frowned, and his eyes narrowed. "Why should I have? The important thing was, you came."

"Do you mean to tell me this was a farce? A selfish, thoughtless means just so you could satisfy your male ego?" Dale asked incredulously, her anger growing in proportion to her dawning realization of what he'd done.

Damon's mouth straightened, and his eyes were sharp and bright in his own growing anger. "Are you suggesting that I...I tricked you into coming here?"

"What would you call it, Doctor?" Dale lashed out, her stored anger of the previous night at last venting itself.

"You've met Tai Chin. She's a reality. Do you call that a trick?"

"You used her! You used *me*! You could have gone to

your own people right here to treat her. Her injury is no better or worse than you or I have seen.''

"We could have handled that, yes!" Damon nodded in admission, his face pale and suddenly angular, the skin seeming to tighten over his bones. "But we couldn't reach her here and here!" he stated, pointing to his head and heart. Her career, and therefore part of her life, is hanging in the balance. You could help her in that way.''

Dale's voice went calm and quiet. "How could you know that, Doctor? You've never seen me work. You know nothing of my credentials and, until two months ago, didn't even know I existed!''

The accusation took hold and settled on Damon like a heavy blanket. Some of his indignation left him, and he blinked at her, having no real answer.

"I asked Boris Teller," he admitted finally. "I called him in New Orleans.''

Dale blanched. "You . . . you got Boris involved in this?" Her voice thinned.

"I told him we had a case here that maybe you could help with,'' Damon said evenly, carefully watching her now.

"That's what he told me. But he never mentioned you'd be here or that you were involved.''

"Maybe he didn't think it was important. Would knowing have made a difference in your decision to come?''

Dale swallowed, and for a moment her eyes looked hurt and pleading. "I don't know," she whispered honestly. "But you didn't have to lie to me.''

"No one lied to you, Dale.''

"All right!" She brushed it aside impatiently. "But you didn't tell me everything. You deliberately kept all the facts from me. Why?''

Damon looked at her, his jaw tensing. Color came back to his face, and his eyes began to soften. Once more he leaned over her desk, bringing them close to each other.

"Because you wouldn't have come if I'd said I wanted very much to see you again. I haven't forgotten New Orleans.''

Dale blushed and dropped her eyes, unable to deal at that moment with the look on his face. She didn't want to bend toward him. She wanted to be angry.

"And I don't believe you've forgotten, either. If you're honest, you'll admit it."

"That has nothing to do with this!"

"You're wrong."

"Damn you!"

"Why? Because I've stirred up feelings in you that you're afraid to feel? Do I make you scared and nervous and insecure? Well, that's what happens when you begin to care," he said astutely but not unkindly. "I for one am glad you're here. I told you so, and I meant it."

Suddenly, Damon straightened up again. Surreptitiously, looking small and like a wounded bird sitting huddled in her chair, Dale watched him. Unaccountably, it annoyed him that she seemed now to shrink from him. His anger at her was unreasonable, and he knew it. She had every right to be indignant and suspicious; he'd only been half honest with her. And if he wasn't being so unreasonable, he also would have seen that some of his annoyance was because he'd, in essence, been found out.

Damon took a deep breath. "I've wanted to make love to you since the moment I met you."

Dale laughed sarcastically. "You've made that plain enough. It's the only thing you've been honest about!"

"And if I'd wanted to," he continued tightly, "I could have taken you to bed that last night in New Orleans, and without any protest or resistance."

Dale's eyes widened in disbelief, and she stared at him. "You're crude!"

"Not crude. Just honestly and openly admitting that I want you."

Dale dropped her head, and her chin quivered. She was now confused and ambivalent in her feelings. "Stop," she pleaded weakly.

"You weren't ready for that," Damon persisted. "You weren't trusting your own feelings yet."

Dale stood up and hurried around the desk. She needed air to breathe. She reached for the doorknob. Damon grabbed her wrist to halt her. He pulled her against his body, but Dale twisted, and it was only a shoulder and part of her back that pressed to him. Damon's arm clamped tightly around her waist, not letting her move, and he continued to hold her wrist, not letting her reach for the door.

"Let me go, Damon. I don't want to hear any more—"

"Listen to me!" he said urgently. "You are very attractive and very desirable."

"No," she whispered brokenly, feeling his wide, warm mouth press against her temple, rubbing into the fine hair. A sudden quaking began in her middle and started spreading to all her limbs.

"I want you." The hand on her waist loosened and slid to her hipbones. He pulled her around to face him.

Dale's breathing shortened. She tucked in her chin, but Damon released her wrist to reach and cup it and raise her face. Quickly, he bent to take her mouth, stopping the angry words, the hurt feelings, the unsure protest. He was skilled and precise, kissing her with a lazy ease that was meant to stroke and soothe and obliterate.

To her own horror and frustration, Dale felt herself melting, giving in to his power. She fought his deliberate, tantalizing embrace, wavered, momentarily lost the battle as she responded, and finally stiffened and jerked away in a resurgence of will.

"I never should have trusted you," she whispered brokenly. Damon let her go.

"That's how people get to know each other."

"Never!" she lashed out at him. Her anger made her eyes change to hazel. "You know nothing about me!"

Damon sighed bleakly. He swept his fingers through his tumbled hair and let out a sigh. "Maybe you're right. The woman I want to make love to is bright as sunshine and warm and a little shy. That's the Dale I want. But there's another one who hides behind being a doctor and a slight limp and is too cautious."

"I don't come in parts, Damon. My being a doctor is a fact." The mention of her leg was offhanded, but it struck a sore nerve. Dale flushed deeply. That slight limp had stood in the path of many things she never had a chance to experience. "And I have every right to be cautious," she went on. "Men like you have...have taught me a good lesson. I don't need your pity."

"Believe me, pity is the last thing you inspire in me!" Damon murmured.

Dale struggled between her pride and an already awakened sense of need that would not now go away but didn't know where there was for her to go with so many raw, untried, painfully exhilarating feelings.

Instinct told Damon not to touch her again, while every part of him wanted to hold her and apologize. And yet another part of him knew it was time to get beyond all barriers. He wanted her. And he wanted her to know it. Tentatively, Damon put a hand to her neck and stroked. Dale stood stiffly, fighting him again. Damon let out a sigh.

"Was it really such an awful risk," he asked softly, "to find out if New Orleans was real or not?"

She turned curiously sad, questioning eyes to Damon. "What do you know of risks?" she asked softly in a hollow little voice. "You have everything. You want honesty from me when you haven't been completely honest yourself. You want surrender without any giving. You want to use what I do without *knowing* what I do, or why." Dale blinked and focused and looked more carefully over his alert face. She watched as her words of truth registered. But it was a small conciliation to be right. "You have Jessica Hilton. And you want me, too."

Damon's jaw muscles worked, and the area around his mouth went white. She had struck home.

"What gives you the right to have everything your way?" Dale asked now in a perfectly reasonable voice. And it grew quiet and soft, merely curious and searching. "Why didn't you tell me about Jessica?"

Damon put his hands into his pockets, jingling the coins, finding the larger one she had given him. He shrugged his shoulders. "There was nothing to tell," he said sternly, looking directly at her. "Jessica has nothing to do with you."

But Dale had, of course, guessed that Damon and the beautiful woman Jessica Hilton had been lovers. Probably still were, she thought in miserable defeat. She felt as though she'd never stood an honest chance.

"I don't think Jessica would agree," Dale told him softly.

"Jessica and I are just friends," Damon insisted.

If it was true that they were just friends, then only Damon thought so. Dale took a deep breath and turned away from him.

"In any case, it doesn't matter. It's none of my business anymore. I think I can see what happened."

"I don't think you do," Damon put in tightly.

"Yes, I do! It's called burning your candle at both ends!" she accused him.

Damon's jaw clenched. "I wanted to see you again. I make no bones about that. But that's not the only reason you're here."

Dale lifted her chin proudly and turned so he couldn't see the trembling of it as he effectively put her in her place, killing her own secret hopes.

"Put your indignation away, Doctor. At the moment, it's out of place." Damon jerked the door open angrily. "I believe you have a patient waiting to see you!" he reminded her. And then the door swished closed gently behind him, and Dale was left feeling more alone than she'd believed possible.

Chapter Eleven

Madge Christensen made her way from the kitchen with a glass of fruit juice for herself in one hand and a cup of coffee for Damon in the other. On top of the coffee mug was also balanced a small plate piled with some of her freshly baked cookies.

"Here you are," Madge said to her son.

The chair Damon was leaning back in came down softly on all four legs, and he sat up straight to accept the plate and cup. "Thanks," he murmured absently, and went back to staring blankly into space, somewhere over Madge's garden wall.

"You need a haircut," Madge said conversationally. His hair and its length was a long-standing bone of contention between mother and son ever since Damon was a teenager. While it used to spark rebellious arguments from him years before, it was now only a private joke. Normally, Damon would throw his mother an affectionate smile, remembering the battles. Right now Madge wasn't even sure Damon had heard her.

Madge settled into her own chair and looked out over her small yard. It was an elevated piece of land in North Oakland that afforded her a stunning view of San Francisco and the Bay beyond its western borders. She had seen the Bay under every imaginable condition over the years. And so had her two sons, raised in that house. The elder, Peter, had always wanted to explore beyond that stretch of water, wanting to know who and what was on the other side. At that very moment, he was off being a journalist in a part of the world somewhere no one had heard of yet. Damon, on the other hand, seemed to have everything he wanted right there. And it was only recently that he seemed to prowl and become restless, as if wanting something to be different or something to change.

"How's the new consultant working out on your case?" Madge asked.

"Mmm..." was Damon's noncommittal comment as he popped a cookie into his mouth and crunched. Madge looked at him quizzically, his response making no sense and proving that his mind was elsewhere.

"What's she like?" Madge tried again.

Damon went back to tilting his chair on two legs, rocking it back and forth, as he did habitually as a youngster. "She's got green eyes...." A hand came up next to his ear, and the fingers twisted and wriggled. "And she has kind of light-brown hair. The color of wheat. You know what I mean."

Madge raised a brow in amusement, alert to her son's odd answers. "No, I'm afraid I don't." It wasn't exactly what Madge had in mind when she asked what the young woman was like. Still, the response was rather telling. "How does she get along with the patient?"

Finally, Damon focused on his mother, seriously considering the question. "Very well. They spend a lot of time together. She's met with the girl's parents and her coach and discovered a number of interesting things."

"Really? Such as?"

"First of all, Tai's father is very angry that this accident happened when it did, preventing his daughter from competing with the team this winter. He's taken it almost as a personal loss." Damon drank the rest of his coffee and frowned at the dregs in the bottom of the cup. "I don't think he'd ever say so, but he's very disappointed in Tai for not being more careful."

"That's a shame," Madge said with feeling. "After all, it's hardly her fault if a car goes out of control and pins her to a wall. She's lucky to be alive!"

Damon shrugged. "Well, Tai is an only child. Her parents had her rather late in life. They're banking a lot on her accomplishments. They've seen to it that she's had the best training. It will all be lost if she can never skate again."

"That's a horrible attitude," Madge said wryly.

"Yeah, but unfortunately you'd be surprised how many

parents feel that way about their talented children. They place a lot of pressure on their kids to do well, and produce. Tai was national champion two years straight for her division and age group, and she placed second in the international finals last summer."

"Poor dear. She must be bitterly disappointed herself."

Damon looked at his mother. "But that's the whole odd thing about her case. I'm not so sure that she *is* so disappointed. And that might be precisely why we haven't been making progress with her up to now."

Madge frowned and sipped from her juice. "I don't think I understand."

"Well, as long as her leg was severely injured and she was off the team, she didn't have to think about it. She didn't have to train or compete or make any decisions about the team for years from now. In other words, the pressure was off!"

"But surely she does want to get better."

"Oh, of course! The question for Tai was, however, how much better. Enough better to work and compete again? Or enough better to just lead a normal life?"

Madge continued to stare at Damon. Finally, her brows cleared and, seeing the logic of it, she smiled in understanding. "Now I see what you mean."

Damon sat back and popped another cookie into his mouth.

"But surely Tai didn't tell you this herself. How old did you say she was?"

"Fifteen," he mumbled around the cookie.

"She didn't work all this out herself. At least not consciously." A kind of amazed faraway look returned to Damon's eyes for a second.

"Dale helped her."

"Dale?" Madge questioned.

"The consultant from New York."

"Oh, yes," Madge said, but she was thoughtfully watching her son. It was the first time in recent memory that Madge could recall hearing actual awe and a certain surprised admiration in his voice.

"Is Dale the one with green eyes and kind of wheat-colored hair?" she asked in a voice quivering with laughter.

Damon stared blankly at her. "What?" he asked, truly not understanding what she meant.

"Oh, never mind!" Madge laughed. "So...tell me some more about this miracle worker. What's going to happen now?"

Damon frowned into the cup again and swept a free hand through his hair. His mother grimaced lovingly at him. "I don't know," he said softly in his deep voice, his thoughts at that instant veering along entirely different lines. Then he jerked upright in his chair and blinked. "I mean...Dale thinks that she needs to find out from Tai what Tai wants to do. That will determine the next step in the treatment."

"Isn't that odd?"

"What is?"

"That she would ask Tai."

Damon laughed derisively. "That's what I said. Tai's whole future may depend on an operation. Why shouldn't she have a say?"

Madge thought about it, and finally chuckled. "Why not indeed?"

Damon slouched back in his chair. He locked his hands behind his head and went back to his rocking, staring out beyond the garden. His visions for the moment were of a slender female doctor moving through the hospital corridors with bouncing wavy hair and an uneven gait. With at least a pleasant smile for everyone and laughing eyes and time for a fifteen-year-old patient, but only hurt looks for him recently.

Damon also remembered the phone call he'd received from Jessica the evening he was to drive into San Francisco for the board meeting. Jessica had been probing and inquisitive about the new Dr. Christensen she'd met that afternoon, and asking why he hadn't told her about her. It was precisely that conversation that had alerted Damon to the change he was going through, just as his return from New Orleans had marked the change in his relationship with Jessica. At that moment, he realized that their relationship was at an end. When Jessica asked if she could accompany him to San Francisco, he said no. And when she poutingly threatened to accept the dinner offer from an interested admirer, Damon wholeheartedly approved. It was time to start the wheels of change before things got complicated. But they already had.

"Mom?"

"Yes, dear."

"Why didn't you ever become a doctor?"

Madge wasn't sure she'd heard right. She sighed. "I suppose you have a perfectly good reason for asking me that now?"

Damon lifted a shoulder and spread his hands. "You were a nurse before you married Dad. According to him, you were a damned good one. Why didn't you go all the way?"

Madge laughed and twisted more comfortably in her chair. "I went as far as I wanted to. Don't forget in my time it was still unusual for a woman to train to be a doctor. You had to be twice as good and twice as determined as any man."

"I'm not so sure it's changed all that much," Damon said thoughtfully. "But didn't you ever think of it at all?"

"No, dear, I didn't. Being a doctor meant being almost nothing else. It takes a lot of time and a lot of work. You should know that. I've heard Jessica complain enough recently about how little she gets to see you."

Damon's eyes darkened, and he grunted.

"And quite honestly, I also wasn't sure I could handle being ostracized by my male colleagues. It was bad enough being a nurse at times. Being a female doctor would have been masochistic!"

Damon wove his strong male fingers together and stared down at them, his jaw working in unconscious tension.

Madge tilted her head. "Also, Damon, it's pretty lonely. That's exactly what a woman doctor would be. Any man under her in position or profession is going to be threatened. Any man on her level is going to be threatened and skeptical. And her superiors are going to be threatened, skeptical and patronizing. It's an almost no-win situation."

"You would have been a good doctor," Damon finally said seriously. But Madge shook her head and laughed softly. "I was a better nurse. And besides—your father might never have married me if I had been a doctor!"

Her meaning became clear. Then he laughed as well.

"Why did you ask me that?" his mother wanted to know now.

He thought a moment. "Just curious, I guess. I don't know many women doctors. I don't know how they think...or feel. They're almost a breed apart."

"But they're not!" Madge contradicted. "They're only female. That's the only difference. What makes you think they *doctor* any differently just because they're women?" Madge had a strong feeling that all of this introspection suddenly had to do with Dale Christensen. She wondered what Dale had done to put her son in such a dither and set him back on his heels. Whatever it was, Madge was sure she was in favor of it.

"So," she began, picking up her empty glass and moving to get Damon's plate and cup, "I hope Dr. Dale Christensen is working out. I hope she's everything you wanted." And she disappeared into the house.

There was quite a long pause after Madge had gone, because it took time for Damon to fully comprehend his mother's words. "I think so," Damon said mysteriously to the empty garden and the Bay beyond the wall.

THE FIRST WEEKEND in Oakland had not been as bad as Dale thought it was going to be. She'd imagined two days of awful quietness in an apartment that wasn't hers, in a city she'd never been to before, where she knew virtually no one. At home she would have gloried in two days alone in her house to fool around in the garden or catch up on reading and small tasks around the house. Instead, she had spent extra time at the hospital working out a design for a joint replacement for Tai. She calibrated, measured and modeled until it seemed to work against markings from Tai's X rays. Then she'd gone to the lab and spoken to the supervisor about the best way to have the model reproduced in the synthetic materials she wanted for the actual operation. All of it could have waited until the start of her second week, but she didn't want to risk being in the apartment if Damon called. She wasn't sure how she'd have responded if he had. But Dale only made matters worse for herself by speculating whether he'd called in her absence.

For the next week Dale attempted to block out the awful

sense of humiliation at having been so duped and to try to stop remembering the feel of being very close to Damon. She didn't want to realize that her sense of fear of him was knowing that he was capable of making her feel things that before him had been unknown to her. The last thing Dale attempted was to work harder with Tai so that she could go back home to her own life in New York.

Dale's findings about Tai's true feelings for amateur competition had been a major breakthrough in working with her. And when Damon had stopped by her office one morning to ask, coolly and professionally, if she'd made any progress, Dale had coolly and professionally explained her findings. They'd discussed Tai for almost half an hour, but Damon had stood staring at her so intently that Dale had begun to wonder if he'd heard anything she'd said. Then Damon had merely nodded and said a vague "That's fine" before going down to see Tai himself.

Tai's coach additionally confirmed Dale's theory. He'd told Dale that Tai was a champion by virtue of very hard work and determination. But he stated that she didn't have the competitive drive and ambition that marked a willingness to do whatever was necessary to win and stay at the top.

"I'm sorry this happened to her. She stood a very good chance of at least capturing the silver medal at next October's games. But maybe this is better. She can do something else with her life. Something she really wants to do."

When Dale had asked Tai, the something had been to be a doctor. Dale was hesitant, somehow understanding that part of Tai's consideration was their friendship. But Dale didn't want to influence Tai's life in that way. She had been casual but graphic in explaining that the years of schooling and work involved didn't leave room for much else. The narrative had served to make Tai decide to think about it a little more before she made any decision.

Tai had looked at Dale for a moment with a question in her shining dark eyes.

"What is it?" Dale asked as she changed some of the leg dressing.

"Well," Tai replied, "I was just thinking that since you've already finished school and you're already a doctor, then you can still get married."

Dale grinned at Tai's simple logic. "I suppose that's true. Except for one small hitch."

"What?"

"Who would I marry?"

Tai thought a second. "Well, you could marry Damon. I think that would be very nice."

Dale blanched, and her heart skipped a beat. "Do you?" she asked in a weak, curious voice.

"Sure. Don't you?"

"I haven't really given it any thought. We...we just work together, after all."

"I know he likes you."

Dale stopped what she was doing to look at Tai. "How do you know that?"

"He comes by to say hello, and we talk. He always asks about you." A thought occurred to Tai. "Doesn't he talk to you anymore?"

Dale dropped her eyes. "W-we have different schedules. I...I don't see him very much these days."

"I told him he should have breakfast with us sometime. I told him I was sure you won't mind. You wouldn't, would you?"

"No, of course not." Dale smiled, her enthusiasm cracking around the edges.

But Damon never did take Tai up on her offer, perhaps sensing that the time was not right yet. Occasionally, Dale caught sight of his tall, handsome body as he walked with long strides down a hall. His lab coat would flap open in the breeze he created, and his tie was invariably pulled askew around his neck. Once they nearly collided outside a lab and had stood staring in surprise at each other. Dale's bright green eyes signaled a fleeting light of joy before fading to wariness. Damon's grew warm and softened at her youthful prettiness.

"Dale, I..." Damon had begun, but suddenly breathless and unnerved, Dale had moved around him.

"Excuse me, please," she'd murmured.

Damon watched her go, sweeping his hand in frustration through his wild hair.

Another afternoon Damon came by her office and heard laughter from within. Dale was on the phone, and from the conversation he surmised the other party was a young boy. Someone named Barry. A cast was coming off his leg soon, and he wanted to know if Dale would be there to do it. Damon listened as Dale promised that she would try, adding she would be back in New York when he began his work with Frances McCann. Dale finally got off the phone with a lingering smile as Damon cautiously stood in the door.

"I didn't mean to eavesdrop, but it sounds like he's very excited about having a simple cast removed."

"It's a little more complicated than that. We more or less have a bet that this time next year he's going to be playing on a Little League team. Getting that cast off is only the first step toward that."

Damon pursed his lips. "And I suppose you're going to supervise his work?"

"Of course," Dale answered, as if it were a foregone conclusion that she saw through all of her cases until the end.

"I thought so," Damon murmured with a slight smile.

"What do you mean by that?" Dale asked suspiciously.

"That was a compliment, Doctor," he said oddly. Then Damon waved briefly and left.

It got to a point where Dale was no longer consciously angry at Damon, although a strange hurt and pain around her heart persisted. She started looking for him again around the hospital center and then, when she finally would see him, could only smile shyly and avoid his eyes.

Damon could detect the thawing in her and was glad. But he was also cautious not to rush her. He'd already put his foot in his mouth once, and he didn't want to risk another conflict with Dale. He wanted something entirely different from her than a cold shoulder. Damon kept remembering her accusation that he had everything. That everything came so easy to him—and he took it all for granted. That, coupled with the conversation he'd had with his mother, had enlightened him uncomfortably. Dale Christensen was not like any other woman he'd ever met and wanted. And his big mistake had been in treating her as if she were. His second big mistake had been in not taking her seriously. The words of Dr. Boris Teller came back to haunt Damon many times during those long two weeks when he and Dale walked wide circles around each other. It was as if her very simplicity and straightforwardness were pointing an accusing finger at him and saying, How dare you be so presumptuous! That had been a thought-provoking, frustrating time for Damon. But he'd come to realize that without either he stood no chance of learning any more about Dale and no chance of a reconciliation with her.

Then, finally, it was two unrelated events that made him realize what a total idiot he'd been. One evening he'd caught a glimpse of Dale dressed in a lovely spring dress of mauve silk, obviously on her way to something special. Her hair was tied back into a loose, full, wavy ponytail with a wide pink ribbon. There was no sign of the daytime professional. At that moment, she was alluring and beautiful—and she was going out with someone else.

"Dammit!" he'd ground out under his breath. Damon was beside himself with the thought that perhaps she'd gotten involved with someone else. He wondered if he'd already lost his chance with her. But the very idea of her being intimate with another man tormented him unmercifully.

The second event was the Friday and Saturday when the emergency room erupted into harried activity. Dale had gotten a call that she was wanted in the emergency room on the first floor. She arrived to find it filled with minor emergencies, as well as more traumatic ones, being wheeled in practically one on top of the other. It was a madhouse.

"Doctor..."

Dale turned from the confusion to Gloria Mendez. Gloria took Dale's arm unceremoniously and pulled her into a treatment room. "Dr. Christensen has been yelling his head off for you. He insisted he needed you down here."

Dale nodded and quickly went into the room to find a screaming two-year-old child wriggling while Damon attempted to place a brace on the child's neck and back. A pale young woman of no more than twenty was huddled in the corner, staring helplessly with rounded eyes. Dale at once went to the child and began murmuring soothing, low words and sounds.

"You're here," Damon said unnecessarily and with relief. "Could you hold him. He was on a motorbike with his mother when she took a spill. The boy might have a back injury. I want to get X rays, but he's very scared and won't lie still." Damon continued to work as he talked.

Dale nodded and continued to talk to the boy. Soon the crying was a whimper as she kept up a low flow of words. Damon only registered part of what she was saying. Something nonsensical about the child's freckles being so many stars.

When he was finished, Damon stood with a worried frown on his face. With the youngster now quieted, Dale stepped aside with Damon as he spoke in a low voice to her, sweeping a hand through his hair.

"I think there might be some real damage to his lower back, and I'm concerned about the possibility of internal cerebral hemorrhaging, however slight."

"I'll take this one if you like. I'll stay with him and see to it that a thorough exam and scan are done and all the necessary tests."

Damon nodded. "Let me know when you get the results. I have a broken hip waiting for me now in OR."

"Of course. I'll see about getting him admitted." She turned away to motion for a nursing aide.

"Oh, and Doctor . . ."

Dale turned to Damon once again, her expression bright with alert inquiry. For a moment, Damon's gaze was soft and personal.

"Thank you," he said evenly.

There was a slight pause before Dale smiled slowly. "You're welcome." And then they each went to do the work at hand.

Dale's young patient proved to have the injuries Damon suspected. It took the entire afternoon to see to all the X rays and tests, and still Dale managed a few hours with Tai. But she never left the hospital, and the hours turned over until she lost track of time. When further results showed the necessity for surgery to relieve pressure, Dale stayed with the child throughout, until he was at last settled in a pediatric ward with his frightened mother at his side.

By twelve noon on Saturday, more than eighteen hours after she'd answered Damon's call, everything had quieted down. Dale found an empty chair in the corridor outside pediatrics and slowly lowered herself into it. She closed her eyes for a weary moment and tilted her head back against the wall. She could smell sweat, blood and sickness mixed with medicines in the stale air. She could hear phones ringing and a doctor being paged over the intercom. Someone was crying softly somewhere.

"Doctor..."

Dale's eyes came reluctantly open. Someone tall and dark swayed in front of her blurry vision. It was Damon. Unknowingly, Dale smiled. His eyes were a little bloodshot, too. His hair was ruffled, and his cheeks and jaw were shadowed with a thin growth of beard. His tie was hanging half out of a pocket, and there were splotches of blood over his shirt and lab coat.

"You look like how I feel," Dale murmured in amusement. A tired smile spread across Damon's mouth.

Dale began to struggle up from her chair, biting her lip at the twinge of pain in her left knee. It was aching from long hours of movement and standing. "Have you seen the little boy?" she asked.

Damon grabbed her arm to steady her, and she accepted it. "He's fine. I brought you some coffee." His other hand offered a Styrofoam cup of the dark brew.

"Thank you." Dale sighed, gratefully taking the cup. She took a small sip as Damon's eyes swept over her flushed, tired features to her hair, now a little tangled and wispy.

Dale raised her eyes to his as they stood close to each other in the near-deserted hallway.

"I think you should go and get some sleep," Damon said softly, his voice husky and low.

"I won't argue that," Dale said with a weak chuckle. She tried to walk and had to stop for a second.

Putting an arm around her waist, Damon helped her into an empty treatment room. Then he bent and lifted her clear off the floor and sat her on the table, her legs stretched out in front of her.

Dale didn't protest as Damon pushed up her skirt and bent to probe around her left knee with tender fingers. She let him, suddenly glad to let someone minister to her for a while.

"It's not swollen," he diagnosed. He lifted his head, his

hands moving against the skin of her leg, sending waves of warmth through her. "Just a bit overworked."

"It...it will be fine after a hot bath," Dale said vaguely, watching his jaw tense, wondering what he was thinking just then. Dale dropped her eyes and in fascination watched the sensual movement of his long fingers on her leg.

"Then I suggest you go and take a hot bath," Damon said. He stood up suddenly and turned to dig among some bottles on a shelf. "Take off your stockings," he commanded.

"What?" Dale asked, surprised. Damon turned back, unscrewing a bottle of rubbing alcohol.

"Take off the stockings. I'm going to massage the knee for a few minutes."

Dale didn't move right away. Then Damon grinned wickedly in understanding and turned his back. Dale put her coffee down and wriggled out of her panty hose. When Damon turned back, she watched as he poured generous amounts of the cool liquid onto his palm and then slowly rubbed his hands on her leg.

He was gentle and methodical, unwittingly curing a multitude of ills and hurts with his attention. Whatever holdover of feelings Dale maintained against him from two weeks before completely melted under his able hands. There was a silence between them that was comfortable but also filled with an expectancy. A crisis situation had closed yet another gap and brought them closer to understanding each other.

Damon suddenly stopped, and Dale was disappointed. "That ought to help a little."

"Thank you, Doctor," she whispered.

Damon came around the side of the table to look into her face long and hard. Then he brought his hands up to cup her face, but he only pressed a light, warm kiss to her forehead.

"You do very good work, Doctor," he stated.

"Don't you need me anymore?" Dale asked simply.

Damon raised his brows and smiled at her. "Yes, I do, but not today" was his response. "You're going home to get some rest."

"What about you?" Dale asked with concern.

"I'll leave in a little while. I want to check on my hip patient."

"Then I'll stay with you to help until then," Dale stated firmly, swinging her legs off the table. Damon braced his hands on either side of her to prevent her moving.

"You'll go home and get some rest like I told you," Damon said quietly but sternly. His eyes, searching over her face again, were more personal. A finger brushed back and forth over her chin. "I'm sending someone with you."

"Damon!" she protested, using his name for the first time in a long while.

"I'd take you myself, but—" With a deep sigh he turned away. "I'm sending an orderly with you."

"You don't need to."

"It's my orders."

"I should go and say hello to Tai first."

"I'll tell Tai you said hello and explain why you won't see her today." Then he took her arm and led her out of the room.

Dale took a step and limped again. Damon caught her around the waist. His breath fanned against her cheek. Reluctantly, he held her away from him. Their eyes were now both showing the same apologies and recriminations.

"Are you still sorry you came to California?" he asked in a deep voice.

Dale gave him a small smile. "I was never sorry I came," she answered.

Damon gave her a lopsided smile and released her to call the orderly. Dale wondered if it was really so bad that he'd admitted he'd wanted to see her again or that she'd been feeling very much the same way, too.

Chapter Twelve

Dale heard the buzzer but couldn't respond to it. She wondered why no one else bothered to turn off the beeper. It was awfully insistent, but at the moment she was busy wrapping bandages around a leg, and she still had yards of gauze to go. Dale looked down at her patient, and it was the face of Boris Teller. He was telling her not to bother with him; he'd be fine. He told her to see to Damon. Dale cringed. Wat was wrong with Damon? She tried to hurry, and the buzzer kept on and on.

"All right, all right!" Dale mumbled, turning over and pushing away her pillow. The dream, with its odd content, faded until she was awake. The phone was silent, and she wondered if the sound had really just been part of the dream, but then it started again. It was the doorbell. Quickly, she untangled herself from the bed linens and reached for her thin cotton robe. She only had one arm in a sleeve as she rushed to the door, the other hand attempting to brush her hair out of her eyes.

"Just a minute," Dale shouted as she reached the door in her bare feet. "Who is it?" she asked cautiously.

"Who do you think it is?" came back the caustic response followed by a deep chuckle.

"Damon!" Dale answered in surprise as she fumbled with the lock and pulled the door open partially. She stared at the sight of him as he stood grinning at her rather cheerfully. He was dressed in very faded denims, a gray sweat shirt and sneakers. He hadn't shaved and hadn't bothered to comb his hair. In his arms there was a grocery bag loaded with food.

Damon's grin softened into a smile of pleasure as he took

in her equally questionable appearance. Her beautiful wavy hair was falling all around her face. One of her cheeks had a creased impression from sleeping on the edge of the sheet. She wore a short nightdress with lace straps that was disturbingly transparent and a robe that was either half off or half on. Dale looked just the way he thought she would in the morning, and it had an immediate effect on his senses. He had the impression that her body would be very warm and soft, and he wanted to put the bag down and crush her to him joyously.

"Good morning," he crooned in a husky voice, watching the color deepen in her face.

"G-good morning," Dale murmured, still filled with surprise at seeing him. And, of course, wondering what it meant.

"I come bearing gifts," Damon announced with a raised brow, patting his brown satchel. "May I come in?"

Dale blinked again. "Oh, y-yes."

Damon looked at her. "Are you sure?" he asked at her odd hesitation.

"Yes! I'm sorry. Please come in."

Dale stepped aside to let him inside. She was still rather a comical sight, with the robe hanging half off around her. Once inside the room, Damon turned to look her over with much more thoroughness. His eyes and smile were laced with amusement and something like tenderness. Finally realizing the source of his reaction, Dale came alert, struggling into the rest of the robe.

"Do you know how long I've been ringing the bell?" he asked.

"I thought it was part of my dream. I don't usually sleep so soundly."

"You probably don't routinely work twenty-hour days, either."

"N-no," Dale said, stifling a yawn and again sweeping her hair from her face. "I guess I was very tired."

He tilted his head at her. "What were you dreaming about?"

Dale blushed and crossed her arms protectively over her chest, looking briefly at him. "It...it was just a dream. It didn't make much sense."

He shrugged. "Most dreams don't. On the other hand, some are very telling."

Dale looked openly at him, almost afraid that he'd guessed it, after all.

Damon put the satchel down on the counter. "Come help me put this stuff away," he said, moving around the counter into the kitchenette, pulling things from the bag.

Dale slowly followed, watching in curiosity. "What is all of this? Why are you here?" She looked around for a clock. "What time is it, anyway?"

Damon laughed softly, holding a plastic bag of bright Delicious apples and a container of juice. "In answer to the third question, it's almost ten o'clock Sunday morning."

Dale's eyes widened. "It can't be! That means I've been sleeping more than twelve hours!"

"Good." Damon grinned, giving her the container. "You needed the rest."

Absently, Dale pulled the refrigerator door open and put the orange juice on the shelf.

"In answer to your second question, I'm here to keep you company. I plan on getting you away from the hospital for the day."

Dale looked at him. "Oh, but you can't do that!" she said in agitation.

"What?" Damon asked with a quizzical smile, now handing her English muffins and a couple of lemons. "I can't keep you company, or I can't take you from the hospital?"

"It's just that... I thought I'd spend some time with Tai this afternoon," Dale said, putting her bundles right back on the counter from which Damon had just removed them. He looked from her to the counter and back to her ruefully.

"Tai is having visitors this afternoon. Some of the girls from her team are coming over in a group to see her. I think it will be very good for her. Getting you away will be very good for you." Damon once more gave her the muffins and lemons. "And you're not being very cooperative, Doctor. Put these away!"

Dale did as she was told. "But you haven't told me what all this is for?" She turned and collided into Damon, who held a half-dozen eggs and a small can of ham. There were no clumsy apologies like the first time, but they did just stand and stare at each other. Damon put down the ham and eggs and put his hands on her arms.

"All of this," he began seriously, "is for breakfast." Damon moved his hands up and down the length of her upper arms, letting his hands slide on the soft fabric of her robe. He tried to smile a little, but the fawn-colored eyes were serious and probing.

"Normally, I'd say beware of someone bearing gifts, but this is really a peace offering. I...I was hoping you weren't still angry with me." He watched her.

His words surprised her and she softened toward him instinctively. He was trying to apologize. Dale lowered her eyes from his expectant expression.

"Am I forgiven for being so...arrogant?" he asked softly.

"Of course you're forgiven," Dale whispered at once.

Damon took hold of her chin, his thumb in the shallow cleft. He raised her face, his eyes still questioning. He examined the brightness of her jade eyes, the smooth, glowing features of her pretty face. "But you haven't forgotten it?" he half stated, half asked.

Dale let him hold her chin but dropped her eyes and bit her lip. "Not completely," she admitted.

The sin Damon had committed had been done without regard for her feelings. But there was no way for Damon to know that Dale was not one to hold a grudge. Dale's hurt where Damon was concerned was to a great extent intertwined with, she recognized, the existence of certain feelings for him. But that was her secret.

Dale raised her clear eyes to him and scanned the rakish, unshaven face with its serious light-brown eyes. "I don't suppose you remember those liberal and gallant words you said to me in New Orleans...about not wanting to seem a chauvinist."

Damon didn't respond, but he frowned and his jaw tensed, and Dale knew he remembered.

"You said you could imagine it hadn't been easy being a female medical student. Well, you were right. It was hard. Sometimes it was downright awful. I always had the feeling I had to work twice as hard and be twice as good just to be accepted. Not all of my professors were so blatantly biased, of course. Boris Teller, for instance, was a gem. But the ones who were prejudiced left their mark.''

"But you didn't buckle under."

"I wouldn't have given them the satisfaction."

"Did you want to prove them wrong? Is that why you stuck with it nevertheless?''

Dale shook her head and smiled at his lack of understanding. She wasn't angry with him. Dale supposed it was hard for people to understand situations that they themselves had never experienced.

"No, Damon. I wanted to prove myself right. I knew I could be a good doctor. And I am. It just infuriates me that even now I might still have to show it, again and again.''

"To me, for example," he added softly.

"Yes," Dale whispered, holding his gaze.

Damon let out a self-derisive little sigh, raising both brows in defeat. "Guilty," he admitted.

Dale smiled. "So am I, I guess—of being overly defensive at times.''

Damon opened a hand and rested it along the curve of her jaw and cheek, the thumb again lifting her face. "Then we'll leave it at that for a while," he whispered. Then he slowly bent forward to kiss her briefly. It was just a brushing of his lips against hers. But from the gentle flaring of his nostrils Dale knew he was holding himself back from wanting much more. Damon moved a step back from Dale in the small space, letting his eyes wander to the opening of her robe and the flesh exposed above her breasts.

"Why don't you go get dressed," he suggested in a husky voice. "I'll get started with breakfast." He turned back to the brown bag now, ignoring her.

"What are we doing after breakfast?" Dale asked.

"I'll tell you while we eat," he said. He looked over his shoulder at her, still standing there. He took her by the shoulders, turned her around and guided her out of the kitchenette. Smiling happily to herself, Dale headed for the bedroom.

"Did you bring jeans with you?" he called after her.

"I think so."

"Good. Wear them—and flat shoes."

Dale took a quick shower and quickly dressed. When she emerged twenty minutes later, she was wearing a blue plaid blouse that complemented her eye color, comfortable jeans and beige canvas shoes. Her hair was combed back, and there was a solid blue scarf folded and tied around her head.

There were wonderful smells filling the air of the small apartment. Dale went back to the living room and saw that Damon had set the coffee table with plates, silverware and glasses. He glanced up briefly and looked her over carefully. Apparently satisfied with what he found, he nodded and turned back to the pan.

"You're just in time."

"Can't I help with something?"

"No. Just sit down and get your salivary glands going!"

She laughed lightly and sat on the floor at one end of the square table. Damon began filling the plates with what turned out to be eggs Benedict and sliced tomatoes. He poured the orange juice last.

Dale smiled at him and did a double take when she realized his face was clear and smooth of hair. While she dressed, he'd availed himself of her razor and the bathroom sink. But he hadn't combed his hair. Or had he?

Damon knew she was watching him. He squatted down next to her and, lifting one of her hands, laid it flat against his face. "Okay?" he teased, knowing her thoughts.

"Yes," Dale admitted, blushing, slowly moving her hand against the hard masculine jaw, somewhat mesmerized by the casual personal touch. Sitting down opposite her, Damon grinned.

"Okay, you can start now," he ordered.

Dale lifted her fork. "I'm impressed!"

Damon nodded sagely and stole a humorous glance at her. "You should be."

"But is it as good as it looks?"

"Even better!" he came back, raising his juice glass to her. They both smiled.

He was a good cook, Dale had to admit, finding that a great surprise in someone like Damon.

The juice was a mixture of orange juice and champagne—a mimosa. The lingering bubbles tickled her nose, and she felt as if they were celebrating something. Once again, when Dale asked what he had in mind for the day, he was vague.

"Well, I have to check up on a patient or two. Then I thought I'd give you an auto tour around the city."

Dale frowned, swallowing a piece of ham. "You're going to see patients dressed like *that*?"

He looked at her with a straight face. "They're very unusual patients."

They ate to small conversation, surreptitiously watching each other. Dale felt happy having breakfast with Damon. It made her feel that she was special and that he wanted to be there with her.

Damon's feelings were a little different. In his mind he realized that he'd never behaved in such a manner with or for any other woman.

When the meal was over, they put everything away. Finally, they stood at the counter having coffee, Dale looking affectionately at his casual dress and stance. She was getting used to him and rather liked the way his hair was left to do as it pleased. It seemed uniquely part of him.

Damon suddenly chuckled and ruffled his hair. "You're looking at me the way my mother used to when she thought I needed a haircut. But you're too polite to say so, right?"

"Well..." Dale hesitated. "Maybe a little trimming would just put it in order."

Damon gave her a half-wicked grin. He put down his coffee, went to a kitchen drawer and began rummaging through it. He turned around with scissors in his hand. He presented them to Dale, handle first, as if presenting a choice of weapons. Dale accepted them hesitantly and looked at Damon.

"Okay, you cut it," he ordered.

"Me! But I...I couldn't do that!"

"Doctor, there isn't that much difference between scissors and a scalpel."

Damon abruptly sat in a chair and turned his back to her. He had fully expected Dale to decline at once, thereby ending the subject of his hair. But there was movement behind him, and he felt a towel being draped around his shoulders. And when he felt her hand softly stroke and push and lift his hair, Damon realized with growing alarm that Dale had every intention of going ahead.

With admirable control, Damon sat and listened to the first snip of the scissors and then the next. Slowly, he resigned himself to having his appearance severely altered.

Fifteen minutes later, when Dale stopped with a sigh and stood back, Damon slowly stood up and walked with cautious steps to the mirror hanging on the wall. What he saw surprised him. His hair had not really been cut at all. It still lay the way it always did. But it was neater. Dale had trimmed the unruly ends that tended to curl wildly and given definite shape to the sides and back. He couldn't help the breath of relief that escaped him as he turned to her. He found her grinning saucily at him.

"Scared you, didn't I?"

"Quite honestly, yes."

"Serves you right," Dale said without sympathy, putting the scissors on the counter, "for trying to be so smart. I cut my father's hair all the time when I visit him." And with that grand announcement she left him, for once without any response, and went to get a jacket, a purse and her medical beeper.

Damon's unusual patients turned out to be several injured players of the Oakland A's baseball team. Instead of a little black bag that doctors traditionally carried, Damon used a small yellow knapsack, looking very much like one of the players himself on the way to get ready for the game.

Dale was banned from the all-male enclave of the locker room and placed in the VIP seats on the field, where she waited for Damon. He eventually appeared with more players. There was a lot of camaraderie and friendship there, and for a while Damon even took batting practice with them. Dale watched, enjoying his display of athletic ability, smiling and waving to him once when he looked her way.

As they were leaving, the team gave her one of their jerseys with the home colors. Dale asked if they'd mind her giving it to a young patient of hers, and the players happily added a ball, as well. Dale caught Damon's eyes on her for a moment and was stopped by the warmly expressive light in his gaze. He was impressed by her thoughtfulness and took hold of her hand to give it a squeeze and keep her near him as they finally left the stadium.

Damon covered the city of Oakland almost in a circle. They left the stadium and drove south, catching glimpses of San Francisco Bay. They made their way to Knowland State Park and got out of the car to walk and explore leisurely, Damon matching the pace of his long legs to that of Dale's. They walked and held hands, enjoying most each other's company.

They drove up to the Oakland Zoo, buying peanuts to feed the chimps and elephants but eating most of them themselves. They drove around Mills College and to the high school that Damon and his brother, Peter, had attended. Dale was oddly moved by that site more than any other. It touched so much on Damon and the person he was. Ideas had been formed there, friendships made, futures planned. He showed her the football field, the annex where student dances were held. Dale had a sudden image of a tall, lanky, youthful Damon being part of a real high school crowd with double-dating and varsity sports, school events and fun—all the things she'd missed out on for the most part. The memory was bittersweet. She had not been without friends, and she did participate when she could. But so much had been denied her.

Dale turned to smile up at Damon as they stood next to the annex and looked over a temporarily deserted playing field.

"You must have had a lot of fun here."

He looked down at her, considering. "Yeah, I did. Academics notwithstanding, I passed a good four years here."

Dale tilted her head. "What kind of student were you?"

Damon grimaced. "The usual kind. Basically indifferent. But I liked science and math. They could have kept the rest."

Dale laughed. Damon took her hand, and they started walking slowly toward the stands where hundreds of students sat on Saturdays to cheer their teams on.

"I had one teacher who promised I wouldn't graduate because I never brought my textbooks to class." Dale could imagine his nonchalant attitude, and her amusement continued. "Two others had an ongoing bet as to how long I'd go before getting a haircut."

"Who won?"

"No one. I got through the semester without one. I finally gave in for a summer job I took working in a lab."

Dale smiled at him. "Somehow I can't imagine you being coerced into doing it," she teased.

Damon raised a brow, giving her a half-serious look. "It's only happened once," he said. Dale knew he referred to that morning's haircut, and she felt pleased. Damon turned and squinted out over the field.

"I also never took notes." His hair had fallen back into the careless windblown effect. Dale loved it. "I think I got through my senior year with a clipboard and two sheets of paper. And that was for five subjects!"

She shook her head woefully, her eyes bleary with tears of laughter. "It's a wonder you got as far as you did!"

Damon chuckled. "I did it on personality alone," he jested.

She could believe that, too. She could believe he always had dates and friends and was always involved, if not at the very center of things.

"And what about you?" he asked suddenly. "Did you like high school? Were you a trial to all your teachers? Although I think not."

Dale's smile softened. She took a deep breath and let it out, looking around the high school complex. "Well, for me it was a little different. I liked the academics. I liked reading to find out things. Believe me, I had a lot of time to read! I spent very little time in a classroom; if I was having more surgery, I had tutors at the hospital and then later at home.

"I was never a cheerleader," she joked, feeling Damon's silent, watchful eyes on her. "And I...I didn't date much. It was too difficult maneuvering braces, crutches and canes. You can imagine what a lousy dancer that made me!" She laughed nervously.

Damon came closer and his hand reached up. It slipped under her full, warm mass of hair and curved around her neck. Dale watched him warily, pleading with her eyes for him not to feel sorry for her.

Damon smiled ruefully. "I can tell you from experience that the only thing you missed was not getting your feet stepped on!"

She relaxed under his hand.

Damon's brows knitted in question, and he frowned at her. "I suppose you also never had a guy breathing hot and heavy, pawing you on the front seat of his father's car."

Dale chuckled, biting her lip to keep the laughter and adolescent pain inside. His fingers rubbed her neck. A lovely sensation radiated through her from each of his fingertips. He was watching her with a long, considering light in his eyes.

"Come with me. I want to show you something," he said. His hand moved to the rounded end of her shoulder, and he held her to his side as they walked away from the field and behind the wooden construction of the bleachers. There was a narrow, dim alleyway with a wall behind it that was a part of the outermost perimeter of the entire field. They stopped in the middle, and Damon turned to her. Dale was curious as to what he would show her there, but she looked trustingly up into his handsome face. Damon put his hands on her shoulders.

"We used to call this spot the 'Love Lagoon.' It usually filled with about six inches of water if it rained, and it seemed like it always rained when we played home games."

Dale frowned, not sure where this was leading. Damon pulled her one step closer to him. His voice dropped to a low, deep, caressing timbre and vibrated along her nerve ends in a curious sensual fashion.

"We used to drag our girlfriends back here for a quick heavy-duty kiss or two—fortification against the cold and the possibility that we might lose the game." His arms dropped from her shoulders and closed around her, bringing Dale against the hard, long length of his body. "You shouldn't miss out on everything," he concluded with surprising feeling. His mouth opened and slowly settled possessively over hers.

But there was no groping, no fevered panting of youth or hasty caresses stolen in a moment. Damon took all the time in the world to explore, to rock back and forth over her parted lips, to probe deeply and stroke with his tongue until she was pliant and dizzy and weak.

Dale held to him in surprise, in growing wonder and need. He was so tender, so sure and deliberate, that she surrendered without a second thought, answering his kiss. His understanding had been poignant and filled her with a sweeping of emotion. No one had ever seen before what all those missed carefree times might have meant to her. She'd never told anyone, but with Damon it was very clear she didn't have to. He knew.

And another feeling came alive, rose within her and surfaced. It flashed in Dale's mind and then her heart that she loved this man. She loved his breezy way, his gentle way—and even his offhand arrogance at times. And she loved the way his strong, capable hands, his understanding touched on her—so sure, yet gentle—and healed.

Chapter Thirteen

Damon knew as he sat in his car next to Dale that he was where he most wanted to be. He occasionally glanced her way to watch her scanning the moving landscape outside her window. Every now and then she'd ask a question, exclaim at something she'd seen, or laugh at some of his nonsensical observations. Her face was rosy and velvet in the late-afternoon light. The wind through the car window played havoc with her hair, billowing it around her head in a fantasy of brown-and-blond-streaked locks.

Damon kept recalling the feel of her in his arms as they stood like teenagers behind the bleachers, kissing. But neither his actions nor her response had belonged to emotions quite so young. She'd felt so soft, so good against him that he'd known an instantaneous urge just to stand there and not move for a long time, while, on the other hand, suddenly wanting to take her somewhere quiet and safe and make gentle love to her. And Damon had also realized a protectiveness that was sudden and fierce. He didn't want anything to hurt her—ever again.

That was a responsibility that he had never assumed for anyone before. He had not been completely sure what it meant as his arms had tightened around her, feeling the soft giving of her chest against his. But when he'd felt her begin to tremble, he released her, cupping her face to examine leisurely every facet of it, as if he'd also just discovered her.

Damon reached out a hand to take one of hers, resting in her lap. Dale turned her head to him at the touch and smiled happily. Damon felt his throat tighten and felt a certain exhilaration. He squeezed her hand for a moment and released it.

"Are you hungry yet?" he asked.

Dale laughed. "I was hungry an hour ago!"

"I thought we'd go somewhere quiet and out of the way for a leisurely dinner."

Dale looked a bit concerned. "Oh, but we're really not dressed for that!"

Damon smiled knowingly at her. "Don't worry about it. I know just the place." They drove another ten minutes, the car gradually climbing to the elevated sector of the city.

Dale watched, puzzled, for the kind of restaurant he would bring them to but only saw quiet, attractive residential homes on quiet, clean streets. Damon turned his white sports car into one of the streets and stopped in front of an unpretentious split-level house whose architecture was of Mediterranean influence. There was a car already in the driveway and another right behind it. Dale turned to Damon.

"This can't be a restaurant. I think someone lives here!"

Damon got out of the car and came all the way around to open her door before he said anything. His expression was a bit closed, and he took another thoughtful look at the car in the driveway. A sleek, well-cared-for Mercedes.

"I know the owner very well. I used to live here."

None of this information settled Dale's uneasiness as she allowed herself to be led up the short flagstone walk to the door. But Damon didn't stop there. He opened the door and, holding Dale's hand, moved right into the foyer. Dale had no time to look around as she followed behind Damon, except to notice the comfortable, warm feel of the house and to get a sense of pleasant colors in the furnishings and decorations. Low stools, a rocker, woven pillows, baskets of dried flowers and potted plants.

They continued out through a glassed-in porch and then a yard. It was a small yard with lovely flowers and shrubbery and a view over the city from a corner wall. There were two youngsters playing with a football and an older, attractive woman with a becoming, short haircut who let Damon kiss her cheek and pull her from her lawn chair. And there was the curly-haired blonde, whom Dale had met several weeks before at the hospital. She stood up, also, her eyes riveted on Dale as if to ask what she was doing there. Oddly, it was the very same question Dale was asking herself as she stood uncomfortably alone for those interminable seconds before Damon returned to her side. The two women came forward, with the children approaching in curiosity, as well. Dale somehow smiled as all eyes turned to her.

"Dale," Damon began, lightly holding her arm, "I want you to meet my mother."

Madge smiled warmly and put out her hand for Dale to take. The grasp was firm and friendly.

"Mrs. Christensen," Dale said softly.

"Oh, please! No formalities. I'm Madge to everyone!"

Dale relaxed a little, liking this pleasant, open woman. Still trying to hold on to her composure, she now turned politely to Jessica.

"And this is Jessica Hilton," Damon said evenly. "I believe you met at the hospital."

Jessica suddenly beamed most charmingly at Dale and shook her hand, too. But she had also positioned herself almost against Damon in a familiar way that sent a chill all through Dale when she remembered how close she'd been to him herself not long before.

"Yes, I remember you! How nice to see you again, Miss Christensen."

Damon looked down at Jessica. "It's *Dr.* Christensen," he corrected smoothly.

Madge's brows went up imperceptibly as she looked from her son to Dale.

"Oh, yes!" Jessica chuckled.

Dale spoke then. "Why don't you just call me Dale, and let's forget titles."

"Good idea." Madge nodded her agreement and turned to the waiting children. "Dale, this is Bobby and Tiffany, Jessica's two children."

Dale smiled at the youngsters, a handsome boy of about ten or eleven and a girl of seven who very much resembled her mother. Tiffany looked up openly at Dale and then moved to lean back against her mother.

"Mommy, is she married to—" Jessica's hand covered her daughter's mouth quickly.

"Don't be rude, Tiffany," she said with a nervous laugh.

Damon put his hands into the front pockets of his close-fitting jeans, and only Dale and Madge exchanged rueful, amused glances.

"I hope you're staying to have dinner?" Madge asked Dale, quickly bypassing the child's question. She turned to her son.

Damon's face was closed, and Dale wondered why he seemed so aloof suddenly. Naïvely, she was not fully aware of the tension he felt being between her and Jessica, as Damon was unaware of the uncertainty and doubts that now began to plague her.

"I'd hoped to," he said carefully.

Madge intervened at that point, more or less guessing the dynamics of the situation. "Jessica stopped by unexpectedly. I invited her and the children to stay. We'll have a nice large gathering around the table." She smiled reassuringly at Dale. "It's nothing fancy."

"Please don't go to any trouble," Dale began.

"Nonsense! Damon's been dropping in and out lately, so I'm prepared for any event!" Madge said.

"What's the matter with your leg?" a tiny high voice piped up. All eyes lowered to Tiffany as she stood gazing at Dale, waiting for an answer.

Jessica covered her eyes, wondering in agony what she'd done to deserve having her child embarrass her that way. But no one was paying any attention to Jessica, least of all her daughter. There was only a small pause of surprise, but Dale looked at the little girl and smiled.

"A pile of logs rolled on top of me when I was a little girl and hurt my knee very badly. My leg never got all better, so now I limp a bit."

It was short, clear and simple. No emotion, just plain facts for the little girl to digest. And once told, she lost interest.

"Oh" was her only response before skipping back to her brother and demanding to be tossed the ball.

"It was a very dull story," Dale joked with a slight lift of her shoulders. Madge laughed in appreciation of her sense of humor.

"Bad knees aren't very interesting, I'm afraid. Walt Disney is still her speed!"

"I hope she didn't put you on the spot and embarrass you with a painful subject," Jessica gushed. "You know how children are."

Dale looked at her with raised brows. "I didn't mind at all. She was just being naturally curious." Dale continued to turn her head to look at Damon, and he winked at her from a straight, calm face. Dale smiled in answer. Catching the exchange, Jessica turned an alluring wide-eyed face to Damon.

"Day, if you don't mind, I'd really like to ask your advice on something. Can we go somewhere—private—and talk?"

Dale's smile began to fade. Day? Is that what she called him? How personal—and special. She looked down at her toes and wriggled them in her scruffy canvas shoes, her hair falling forward to hide her face.

"If you insist" was Damon's even response, not at all liking the idea of going off somewhere with Jessica and leaving Dale alone. But he knew Jessica. If he put her off for the moment, it would only come up again later. He turned doubtful eyes to Dale, concerned now about what she would think.

Madge touched Dale's arm, commanding her attention. "I have to see to dinner. Would you like to keep me company, or would you rather stay in the yard?" she asked softly.

Dale gave a wan smile. "I . . . I think I'll stay here if it's all right."

"Of course it is. Make yourself comfortable, and I'll be back shortly." She patted Dale's arm comfortingly and walked into the house. Jessica followed, moving with a familiarity that stated she'd been there often before.

Damon turned to Dale, scanning her face and expression with a worried frown. "I'm sorry. I—"

Dale shook her head and gave him what she hoped was a calm smile. "I'm fine. There's a gorgeous view over that far wall, and I'm going to take advantage of it for a while."

Finally, he gave her shoulder a brief squeeze and also went into the house. A frown replaced Dale's weak attempt at smiling, and she looked thoughtfully after the three retreating adults. Chewing her lip, she slowly made her way to the wall and looked over into the wonder of San Francisco as night approached. But she only registered a little of what she saw. Inside, Dale was assailed by doubts, and much of her earlier joy of that day alone with Damon was severely shaken in the presence of the stunning Jessica.

Dale could see the pretty blond head with its soft fluffy curls as she turned doe eyes up to Damon. And she was so meticulously dressed in sparkling white slacks and a yellow and white horizontally striped top that made her look like sunshine. The small soft hands had been manicured, the nails gracefully tapered and lacquered. Dale looked down at her own slender hands. They were nice hands, smooth, the nails even and rounded at the ends. She couldn't afford the luxury of long nails. She had hands that worked.

Her jeans were well worn and not of a designer cut. Her blouse was not fashionable. Just a serviceable plaid with colors that suited her eyes. Dale wondered more than ever why Damon should trouble with her when there was someone so fantastic and obviously interested in him like Jessica.

"Do you want to play with us?"

Dale blinked and turned around to face Bobby.

"Do you know how to catch a football?"

"I...I think so." Dale chuckled, for the moment diverted.

"Okay, come on," Bobby ordered, turning away to the spot where he'd been playing with his sister. Dale lifted a corner of her mouth in a smile and followed.

Soon she found herself caught up in a three-person game of touch football. It was absurdly uneven, with Tiffany squealing in delight at just being able to catch the ball and making no attempt to score points. Dale and Bobby, however, dodged each other to reach mock goals indicated by a lawn chair at one end of the yard and a potted plant at the other. It wasn't a very vigorous game, and Dale suspected with amusement that Bobby was showing respect for her gender and age. But then he did tackle her before she reached her goal. Dale's toe stubbed over a clump of hard earth, and she went sprawling, with Bobby and Tiffany on top of her. She winced as her arm scraped over something hard and sharp. Tiffany thought it all great fun and started giggling. Soon Dale was laughing helplessly at the sight they must appear, and Bobby, at first aghast that he'd knocked a grown-up to the ground, was soon laughing, too.

At first, they didn't hear the voices from the house, but then bodies were being pulled off Dale, and a pair of familiar strong arms were lifting her to her feet. Dale suddenly thought that Damon always seemed to be pulling her to her feet from some disaster or other, and she laughed all over again.

Madge let out a sigh of relief when she saw that Dale wasn't hurt, and she was surprised by the young woman's amusement over the whole incident. Damon's face had positively gone stiff when he'd heard the noise from the yard and ran to see Dale flat on her back. All he could think of was that she was in some way hurt. But he didn't know what to think when he found all three bodies on the ground in hysterical laughter. She was a bit disheveled, her hair wild and out of place, loose blades of grass on her jeans and blouse, but she was laughing joyously, just like the children.

"Did you hurt yourself?" Damon asked, concerned.

Dale shook her head. "I'm okay. I guess I must look awful!" She began brushing herself off.

Tiffany came over to her and pointed. "Look! Your arm is bleeding!"

Dale lifted the arm to discover a nasty scratch about four inches long on her arm below an elbow.

"I guess I am," she said absently.

"Tiffany, come away before you get it all over yourself!" Jessica said sternly, with slight distaste. Madge bent and retrieved a small hand spade, now rusted and dirty, that she'd given Tiffany months before to play with.

"Here's the culprit," Madge said, holding the spade up.

Damon reached for Dale's arm, but Madge stepped in front of him. "Why don't I take Dale to clean that up. Dinner will be ready in a moment. Damon, why don't you all just go on into the dining room. And see that the kids wash their hands."

Damon started to argue, but a look on his mother's face stopped him, and without further hesitation they did as Madge ordered. She then turned a smiling face to Dale, her eyes brimming over with controlled laughter.

"That's the most fun I've ever seen those kids have. Jessica is so afraid they'll get dirty or hurt themselves.''

Madge led Dale into a small bathroom just off the enclosed porch. Dale sighed. ''That's too bad. Kids are supposed to get dirty and hurt themselves.''

Madge cleaned the arm expertly for Dale, since the scratch was in an awkward place. Dale, for a dreamy moment, recalled Damon's gentle ministrations to her knee in New Orleans and the warm, wonderful feeling his touch had begun in her, which had now developed into something much deeper and stronger.

Dale found herself avoiding Damon's eyes when she reached the dining room with his mother. Madge and Damon took the end seats, and Madge, taking control, sat Dale to his left and Bobby to his right. Dale's knees touched Damon's under the table as she drew her chair in closer, and he gave her a small conspiratorial smile.

Dinner conversation centered around the news Madge had received that her older son, Peter, was due in California at the beginning of June. Dale was suddenly stilled at the announcement, but only because she realized that she would very likely be back in New York by then. She tried to take part in the conversation, but a vague depression began to settle on her as she realized the contradiction in her situation.

She'd never thought she'd fall in love. She'd never thought it would happen so quickly or that she'd feel so sure about it. The love in her for Damon created another person who was called Dale. But she had not yet begun to consolidate that new person into the one who was a doctor with responsibilities the width of the continent away. And, as far as she knew, the love was all one-sided.

Suddenly, Dale knew as clear as day why she'd been so frightened of him when they'd first met. He had the power to arouse her emotions, and she was afraid of the feelings. But now that they were there, real and upon her, she was even more afraid. For what was she to do with them once she was back in New York?

Covertly, Dale looked at Jessica—a lovely woman who had a place there. Dale really was the outsider. She was temporary, and when she was gone, Jessica would remain. Dale began to feel bleak and helpless. How foolish of her to think she meant anything to someone like Damon, who could have anyone he wanted. What was she doing at a dinner table with his mother and one of his female friends?

The delicious simple meal that Madge had prepared refused to go down her throat. Dale consumed three glasses of water trying to make it easier. She answered questions and made comments, but her mind and spirit were elsewhere.

NONE OF DALE'S CONCERNS would have been solved, but at least one question would have been answered if she could have known the gist of the conversation between Damon and Jessica just before dinner. Jessica had asked if he'd been away from the hospital all day, since she'd been unable to reach him there or at home.

"Quite frankly, I've been with Dale all day. I've been showing her some of Oakland."

"That's nice of you, Damon. Showing her a good time before she has to leave to go back home!"

Damon's jaw tensed, and his mouth became a firm straight line. "I wasn't just being nice, Jessica," Damon informed her calmly.

Jessica laughed softly, tilting her head coyly. "If I'd known, I would have been happy to take her around. I just thought she was here to help with a case."

Damon seriously doubted if Jessica would have done any such thing. She was not a mean person, but her thoughts didn't generally run to anyone's feelings but her own. It was a form of protection, and Damon understood that, even though he found it one of her less endearing qualities. He knew Dale's being there went a lot deeper than just the case. But that was not Jessica's concern.

"True. She is here as a consultant. But that's no reason why she shouldn't also enjoy herself." Damon turned back to Jessica and looked hard and long at her.

"And I wanted to spend the time with her, Jessica."

Jessica's eyes flashed, and her chin lifted. "I see," she whispered.

"Do you?" Damon asked, frowning.

"I think I do." She nodded. "Now I understand why you tried to encourage me to see other men. It's so you could see other women."

"Even if that was true, and it's not, I would still feel it's time for you to see other men."

"Well, I have been seeing other men!" she said almost defiantly, but Damon didn't in the least rise to the bait. He only showed polite interest and said nothing. Finally, Jessica stopped her posturing and made an impatient, vague motion with her hand in the air. "Oh, I guess I should have known this would happen."

"What you're looking for is not me," he said softly.

"I'm just finding it a little hard to let go," she said honestly. Suddenly, at that moment, she was the hurt, skittish Jessica he'd first met who'd seen a hard time with an insensitive older husband and was just beginning to enjoy being free of him and attractive to someone else.

"I know that," Damon answered evenly. He didn't want to say anything to embarrass her or make her feel small. They'd had a comfortable relationship on and off for almost two years. But it had run its course for both of them. Damon had known that months ago.

"For a long time I didn't think anyone would ever find me attractive again. Not until you."

"And now men are swarming all over you," he teased.

Jessica shook her head in exasperation. "Aren't you even just a little bit jealous?"

"No, I'm not. You're not in love with me. You never have been. Someday when you're completely over your first experience, you're going to want to get married again."

Jessica listened quietly to Damon's little speech, but she didn't respond to it. "Are you in love with her?" Jessica asked bluntly. There was no mistaking whom she referred to.

Damon crossed his arms over his chest. He felt something he'd never known before. He liked being with Dale. He was a different person when they were together, and he longed to make love to her and discover the womanly passion he knew existed in her. He sought her opinions and depended on her strengths, forgetting quickly that he'd ever held them lightly. She was the only woman in his adult life that he couldn't wait for his mother to meet. Still...

"I don't know" was all he had said in answer to Jessica's question.

DINNER WAS finally over, and Jessica decided it was time to go. But despite Jessica's announcement, Dale stood forlornly to the side as Madge and Damon said good-night to Jessica and her kids. Tiffany hugged Damon and gave him a wet kiss on the cheek. Dale felt dismally aware of not being part of that intimate group.

DALE INSISTED on helping Madge with the dishes. They talked easily and at length about gardens, and they'd almost forgotten about Damon until he came into the kitchen to lean in the doorway, watching them.

"I think he's trying to tell us something," Madge whispered to Dale like a conspirator. "Did you want something?" she asked her son, and watched him scowl.

"Yes, company."

Madge led the way back to the living room. Damon stretched and rotated his shoulders and neck as he walked. Dale realized he had to be as tired as she was. They'd been out all day after having worked very long hours the morning before.

"I see you took my advice and got a haircut," Madge observed, sitting on the flowered chintz sofa and patting a space next to her for Dale.

Damon ran his fingers through his hair, not helping its state any. "Yes, I thought it needed some order," he said caustically, while Dale hid her smile and avoided his gaze.

"Well, it makes you look less like a pirate, I must say!" Madge turned to Dale. "People wouldn't really suspect him of being a doctor, would they?" she asked, smiling.

Dale gave Damon a quick amused glance. "I suppose it doesn't really matter. No one thinks I'm a doctor, either. Even Damon has trouble deciding about me." She laughed easily, but the look she gave Damon was wicked, and he grunted and shifted in his chair.

Madge laughed shortly. "I'm surprised that he would, but he's been known to behave as if he were blind as a bat."

"I don't know if I appreciate being talked about like this!" he complained.

"That's because you have a guilty conscience," his mother said easily, and then turned back to Dale. "Had you always wanted to be a doctor?"

Dale laced her fingers together and pressed them into her lap. She clearly remembered Damon's asking about her motivation in New Orleans. She didn't think about it too much herself anymore. It seemed that doctors and medicine had so long been a part of her life that there had never been anything else. She remembered now that she never had answered him.

"Once I wanted to be an actress. Oh...for about a month. It was after I saw Audrey Hepburn in *My Fair Lady*. But when I tried performing in front of my brother David, he told me I was a terrible actress."

Madge smiled, and Damon watched her thoughtfully. His elbows were braced on the arms of his chair, and his clasped hands rested against his mouth and chin so that only his fawn eyes were visible to her. She couldn't tell what he was thinking.

"Then I thought I'd be a lawyer, because my mother said it was perfectly okay for girls to be lawyers."

"Good for your mother," Madge murmured.

"But I hated fighting and arguing over things. So I scratched that idea. I guess I really became interested in being a doctor while I spent so much time in the hospital. I was fascinated that people could learn to cure other people and save lives. I wanted to be able to do that, too."

There was a silence when she stopped talking, and Dale felt embarrassed and too much as if all eyes were focused on her. But the pause was very slight, and Madge reached to touch her arm.

"I don't think I've ever heard it stated as nicely," she said.

"Or as sincerely," Damon added, almost to himself. And from his eyes Dale could see a spark of light that held— what? Surprise, pleasure, awe? It encompassed her and was private between the two of them. And although it was only seconds long, Madge was completely aware of the exchange, and she smiled complacently.

She very much liked the unpretentious and straightforward young woman who had managed to strip away some of her younger son's arrogance and assurance and pride. Although he was as yet unaware of it.

Chapter Fourteen

Damon and Dale left shortly afterward, remembering that they both had to work the next day. Madge gave Dale's hands a very warm, very affectionate squeeze and said they should get together again soon. Dale would have liked that very much, but she only smiled wanly, realizing that she'd be leaving soon to go back to New York.

In her insecurity, Dale didn't attach any significance to the fact that Damon had brought her home to his mother. In any case, her pleasure in the occasion had been marred by the presence of Jessica.

But Dale liked Madge very much. She reminded Dale a little of Grandma Lacy, her maternal grandmother, who was always so kind and always had a ready smile for everyone. It was lovely to think that Madge's son was someone she could love so much. But Dale's depression gained strength and fastened itself to her. She no longer remembered at what point the protective barrier surrounding her had developed a crack through which Damon had managed to slip in. Perhaps, after having met him, she hadn't tried very hard to keep him at arm's length. And it didn't matter anymore—the damage was done.

Damon had touched her. He had been gentle and caring. And even though his methods of getting her to California were questionable, she was there in part for him and stayed because of him. He had held her within the circle of his arms with passion and had awakened desires she'd never thought she had. Never had she felt more like a woman.

Next to her, Dale saw Damon lift a shoulder and grimace, arch his back and try to slip a hand between it and his seat to rub the muscles.

"Are you tired?" she asked solicitously.

"Yeah, that, too," he murmured. "But I think old age is just beating my brains out!"

Dale laughed. "You're right. You are getting old. I feel fine!" She made a face. "Well, actually, I guess I'm a little tired, too."

"How's your arm?"

Dale touched the sore scratch gingerly. "It's very tender and just starting to feel stiff."

He looked at her again and back to the road. "Look, I'm probably being overcautious, but I'd like to give you a tetanus shot."

Dale nodded. "All right, if you think it's necessary. Shall we stop in at the hospital?"

Damon hesitated. "No, my apartment is closer. I can give you the injection there before I take you back to the complex."

He said it casually, but already Dale could feel the air vibrate between them in anticipation.

"Is that all right with you?" he questioned quietly.

"Yes," Dale answered, although her voice was a bit thin and breathless.

The rest of the ride was devoted to trivialities about the traffic and the city. Damon's building overlooked Lake Merritt, Lakeside Park and the sailboat clubhouse. His apartment was fairly large, with a living room, dining room, off which was a terrace and a small kitchen. There was a long hallway with two more rooms off to the side.

What she saw was simply but tastefully decorated. The colors were predominately blue and brown, with touches of green and yellow. It was an earthy combination. The carpeting was powder blue, his sofa a rich chocolate brown in brushed cotton. There were several framed lithographs in sepia ink of large game animals that adorned the off-white walls. Dale spotted a bentwood rocker she judged to be a real antique, modern side chairs, a glass coffee table and a basket piled with medical journals and newsletters.

The rooms looked like Damon. Open and uncluttered. Comfortable but lived in. There was a sports jacket over the back of a dining-room chair, a pair of loafers under the coffee table, and his lab coat and stethoscope hung on a doorknob. There was nothing she would change.

When they entered the apartment, he said he wanted to check in with his answering service. He'd switched on a light, told her to be comfortable and disappeared down the long hallway. She stepped through the partially opened glass doors to the terrace and looked out over the railing into the night. She was trying to imagine Jessica there, as Dale knew she must have been often. She speculated on whether Jessica fit in and belonged there more than she herself did. Dale had never concerned herself with such comparisons before. The idea of love, and someone loving her, was foreign, unlikely, avoided. The idea of her loving anyone had been exactly the same. Now she was different. Love made people different. It made them want things they couldn't have, be something they couldn't be. Dale wanted to be someone special to Damon.

She laughed softly to herself. She really had changed. Whatever happened to the strong, dedicated doctor who had been too busy for involvements?

Dale wandered back inside and glanced at a bookcase. On top were three framed photographs. One was a picture Dale judged to be fairly recent of Madge. Another showed Madge and an older, strikingly handsome man that could only have been her husband, Damon's father. Dale bent closer to study the image, looking for the son in the father—and it was there. The same-shaped face and jawline, although the elder Michael Christensen's seemed more angular and chiseled. A face of authority and power. His hair was thick and curlier than Damon's.

The third picture showed Damon standing with another man. Perhaps a few years older and slightly shorter. The face was handsome in a sensitive, thoughtful way. Dale knew it was Peter, Damon's older brother.

"So what do you think of my family?" came a quiet, deep voice behind her. Dale didn't turn, enjoying the moment of seeing Damon's family. She felt Damon rest a hand on the small of her back and she smiled at the touch. Whenever he touched her, he brought her closer to him in so many ways.

"It looks like a close, happy family," she responded softly. "Your father was a very handsome man."

She heard a deep chuckle. "My mother would be the first

to agree with you. He was also a damned good doctor," Damon said evenly.

Dale tilted her head. "Was your mother a nurse at his hospital? Is that how they met?"

Damon looked down into her face. "How did you know she was a nurse? Did she tell you?"

"No, she didn't. But I could tell by the way she dressed my arm. There's a certain order to things, and habits are hard to lose."

Damon just stood looking at her. He began to smile as he reached up a hand to curl a lock of her hair around his finger. "She was a private nurse for a patient my father was treating at the time. The patient eventually suffered a heart attack and died. My father persuaded Madge to come work at the hospital. The rest is history."

Dale looked over her shoulder at him and arched a brow. "Sounds vaguely familiar," she said.

"It does, doesn't it?" he commented blandly. Dale turned back to the pictures.

"Damon?"

"Mmm?"

"What's Peter like?"

He frowned. "Peter?"

"Yes. Is he anything like you?"

Damon laughed softly, putting his hand to her back again, rubbing absently against her spine. "And just what am I like?"

"Let's not change the subject!" Dale murmured, poking him gently with her elbow.

"He's thoughtful," Damon began. "Introspective is what I mean. Everything has deep, hidden meanings for Pete. He asks a lot of questions. And he's very serious. I suppose that's why he's a journalist doing investigative reporting. He wants to know everything." Damon looked affectionately at the photo. "We're not anything alike, but we've always been very close."

"Is there nothing deeply hidden for you?" Dale asked seriously in a low voice. "Is everything always so clear and understandable?"

Damon's hand on her back moved, manipulating her to face him more. "No, not everything," he said in a drawl, his voice deep. "Some things I'm not sure of at all. Why did you want to know about Pete?"

Dale dropped her eyes. "I...I just wondered if he had the same kind of concern for people that you do."

"Peter is concerned for the world. I'm a little more selective. And probably a good deal more selfish." He touched his lips to her forehead, and Dale raised her face, knowing he would kiss her. The phone rang.

With a groan of exasperation, Damon released her and sat on a chair, picking up the extension in the living room. It was Dr. Anders, and Damon made a face when he hung up. "Meeting tomorrow morning." He sat looking her up and down slowly. "Now, where were we before the phone rang?"

"I believe you were going to give me a tetanus shot," Dale supplied innocently.

Damon raised a brow and a corner of his mouth. "That's not quite how I remember it, but okay. The shot first." He groaned again as he pulled himself out of the chair and stepped briefly into one of the side rooms off the hallway.

Dale laughed in amusement at the exaggeration of his tender muscles. Damon returned with a bottle of alcohol in one hand and a hypodermic and cotton balls in the other.

"I hope that laugh doesn't mean you're getting hysterical just because of a little needle," he said, putting his supplies on the coffee table and reaching for her arm.

"What little needle?" Dale asked dryly. "I remember them as being about two feet long and very sharp."

Damon laughed, pushing the sleeve of her blouse up. "You were a lot smaller and younger at the time."

"Well, I'm bigger now, and I still don't like them!"

Damon looked at her almost as if he weren't sure whether to believe her or not. But his eyes began to twinkle, and he let go of her arm. "I'll be right back," he said, and marched off down the hall again. Dale frowned after him, but he was already walking toward her with his long stride, the well-developed thigh muscles working under the close-fitting denim jeans. "Now, if I give you this, you have to behave," he said, stopping in front of her.

"Give me what? What are you talking about?"

"First you promise to behave," he said in a stern authoritarian voice, tilting his head back and looking down at her.

Dale pursed her lips. "Oh, all right. I promise!"

Damon produced a lemon lollipop from behind his back. Dale stared at it blankly, thinking he was out of his mind. And then she started to laugh as Damon began peeling the cellophane from the candy. While she was still laughing, he popped it into her mouth. Dale's amusement choked on the mouthful of sweetness as Damon quickly swabbed her arm and administered the shots.

"Every now and then a patient will bring a squirming toddler along to an examination. These are guaranteed to keep them happy for a while."

"How clever of you, Doctor," Dale said softly. Suddenly, she tried to visualize Damon interacting with a child. She imagined him playing and rolling around on a floor with a spirited two- or three-year-old or comforting a tearful hurt. Instinct told her he'd be wonderful and caring. "But are you trying to tell me what a baby I'm being about this?"

Damon grinned wickedly at her. "If I thought you were, believe me, I'd have an entirely different treatment in mind!" Damon stood grinning at her. "Okay now?" he asked.

Dale lifted a shoulder haughtily and turned away. "I was going to offer to give you a back rub in return."

"I could really use a good back rub," Damon said in a coaxing, half-serious voice. "Would you?"

Dale turned back to face him, seeing that he was indeed asking. She took the lollipop out of her mouth and twirled the stick between her fingers. "If...if you like," she said quietly.

"Are you any good?" he asked impertinently.

"I think so. I learned from a physical therapist."

He nodded. "Okay." He walked into the nearby bathroom and came back with a large royal-blue bath sheet. As he shifted the coffee table to the side and spread the towel on the floor, Dale watched, mesmerized, her heart beating faster when he pulled his sweat shirt over his head and began freeing his strong arms from the sleeves. It all seemed to be happening in slow motion in her eyes so that she could openly enjoy the moment.

His chest was just as broad, just as firm and developed, as she'd been able to feel with her hands those times that he'd held her close enough. His chest hair was even and dark across his breastplate, not curly but silken and smoothly flat. It tapered down his torso in a fine, straight, dark line to disappear provocatively below the waist of his jeans.

Dale felt herself go limp inside, and there was a tension in her stomach and groin that was readily recognizable as her own desire for him. He was entirely too virile to be believed, and she wondered if any woman had ever been able to resist him.

Damon tossed the shirt on the sofa and bent to pick up the alcohol. Dale loved the rippling of muscles in his arms and back and the way his stomach stayed smooth and flat as he bent from the waist. He passed her the bottle.

"I'm in your hands, Doctor," he teased, and proceeded to stretch out on the towel, stomach down, his head pillowed on his folded arms. Dale snapped out of her lethargy and knelt on the towel next to him, kicking off her canvas shoes. She finished the last of her candy and put the stick on top of the used cotton swab. Pouring the alcohol into the palm of her hand, Dale slowly and hesitantly began at his neck and the rolling ridge of his shoulders to press with her fingertips.

"Straddle my back if it's more comfortable," Damon said easily. But Dale knew she couldn't bring herself to do something so intimate, even with his say-so.

"It...it's not necessary. I'm fine this way." She lost herself in the wonderful feel of her hands gliding easily over his back. Her movements became rhythmic and steady, rubbing and kneading and twisting slowly over the valleys and planes. He was conditioned and firm—but sore. Every now and then he'd groan softly as she hit a spot that particularly needed working, and she'd stop to give it extra attention.

Dale couldn't help smiling as she worked and listened; there was no other sound between them. It seemed so natural, so right. The silence seemed filled with heated sensuality, with her hands moving intimately over his body. Her active imagination began to wonder what the rest of him looked like. Dale bit down on her lip and slowly expelled the air she'd caught in her throat at the thought.

"Mmm," Damon moaned softly, and Dale's insides tightened. It was a sound of pleasure. She thought of stopping but didn't want to. "You were taught well," he mumbled drowsily into the towel. He grunted and shifted positions slightly.

Dale smiled. "Thank you. I learned so that I could help my kids."

"Will you also stay to help Tai after her surgery?"

Dale's hands stopped. "N-no, I won't. I can't be away from my practice that long. I have other patients," she said somewhat grimly. It was one of the things she realized would have to be sacrificed. But Tai was older than most of Dale's patients and would understand. Dale knew that her going meant leaving Damon, and the sudden constriction around her heart at the thought was painful. It was going to take a long time to forget.

Dale's hands moved again, working their way down his spine to the lower part of his back. She watched, fascinated, as his upper back flexed and stretched.

"I'd almost forgotten," Damon said softly. "You seem to belong at the hospital."

Dale's hands slowed. "But I don't. I'm not indispensable, you know. You could always have done without me."

Her choice of words was deliberate, and Damon reacted to them. He began to lift his body and roll onto his back. Dale sat back on her heels, feeling a twinge of discomfort in the left knee. Already she missed the contact with his body. Damon lay on his back and looked up at her closely, thoroughly, his nostrils flaring and his jaw tensing.

"That was probably true at the beginning," he answered. Then he reached out to take her hands, wrapping his fingers around her wrists. "You haven't been unhappy here," he stated rather than asked. Dale shook her head. "And you will be sorry to leave."

Dale looked at him. His eyes were dark, his mouth curved, and for a frantic moment she thought he could see right into the center of her and guess her secret. Would Damon be able to see the love in her, the love that was meant for him alone? "I will be very sorry to leave," she admitted, her voice low and broken with emotion.

Damon continued just to look at her. Too late Dale realized what was wrong. Too late she saw that her gentle ministrations to Damon's tired back had soothed and relaxed him...and then aroused him. He was almost slumbrous; his look was seductive, his breathing shallow. Dale caught her own breath as she sensed how vulnerable they both were and how susceptible she would be to his lovemaking.

"You have wonderful hands," he crooned, holding her gaze locked in his.

"They—they're doctor's hands," Dale said vaguely.

Damon began to pull her down to him. "They're a woman's hands," he corrected.

Dale had very little leverage, and in any case, Damon was infinitely stronger. He held her firmly, bracing his arms and controlling the descent of her weight until she was lying half across his chest. Her breasts were pressed flat against him.

Dale could see the topaz flecks in his eyes, the faint laugh lines around them and the laugh lines next to his mouth. But there was no laugh and no smile. Only open desire and physical insinuations as their breath mixed warmly.

Damon lifted a knee, and Dale's body shifted until she was virtually nestled between his legs. Her hands clenched on his warm chest, and she gasped when she felt him hard and fully aroused against her middle.

"Dale, nothing has changed. I still want to make love to you."

He was watching her agitation, the slightly parted lips, the cleft accented in her rounded chin. Damon's arms closed around her back, making her undeniably aware of him, of his strength, power and desire. He lifted his head from the floor just enough to ply an experimental kiss from her, his tongue brazenly brushing over her mouth. His hands began to pull her blouse free of her jeans as he worked his hands under the material. His touch evoked a quiver and goose bumps on her flesh before it warmed under his hands. Slowly, she relaxed to enjoy his gentle massage of her back and spine.

Her head seemed to lower of its own will until their lips could meet again, Damon at once seeking entry. He was very slow and methodical, as if he had all the time in the world. But the pace served to build up an expectancy and tension in Dale that made her feel dizzy, as if she weren't getting enough air. She went limp, liquid inside, a nagging ache twisting in her loins that seemed as much pain as pleasure. It made her squirm against Damon. Shuddering with a moan, Damon slid his hands down her back to press the length of her even closer.

Suddenly, Dale desired him unashamedly. Her hand lovingly stroked a strong masculine cheek, slightly roughened with nighttime hair. She wanted to be part of him, feel him deep within to release all her feelings out. He couldn't guess her feelings for him, and she had no hold on him except for the moment. She would be satisfied with that. Nonetheless, she quaked, and Damon knew at once a hesitancy in her against all she was now feeling and wanting. He released her mouth and brushed his lips along her jaw, to her ear. Her heart was pounding against his naked chest.

"What's the matter?" he asked hoarsely. Dale's head shook in the negative, her rich wavy hair fluffy against his face. He rubbed his cheek against hers and, bringing his hands to her rib cage, moved and rolled Dale onto her back, reversing their positions. He leaned back to see into her sparkling green eyes, the face pink and glowing, the mouth quivering from kisses.

Damon felt awe. She just seemed so young lying there watching him with trust, so different from the woman with such hurt pride and indignation of weeks before, when he'd been so thoughtless and stupid. Had a mere month changed so much? He allowed a hand to travel up her torso beneath the blouse and surround a heaving breast. He could see the intake of a sharp breath, feel her rounded flesh expand into his palm. He burned all inside to have her completely. But he suddenly felt the most incredible need to be slow and gentle with her.

"I love the way you feel when I touch you." His thumb could feel her erect nipple through the thin nylon bra. He absently made little circles around it. Dale barely whispered his name before he bent with a groan to kiss her again, feeling her back arch so that he could easily curve her into him.

Dale gave in. She'd decided that she needed to have something of him. If it couldn't be love *for* her, then let it be love *of* her for the moment. Perhaps it would relieve the ache and assuage the need. Perhaps it would obliterate Jessica. Love was a gift, to be given freely, and though Dale knew in the end it could cost her dearly, she wanted to give it to Damon.

But her decision was all for nothing. All at once, Damon forced himself to stop. He lay heavily across her for a long, shuddering, agonizing moment. He gathered her tightly against him to keep them both still and buried his face in her neck, kissing and nuzzling the skin. She smelled sweet, vaguely of honey, flowers and a spring night. He wanted her so badly it was almost unbearable. And he realized that if he continued right now to make love to her, he could have her without question or protest, and that's what stopped him cold.

Now Damon understood what was different. It was, essentially, the way he saw Dale. Suddenly, it *was* important that she think well of him, that she trust him. Damon didn't want her to surrender. In New Orleans he would have settled for that. Now he wanted more. He wanted her to give not because their passion compelled her to but because it would be right with him and good.

His motives, however, had not communicated themselves to Dale, and when he stopped his caressing of her, she grew anxious, seeing it as rejection. Damon let out a great sigh and looked into her puzzled and bright eyes.

"You're having a very strange effect on me," he whispered. Dale blushed and closed her eyes. Damon grinned and gave her a gentle, swift kiss. "That's not what I mean," he said in a husky voice, and boldly pressed his hips to hers. "I mean I've developed a conscience."

He moved to sit up, bringing Dale with him, holding her in his arms. "I'd like nothing better than to have you share my bed tonight. But I've run you ragged all day, and we're both tired." Tensing his jaw against his physical instincts of the moment, Damon began helping to pull her clothing to rights, lingering for a delicious moment with a hand to her breasts.

Dale burned with embarrassment. She had been wantonly prepared to give herself to him. She didn't want to think what it meant that he hadn't made love to her.

"You're right. You have developed a conscience. Either that or—"

Damon cupped her face and forced her to look at him. "I'm taking you home because I care what you think. And tomorrow morning you'd have regrets."

Dale shook her head and bit her lip. "I . . . I don't know."

"Well, I do. I don't want to hurt you."

Dale looked closely at him, letting out a sigh of relief. She was seeing a different Damon. She was pleased that he might care. Pleased that he might think beyond the one night with her. "All right." She nodded, and Damon helped her to her feet. Dale's eyes lowered to hide a myriad of emotions. She spotted a number of coins on the floor at their feet. She bent to pick them up, knowing they'd rolled out of Damon's pocket. Among them was the pewter Mardi Gras coin she'd given him in February. Dale rubbed her fingers over it in disbelief. He'd kept it! Not only that but carried it with him all the time.

All at once, Dale was convinced of his sincerity. Damon was not a frivolous person, though he had a lighthearted sense of humor. He sometimes had an offhanded attitude, though he was not indifferent. He was not sentimental, although there were people and things important to him.

She looked up at him, her eyes bright and questioning. "Damon," she whispered, wanting an explanation.

"I haven't stopped wanting you," he said, taking the coin back. Then, pulling her to him again, he gave her a slow, promising kiss. "The medallion is my raincheck," he said against her cheek, and put the coin back in his pocket.

Chapter Fifteen

Dale ducked her head, trying to see into Tai's partially averted face. Their morning together had not gone well, and Dale thought rather anxiously that it was all because she'd spent no time with the girl the day before. Tai's good morning to her had been mumbled, and she seemed aloof. She didn't respond to Dale's teasing claim that it must have been much more fun spending time with her own friends, but if anything, Tai seemed displeased at the mention of them. What had happened between Friday afternoon and Monday morning to make such a difference?

Sighing softly, Dale shifted aside Tai's half-eaten breakfast and touched Tai's arm. "You know I'm going to operate on Thursday, don't you?"

"Yes" was the uninterested answer.

"It's going to take about four or five hours."

Tai nodded, staring down at her hands. Then, slowly, she lifted her head so that her glowing dark eyes peered questioningly up at Dale. Encouraged that she was not being totally locked out and ignored, Dale smiled warmly at the girl, unconsciously reaching to lay flat the Peter Pan collar of her pajama top.

"Is—is it going to hurt a lot?" Tai asked, and Dale realized, as she should have, that the pain afterward would be of concern to the girl. She also knew she couldn't underplay it.

"Yes, I'm afraid so. You're going to be uncomfortable for several days."

Tai nodded grimly.

"I'll try not to let it bother you too much. We'll give you something to ease the pain."

Tai's voice dropped to a shy, hesitant whisper. "Did your leg hurt a lot?"

Dale raised a brow. Tai had never made reference to Dale's limp before. "Did it ever!" Dale grimaced. "I was younger than you at the time, and I remember feeling that it would never stop. But the pain did go away."

"Will I have to stay in the hospital for a long time?"

Dale shook her head and smiled. "No, as a matter of fact, we're going to try and get you home as soon as possible. You'll probably be happier with your family and friends around you." There was no further response; Dale sighed.

She racked her brain trying to think what she could do, feeling helpless as her rapport and ease with Tai dissolved and slipped away.

"Would you like Dr. Christen—Damon to be there, too, on Thursday?"

Tai nodded.

"Tai, you can talk to me. Whatever it is that's bothering you, I'll try to understand. If you're afraid, there's really nothing to be afraid of. But tomorrow I'll bring by the replacement we'll use so you can see and feel it."

"It's not that!" Tai suddenly interrupted in a broken voice.

Dale looked blankly at her.

"I wish my friends had never come. I wish they'd stayed away from me!" And then her thin body began to shake with sobs. Dale automatically reached out to pull Tai against her and soothe her. She could see it was pointless to ask any questions right now.

Yet a pang of worry grabbed at Dale. She hoped Tai wasn't having second thoughts about the operation. Her parents had agreed at once, signing the necessary forms. But Tai was the patient. If Dale didn't have her consent and cooperation, then it was almost useless to go on. They'd discussed it many times in the past several weeks. Tai might not ever qualify for a championship skating team again, but she would be able to skate. She would be able, as a matter of fact, to do anything she wanted to. Her options were much greater in number than Dale's had been. But all of them would take time.

Time. Dale gnawed at her lip as she held the now-quieted

girl. Somehow that had clicked in her mind as a clue to what was bothering Tai. Perhaps the next day, when she'd had a night to think about it, she would tell Dale what was wrong.

"It's all right," Dale murmured. "I think you're just a little nervous. I am, too, you know. We won't talk about it anymore today. But if you need me later, I'll come right over."

"You don't have to do that." Tai sniffed softly. "I'm not a baby!"

"Of course not," Dale agreed evenly. "But sometimes you just have girl stuff to talk about. I'm a girl, too!"

Surprisingly, Tai giggled. "No, you're not. You're a doctor. That's different."

Dale shook her head ruefully, both amused and exasperated. She wondered how the two terms became mutually exclusive all of a sudden. "Still, if you need me, I'll come. Okay?"

"Okay."

Dale left her a few minutes later, so intent on figuring out how to reach Tai that she nearly ran right into Gloria Mendez.

"I see you made it in today!" Gloria commented as they started walking down the hall.

Dale looked at her quizzically.

"After that crazy foray Friday and Saturday, I thought you might have given up on us and gone back to New York!"

"Oh, I don't scare that easily."

"They told me yesterday you'd be out for the day. I hope you got some rest and managed to enjoy part of the day?"

Dale smiled dreamily, a pretty glow brightening her features. "Yes, I had a wonderful day off, thank you."

Gloria shook her head. "Well, whatever it was about yesterday must have been catching."

"What do you mean?"

"Damon Christensen was in early this morning for a meeting, and from the looks on his face, I'd say he had a wonderful day off, too!"

Dale blushed, opening her mouth to comment but unable to think of a thing to say offhandedly. Gloria touched her arm.

"You know, I think it's great if you two spent it together."

"Oh, you do, do you?" Dale said suspiciously.

"Sure! Everyone around here thinks you're doing great work with Tai. It won't hurt Dr. C. to be brought down a peg or two for his manner with women doctors. You're every bit as good as he is."

"Thank you," Dale said weakly. "But what has this to do with whether or not we were together yesterday?"

Gloria shrugged. "I just put one and one together, and guess what I came up with? And besides, half the staff is convinced you're secretly married and just not telling anyone."

Dale stopped and gasped. "Gloria, you're joking!"

"Would I joke about a thing like that?"

"Yes!"

Gloria laughed. "Well, maybe. Actually, it's just good-natured teasing. I hope you don't feel offended," she finished, watching Dale nonetheless to see just what her reaction would really be.

Dale laughed in irony. "Why should I be offended? You're not the first or only one to think that of Damon and me."

"Well, it's obvious he likes you and thinks highly of you."

"May I ask how you came to that conclusion?"

"You know that toddler with the spinal problem you offered to see this afternoon?"

Dale nodded.

"Well, Damon Christensen told the parents he wanted a 'visiting specialist' to see the child first. That's you!"

Dale was surprised. She had no idea.

"And he has a rather tricky operation scheduled for tomorrow morning. He told me he thought you should be there to see it. He didn't ask for any other assist."

Dale's throat tightened, and she was overcome with pleasure. But she tried to appear indifferent. "He's only being professional."

"He's only being very particular!" Gloria corrected.

But Dale began to feel uncomfortable with the conversation, and Gloria saw her begin to withdraw protectively behind a demeanor of professional aloofness.

"Look," Gloria said in a low, serious voice, "I apologize if I'm getting personal. I'm way out of line—"

"Forget it," Dale said softly, taking a deep breath of air. The whole situation was so full of irony that her humor was restored, and she chuckled wryly. "You know, I'm starting to feel like a character on 'General Hospital'!"

Still, Gloria realized that she may have pushed a bit too far and reverted at once to a professional attitude. "I hope your problems aren't that bad! There's nothing else, is there?"

Dale frowned and rubbed her forehead absently. "I hope not. Something is bothering Tai Chin. She won't talk about it, and I think it has to do with her surgery on Thursday."

"Has she changed her mind? It's happened, you know, especially with someone that young. Time starts closing in, and they start to bolt!"

Dale wasn't convinced it was that simple. "No, I don't think that's it."

"Would it help to talk to her parents?"

"I don't think so." Dale sighed in frustration. "I have a feeling about this, but I just can't put my finger on it right now."

They stopped near the elevators. "Well, what next?" Gloria asked.

"I'm not sure, quite honestly. Maybe tomorrow she will have settled down. In the meantime, could you double-check my use of Operating Room Three for Thursday afternoon?"

"Sure. Anything else I can do to help?"

"Have you seen Damon Christensen lately?"

"He's been in and out of meetings all day with the board and chief of staff. The departmental budgets are due, and there's also some sort of fund raiser this week."

Dale bit her lip.

"Can I relay a message?" Gloria offered.

"Just have him call me when he gets the time."

Gloria chuckled and said almost to herself, "Doctor, he'll *make* the time!"

DAMON WAS somewhat slouched in his chair at the end of the conference table. The legal pad in front of him held several pages of data, numbers, money amounts and totals. The pages were also liberally scribbled with unrecognizable doodles, cryptic quotes and, if one looked carefully, the name DALE spelled out clearly and then hastily scratched out.

Anyone seeing him in that instant could easily assume he was bored, tired or disgusted. Only his surrounding professional colleagues knew that he was none of those and was very much aware of the happenings at the meeting. It was evident in his sharp questions and verbal observations, strong rebuttals and suggestions.

But it was nearly six o'clock Monday evening, and given a choice, he'd rather have been elsewhere. More specifically, he wanted to be with Dale. He needed to see her, talk to her, hold her just for a little while. And if the damned meeting didn't break again soon, he was going to excuse himself long enough to do one of the three.

Dr. Anders saved Damon the effort, however, by announcing they would break for an hour and then come back. Damon pulled his tie loose and headed for the door. Dr. Anders, chewing on his empty unlit pipe, called out his name. Almost reluctantly, Damon returned to the table.

"How's Dale Christensen making out?"

At the mention of her name, Damon at once took the defensive, thinking Dr. Anders had some criticism of her. Damon straightened tall and put his hands into his trouser pockets, his arms pinning his white lab coat open. "I believe very well. She's scheduled surgery with the Chin girl for Thursday."

Dr. Anders nodded, puffing on the memory of his beloved cherry tobacco. "Good! I understand you've taken her under your wing?"

Damon tensed again, but Dr. Anders was as bland as plain rice.

"I guess you can say so," Damon answered at last.

Dr. Anders shook his head. "I'm sorry to say there's been no time to really get to know her. My wife and I picked her up at the hospital her first week here and took her to dinner."

Damon remembered that night. It was the first time he'd been swept with a strong wave of jealousy at the thought of her dating someone else. A self-derisive smirk lifted a corner of his mouth.

"The poor woman has probably not seen a thing of Oakland outside of this hospital in a month!" Dr. Anders went on.

Damon lowered his head to hide a satisfied grin as he remembered the pleasure of Sunday with her. Dr. Anders tapped the stem of his pipe against his teeth.

"Very interesting young woman, full of enthusiasm and ideas. I like that."

Now Damon did allow himself to smile. Rather proudly if it were to be analyzed. He liked that in her, too. "Yes, we've spoken about some of them."

"What do you think of her?" Dr. Anders asked so suddenly that Damon stared, speechless, for a long moment. Hadn't he been asking himself that since he met her? He thought she was a good doctor. She was caring, dependable and smart. He thought her cheerful, gentle and loving. He also thought her very attractive, soft and sensual. Damon coughed a little.

"I'm very impressed with her" was his answer.

"Dr. Anders nodded. "So am I. I'm hearing very positive things about her. I tell you, I think I'm going to be sorry when she leaves!"

Damon's eyes grew dark and clouded. His mouth was clamped closed over a series of denials and conflicting utterances. He removed a hand from his pocket and absently ran it through his hair. He never did respond.

"Look," Dr. Anders continued, "we're hosting a garden party on Sunday next. Why don't you plan on coming and bringing Dale with you. There will be people there I'd like her to meet. Do you think she'll come?"

Damon smiled slightly, "I'm sure she'd love to."

Damon finally got out of the conference room, and with an urgency that was frightening as well as intense, he made his way up to Dale's cubicle of an office. He was prepared to be very unreasonably annoyed if she wasn't there or had left to go back to her apartment. When he got off the elevator and found the office door open, he knew a relief that was just as intense as his urgency of a moment before.

Dale looked up at once when he stepped through the

door. She'd been hoping to see Damon all day. Her continual worry not only over Tai but because of the obvious hospital gossip about her and Damon quickly faded from her brow and was replaced with a soft shyness that was Damon's undoing. Dale took in the loose tie, the forever unruly hair, the dear strong face with shadows of weariness, and she wanted to touch and caress his cheeks and make him smile. Seeing her now, he did just that.

Damon held her green eyes locked to his as he approached the front of her desk. Then he took his time about putting his hands on the top of the desk and slowly bending toward her. Her chin came obligingly upward so that their mouths readily met in a sensual, eloquent kiss of longing.

Damon held her mouth and manipulated it, tasting and nibbling and stroking until the erotic suggestion of it forced Dale to pull her mouth away. "Damon," she whispered brokenly, "th-the door is open."

"Shall I close it?" he asked in a low, deep tone from his bent position.

"No!" Dale said firmly, but nonetheless Damon reached behind him and closed the door at least partially. He turned back to her, his eyes and mouth and tensing jaw speaking volumes.

"We have to stop meeting like this," he crooned in a teasing voice.

"Yes," she agreed nervously, brushing her hair. She looked up as she distinctly heard him groan.

"I must have been crazy last night not to keep you with me," he said sincerely, with feeling.

"Perhaps it was for the best," Dale offered softly, remembering she would gladly have stayed with him, no questions asked.

Damon sighed. "I'm not sure I've done that many unselfish things in my life. That was probably one of them. Only—"

"Only, what?"

"Right now I wish I'd been selfish." He bent to kiss her again, but Dale put her hands to his shoulders to stay him.

"You don't have enough time!" she quipped back, putting an end to the frustrating conversation. "Aren't you supposed to be in a meeting or something?"

"Yeah, and I have to go back soon." His voice lowered. "I just came to see you."

Dale gave him a warm smile. "I realize you've been busy. You didn't have to leave the meeting."

"Oh, yes, I did," Damon said firmly, narrowing his eyes. "I missed you all day."

She loved the special intimate look he was giving her and the subtle change in his face, and although he said nothing, he could see from her face that she still had not had enough rest. Absently, he reached out a hand to touch the corner of her mouth. Dale blinked and came out of her dreamy state. "Did Gloria give you my message?"

"Gloria Mendez?" he asked, puzzled. "I haven't seen Gloria since this morning. What was the message?"

"That I had to see you."

Damon's eyes looked over her face, down her long neck to the opening of her white blouse. "Me, too," he whispered.

"It—it's about Tai."

Damon came alert. "Is something wrong?"

Dale shrugged. "It may be the idea of the surgery. She seems on edge. I guess I'm a bit on edge myself." She chuckled nervously. She looked up at Damon, her eyes large and round. "I...I was just wondering... Could you assist me on Thursday?"

Damon nodded without hesitation. "Yes, if you want me to."

Dale let out a sigh. "Oh, yes! I do!" she answered in relief.

Damon took her hand and squeezed the slender fingers. "I'm very pleased to hear it," he said, glad with her answer for a number of reasons.

DAMON PUT DOWN his cocktail glass and excused himself from the elderly banker he'd been listening to for the last half hour. With a frown that had creased his forehead all evening, he once again looked at his watch. Hoping to find a telephone to call Oakland Central, he weaved his way through the formally dressed people milling about him. But his arm was suddenly grabbed by a robust older woman with tinted blue-gray hair in a style that hadn't been worn

by women in nearly twenty years. Her fingers and ears were
a glitter of opals and diamonds, and her sequined dress fit
her more than amply curved body as though she had been
poured into it.

"Here you are! I've been looking for you, Dr. Christensen," she gushed.

Damon smiled graciously down at the woman—and at
the gentleman she held with equal vigor by her other hand.
"I haven't been that hard to find, have I?" he asked. The
woman laughed in a high birdlike voice.

"Not at all. But you have been so popular this evening.
I've been wanting you to meet Samuel Harvey, of the
Harvey-Smithers Foundation. They're *very* active in philanthropic funding," the woman said significantly, and turned
a toothy smile to the man. "I've been telling Mr. Harvey all
about the special orthopedic programs you're hoping to
start at Oakland Central, but I'm sure you can do a much
better job. So I'll just leave you two to get acquainted while
I see to my other guests. Gentlemen..."

Damon watched her thump away in her heavy low-heeled shoes. He had to give her credit for wanting to help
her good friend Dr. Anders by hosting a fund raiser for the
hospital, but at the moment Damon himself was not feeling
particularly charitable.

Under the best of circumstances Damon was not fond of
soliciting. But the timing that year was especially bad. He'd
found out at lunch that afternoon that Dr. Anders needed
him to take his place at the fund raiser. Damon had tried to
get out of it, explaining that he was to assist in surgery with
Dale Christensen. Dr. Anders had been sympathetic to the
situation of its being Tai Chin's operation but held firmly to
his decision that Damon was the best replacement and that
someone else would have to assist Dale.

Damon had been angry enough to argue the point but
had given in when reminded that the funds they were seeking were for programs that he'd submitted proposals for. It
was his baby and in his hands.

Damon sat down on a sofa with Mr. Harvey and, after the
usual harmless amenities, began for the tenth or twelfth
time to explain Oakland Central's services and the part he
played in them. There was a certain formula in the way such

occasions went, and Damon had been to enough of them to be able to speak, listen and answer questions while his annoyance continued to bubble below the surface and his mind functioned elsewhere. His confrontation with Dr. Anders had a certain predictability to it that he would eventually get over. But having to tell Dale had been very hard to do, and the results had left him angry, disappointed and anxious.

At four-thirty, Damon returned to Oakland Central and went to Dale's office at once, only to find it empty. Damon went down to the ward floor and found her giving instructions to Gloria Mendez outside the door to Tai's room.

Dale's eyes looked over Gloria's shoulder, and he saw the sparkle of recognition and surprise, even as she continued to talk to Gloria. Soon Gloria walked away, and Dale turned to face Damon, her face lighting up. He gave her a lopsided grin.

"You're here early!" Dale smiled. "I'm glad. Now I can go over what I have in mind. I'm open to suggestions, so if you..." Dale's voice trailed off, and her eyes grew questioning. Damon didn't say anything. "You—you won't be operating with me, will you?" she asked in a soft but curious voice.

Damon tensed his jaw. His hands in his pockets played with their contents. He located the pewter coin. "I *can't* operate with you," he corrected bleakly.

Dale looked at him. Only then, as she became aware that he would not be there to help her, did she realize how she was looking forward to it.

"I've been commandeered to attend an important fund raiser for the hospital." There was no point in telling her about the argument that had ensued. The details seemed irrelevant now.

Understanding came to Dale's face, replacing the startled, surprised look.

"Believe me, Dale, this wasn't my idea. But as was pointed out," Damon said bitterly, "the funding is for my department."

Dale wanted to shout, *Yes, and what better way to emphasize that than to say I can't attend a fund raiser because I'm busy this evening practicing what I preach!* She was shocked at the sudden anger she felt and was even more overwhelmed by her disappointment. She'd wanted him there. Needed him to reassure Tai. But she needed his reassurance for herself, as well.

And she knew about fund raising and soliciting for money. Knew about the politics and the exchange of services that made so much more possible. She knew all about that, knew that Damon had not been given a choice. But the light went out of her eyes.

"I'm not very good when backed into a corner," Damon said angrily, "but that's what they've done. There's more than just me or Tai or you involved here. The outcome of tonight could affect the whole hospital."

Dale nodded with a wan smile. "I understand," she said evenly, seeming to stand taller and raising her chin proudly. "Sometimes we don't have a choice."

But Damon was concerned. She was withdrawing. She was too understanding, and he couldn't for the moment tell what she was really thinking or feeling. If he hadn't been feeling so disappointed himself, perhaps he would have dug beneath the façade and seen her sudden uncertainty, seen not the competent, able physician but a young woman whose confidence was a bit shaken.

Damon put his hands on her shoulder. He could feel a tension in her that held her stiff. It worried him. "Look, I'll try to get away as soon as I can tonight and come back."

Dale shook her head, not meeting his gaze. Her face was suddenly very pale and drawn. "You don't have to. I'm sure the surgery will go well."

"I'm sure it will, too," Damon said impatiently. "But I'm talking about coming back to you."

Dale slowly looked up. He did seem concerned. For a second, her eyes softened and pleaded. Damon's hands squeezed her shoulders. But Dale blinked and let out a small sigh. "I'll be okay."

Damon reluctantly dropped his hands. "Have you found out what's bothering Tai?" he asked.

"No, I haven't. But she seems prepared for this afternoon. I'm going in to see her for a few minutes more now."

"I'd like to talk to her, also," Damon murmured, turning toward the door.

"No, don't!" Dale said anxiously. Damon looked puzzled at her. "Please don't," Dale repeated in a low tone.

"Why not?"

"I . . . I told her you were going to assist me. She was very happy to hear that."

Damon's mouth became a grim straight line. "I'm sorry about that. Look, I should explain to her, also."

Dale touched his arm. "No, Damon! I can understand the necessity of this evening to you and the hospital. Tai isn't going to. And at the moment there's no reason why she should. She's frightened enough as it is."

Damon frowned at Dale. He covered the hand on his arm with his own and held tightly. "Are *you* sure you understand?" he asked.

Dale smiled but gently pulled her hand away. "Yes, I do. I've been there myself." She looked at her watch. "I really have to be going. There's a lot to see to yet—"

"Dale—"

"And I have to get the X rays upstairs."

Damon grabbed her arm. "Dale!" Dale gasped and looked at him. There were so many things in his eyes, some that called out to her and touched her deeply inside. She wanted him to hold her. Kiss her, love her. Unconcerned that anyone would see, she touched his tensed hard jaw.

"It's all right," she whispered, and then quickly turned to go to Tai's room, leaving Damon alone.

ONCE MORE Damon found himself putting down a glass. He stood up and shook hands with Mr. Harvey. And not caring anymore how much more money the hospital may have gained, he bade a determined good night over the hostess's objections and left.

It was nearly ten-thirty, and he knew the operation should be over. But when he got to the OR floor, it was clear that the surgery wasn't over.

Damon hoped it was all right. God, he wished the evening had been different. He wished that when the doors opened and Dale came through, he could have been next to her, feeling pleased, proud and triumphant. Impatiently, he paced the floor. He absently pulled his black bow tie loose and undid the top buttons of his shirt. He spotted Tai's parents in a side room and sat down to speak to them and reassure them. And then he left them to pace some more.

It was nearly an hour later that Dale came through the outer OR doors, clad in surgical greens, her hair bunched and stuffed under a green cap. Damon stopped his pacing and turned to her. He watched her wipe her hands over her face, rubbing the tired eyes. She bent and straightened her left knee a number of times as if to ease an ache. The greens were ill-fitting and absurd, and she seemed lost in the outfit. She also looked exhausted and a little dazed. Damon felt tight in his chest, dry in his mouth. Hands clenching, he wanted to go immediately to her, sweep her into his arms and get her out of there and away to himself.

And now Damon also understood what was different about himself. Now he understood the restlessness and the preoccupation with her as far back as New Orleans. Finding out was so much more simple than Damon thought it would be. He watched as a set of anxious parents came quietly and politely from the waiting room and approached Dale. Upon seeing them, Dale at once forgot her weariness and gave the Chins a warm smile of hope and confidence. She spoke quietly for several moments. The Chins nodded profuse thanks and quietly departed to go home. Dale's eyes followed them until she realized Damon was standing just in her line of vision in the now dimly lit hallway. They stared silently at each other.

Dale was caught in the ambivalent state of continual disappointment that he had not been there earlier and her instant joy that he was there now. And seeing him stand there so unruffled and at ease made her own anxiety over the evening seem so out of place. But she was wrong. The distance between them created the deception. Damon had never felt so uncertain in his life.

She stood so proud, yet so forlorn, he was afraid to move. Two things became crystal clear to him as he considered his next move. One was that he loved her, and it didn't come as a total surprise. The second was that he never should have left her that evening as he reflected that now she might not need him at all.

Chapter Sixteen

Damon walked slowly forward and stopped very close to Dale. He didn't like seeing the tightly drawn mouth. He didn't like the weary but alert look in her eyes or the dark shadows beneath them.

"You didn't have to come back," Dale said in a vacant, indifferent voice.

Damon's jaw clenched. He thought he'd gotten beyond her barriers. But she'd put one up again, just since the last time he'd seen her. Dammit! Didn't she know yet that he always came back to her because he wanted to be with her? "How did the surgery go?" he responded evenly.

Dale frowned. "It was long, much longer than I thought it would be."

"Were you satisfied afterward?" he asked, watching the exhaustion slowly seeping into every corner of her.

"Yes..." But there was a certain hesitancy in her reply.

Damon saw her sway a little. At once, his hand came up to take her arm, while the other reached to pull the green cap from her head. All of her hair had been fastened by a clip to the back of her head. Damon felt himself fighting the instinct that preferred just to gather her against him and hold her in comfort and understanding.

"Come on. I'm taking you back to the apartment."

Dale resisted. "I can't. I have to stay," she said stonily.

"Is Tai in recovery?"

She nodded. "Yes, she'll come out of it tomorrow morning, but—"

"No buts," Damon said firmly. "There's nothing more you can do tonight." He began to pull her again.

"No, I can't!" Dale said in agitation.

Damon suddenly got angry. She was more concerned for everyone else than she was for herself. His hand closed more tightly around her arm until she gasped in surprised pain. Damon's jaw worked, and his mouth was straight and uncompromising. Dale was momentarily shocked.

"The hell you can't!" Damon managed to say between his gritted teeth. "You're going home before you collapse. You'll be no good to anyone if you're out cold!"

Immediately, Dale got defensive. She didn't need criticism from anyone right now, least of all Damon. "Let me go! I don't need you to—" Dale drew a sharp breath and stopped. That wasn't true. She turned bleak, unsure eyes to Damon's hard-closed face.

"We'll discuss this in private," he said smoothly. "I'm very aware of the fact that you manage well alone."

Dale felt oddly unhappy about his statement. She wanted to shout that it was not true. She wasn't that way at all. Maybe she only used to be.

"Nonetheless, you're going home. Everything else, including Tai, will have to wait until tomorrow," he concluded.

Not allowing her even to change from her surgical garment, Damon led her with determination and a firm hand from the hospital. Her limp was very pronounced, and he knew her leg must be hurting. He kept the pace to suit her, and that was the only concession he made and the only one he knew she'd accept right now.

He was feeling so many different things in that silent walk to her building. He felt vulnerable in his sudden overwhelming love for her. Right now he had to be so careful of what he said or did. He stole a glance at Dale as she walked next to him, her chin raised and defiant. He knew she was strong. Too damned strong for her own good at times.

They got to the apartment with not a word spoken between them. But once the door had closed behind them, Damon had no intention of letting her ignore him. Dale moved slowly into the center of the living room and stood hugging herself. She ached all over, particularly her knee. She ached from wanting and needing, and it made her both weak and angry. She had been too long her own source of strength. Yet it unnerved her that her love for Damon could make her lean toward him, leave her open and raw, make her feel fragile and helpless.

She felt she had to prove during the operation that she could manage without him, as she'd always done before. When she'd said good night to Tai's parents and found him standing there, she wanted to run to him and bury herself in his arms and ask him to be strong for both of them. But she didn't know how. Why couldn't she love him and keep her pride, too?

"Why don't you just leave me alone..." she said impatiently. But her voice was low and shaky. Damon made no further move to touch her, but he was beginning to see what her behavior and hostility toward him was all about.

Dale put her hands up to her face, and they were trembling. A short, dry laugh escaped her. "Well, you were right!"

"About what?" Damon asked, watching her closely, coming imperceptibly nearer.

Dale shook her head from side to side. "I...I just couldn't go the distance."

Damon slipped out of his dinner jacket, throwing it over the kitchenette counter and adding his tie to it. "What is it you think you couldn't do?" he asked softly. His heart constricted painfully when Dale turned a tremulous face and enormous eyes to him.

"I'm not sure that I've been of any help to Tai at all. How arrogant of me to think I had anything special to offer her!"

"Then you'd be wrong. You gave her the time needed for her to understand what was happening and to come to grips with what it means for her future. You gave her your skills to make her better. You gave her everything it was possible to give her, Dale. There is no more. The rest is up to Tai."

"But something is still troubling her."

"Then maybe she needs to work it out for herself."

"But what if I missed something important? Or something basic?"

"For God's sake, Dale, stop being so professional! Stop hiding behind your lab coat!" Damon said firmly, his eyes dark and seeking to make her aware.

Dale stiffened. "What else should I be?"

"Scared! And unsure. I already know you are at this moment. You're so good at caring for everyone's hurt but your own." Damon slowly reached out a hand. Dale turned away from him. Foolishly, she felt as if she were going to cry, and she didn't want him to see. She didn't want him to think her weak. Yet even Damon would have told her that it was better to cry now and then, that we're all better off when we're not too sure of ourselves. Hadn't he been learning that all these weeks around her? "Don't you ever think to ask for something just for yourself alone?"

"L-Like what?" was her whispered query.

Damon wanted to say, "Like me," but something told him he still had to make up in some way for not being there earlier when she needed him. "Let's start with something simple. How about a pair of reasonably strong shoulders to lean on?"

The tears slipped slowly then, poignantly, down her cheeks, but not a sound came from her. It was a trick she'd learned as a child so that no one would know of her horrible pain and scoff at her to be a big girl and be brave. She didn't want to be brave—then or now. She hurt.

Dale stiffened the minute she felt Damon's hands touch her shoulder.

"Don't..." Her voice came in a whisper, but he paid no heed. With insight, Damon recognized that being left alone was not what she wanted at all. Damon's arms slipped around her securely, tightening, drawing her back against his chest. She made no attempt to pull away, but neither did she let herself go. Her complete undoing, however, was a gentle kiss pressed to her tangled hair and a deep masculine voice saying to her, "It's going to be all right."

Damon swung her around and pressed her face into his shoulder, holding the back of her head. He felt her body quake, and within minutes the front of his shirt was all wet. Wisely, he offered no advice, no further words of empathy or understanding. He simply held her, because that's what she needed most of all. He was overwhelmed by her emotions and the depths of her despair. But he knew that some of that had been triggered by worry and anxiety, both of which would resolve themselves now that the surgery was over. And the anxiety and worry had made her less sure of herself and therefore powerless. He wanted to say to her that her care and gentleness were her greatest strengths.

Overcome with his own sense of inadequacy, Damon pressed tender kisses to her hair, her ear and her cheeks, wet with tears, down to her quivering mouth, capturing and drawing her anguish right out of her. Dale's eyes opened and stared from their watery green depths into his. Never in his life had he wanted so much to give of himself to anyone.

Their breath mixed. Their mouths touched and played. Dale stopped crying as Damon's hands cupped her face, the thumbs rubbing away the tears. "You need someone to think about you for a change. I've elected myself the person most likely to."

"You? Why?"

Damon pulled her to him again and whispered near her ear. "Easy...I'm the one who thinks about you *all* the time. I'm the one who notices when you work too hard. And I always know when you're in pain from your knee. Like now."

Damon felt her head nod against his shoulder. Dale lost all of her defenses in the face of Damon's insights. She even forgot to be angry with herself for needing him, because it felt so good to be in his arms, listening to his soothing voice.

"You're going to forget all about Tai for the rest of the night. You're going to take off this very unattractive outfit you have on and take a shower. Then you're going to take some aspirin for your knee and go to bed and get some sleep."

Dale didn't want him to let her go. But Damon held her arms and stepped back. Dale resisted. Damon read her thoughts, feeling pleased and hopeful—but firm. "I'll wait here until you're done." He spoke softly, stroking the back of his hand along her cheek. His eyes held a new concern that she had never seen before. Dale nodded and turned away. But she wasn't even feeling nearly as tired as she had been a half hour earlier. She closed herself in the bathroom, and Damon next heard the hissing spray of the shower.

He thrust his hands into his pockets and walked to the one window in the living room and looked moodily out into the quiet night.

It took Dale a long time to dry her hair. And then she reached for a gown and robe, only to realize they were in the bedroom where she usually left them in the mornings. She looked doubtfully at her forest-green bath towel and decided it would have to do until she got to the room.

Dale opened the bathroom door and stepped into the minuscule hallway. Damon turned from the window where he'd been standing and stared at her against the light from the bathroom. Damon himself was a dim outline against the window. She couldn't see his face clearly, so she didn't know what he was thinking in the soft, closed-in silence of the moment.

Damon noticed first that she only had the large bath sheet wrapped around her; her shoulders and arms, legs and feet were bare. Her hair was shiny and wavy and gloriously billowed out around her oval face. Unconsciously, he turned toward her, but just until he could clearly see the velvet depths of her eyes, right now so like the color of the towel. Dale stood as if mesmerized, her lips slightly parted, both hands clutching the towel. She noticed a pensive, deep look on his face. "Did you take those aspirin?" he asked in an odd husky voice.

Dale merely shook her head. She didn't want to talk and break her sudden sense of his male presence as she stood unclothed in front of him.

"If you have any aspirin, get them," Damon softly ordered, and then moved into the kitchenette to run a glass of water.

Dale blinked at his moving form, trying to understand his aloofness, but she did turn back into the bathroom and removed an aspirin bottle from the medicine chest. She met Damon in the hallway, holding a glass out to her. Dale looked up inquiringly into the handsome face, but Damon's expression at the moment gave nothing away.

He was actually thinking how easy it would be to take her in his arms right now and love her. How desperately he wanted to. But he also felt it would be unfair, because she'd just been through too much. And it was unfair to him because he wanted her totally, not just a little time with her or a small part of her.

Their eyes held as Dale placed the tablets on her tongue

and drank half the glass of water. Damon returned the glass to the counter. Dale followed his every move, her heart beating faster in excitement. The air around her became electrified with her feelings and a curious need that had not yet communicated itself to Damon. She wondered why he didn't hold her again. And then she frowned in disappointment when Damon picked up his tie and jacket.

"I think you'd better get into bed and rest. And I want you to sleep late tomorrow morning. You need a little recovery time yourself."

There was something wonderfully protective about the way he stood issuing his orders. But it was also disturbingly impersonal. "Is that the doctor speaking or you?" she asked softly.

"It's me," he answered. There was a silence. Dale held her towel tightly.

"Is that all?"

"For tonight, yes. Good night, Dale."

He was going to leave. He was going to walk out the door, and she'd be left with all this feeling and confusion. He was at the door when Dale knew her heart would burst if he walked out and nothing would ever be the same.

"Damon!" She spoke his name pleadingly, and it was wrenched painfully from her. Yet she also felt relieved. Why shouldn't she have something just for herself? She wanted him to love her, even if he would only do so for the night. But it would be hers.

Damon stopped in the movement of opening the door and turned back to look at her. He couldn't recall ever seeing her look more helpless and vulnerable or more lovely and desirable.

"Damon..." His name was a whisper now, but he felt its urgency grab at his insides and touch his own, and he turned back. He dropped his coat and tie onto the sofa. He came to stand close to her. His eyes swept and searched over her face intently.

Dale tilted her head to look up at him, drinking in his entire masculine appeal.

"Are you sure?" he drawled. Dale attempted a smile, her heart racing, her whole body warming up and melting.

"There was a time when you wouldn't have questioned

it," she said in a shy whisper. Damon took a deep breath, and a hand slipped under her hair to caress her neck, a motion that was uniquely his. A shiver coursed through Dale, and she melted even more.

"You're right. But things have changed quite a bit," he said.

At the moment, Dale was concerned only that he still wanted her. "I—I suppose you don't feel exactly the same now." She lowered her eyes. "But I'm sure. I...I don't want you to leave."

It was on the tip of Damon's tongue to ask why now, but he was busy experiencing a surprised joy that she wanted him to stay, without any pressure from him. Damon bent and lightly pressed a kiss to her mouth. Their noses touched. He tilted his head and kissed her again, applying some pressure to her neck. She smelled clean and fresh and intoxicatingly open. His excitement began to build. He continued to press a series of light, playful kisses on her mouth and face. Then he felt Dale's hand on his chest, felt her fingers fumble for the buttons on his shirt, and he stopped to look down at her.

Bright pink spots colored her cheeks, but she kept her eyes on her task, not looking to meet his tender gaze or smile. She stopped when her fingers reached the band of his slacks. Damon waited to see her next move, but she stood still and so close he could feel her hurried breathing on his chest.

Damon rubbed her neck again, evoking goose bumps on her exposed shoulders and arms. He bent to press his lips reverently to her forehead. "Dale," he said evenly, as if to again ask if she was sure, as if to warn her he would not stop this time. Dale gave him her answer by pressing a light, gentle kiss through the opening of his shirt to the silky hairs beneath. His hand squeezed her neck. She shivered.

"I...I'm cold," she whispered. Damon then smoothed her hair from her face so he could once again see her eyes. He was overcome with emotion at the light he saw there, the calm—and trust. Damon turned her by her shoulders.

"Go get under the covers," he said, moving her ahead of him into the bedroom. He turned off the bathroom light, and the apartment was plunged into semidarkness.

Dale pulled back the coverlet and top sheet but did not

get under them. She sat instead on the edge of the bed, holding the towel to her loosely, her toes pressed tightly against the floor to keep her knees from shaking. Damon pulled his shirt free of the pants, loosened the cuffs and slowly slipped it off, tossing it onto a nearby chair.

Dale watched and waited, curious, shy, excited and anxious. But Damon was in no hurry. He had waited so long to have her, wanted her so badly, that now *he* was almost afraid. He thought with wry amusement how love indeed made all the difference. It suddenly made him a person with strength, patience, caring—immortality.

He came to her, slowly reaching for her hands and pulling her to her feet. In excruciating slow motion, the towel wormed its way loose and simply dropped away from her body to the floor. Dale gasped as she stood naked before him, her breasts firm and rounded, moving with her shallow breathing. She could feel the tension in him. Damon released her hands and took a step forward to bring them together, sliding his hands on her smooth, soft back. When she lifted her head, it was a signal for Damon to bend and kiss her, and finally it all began.

After a long, intense kiss that clearly stated both their needs, Damon lifted her and laid her full-length on the bed. Dale watched in open fascination as he removed the remainder of his clothing, revealing a firm muscled body already indicating his desire. She slid over to make room for him next to her. Damon stretched out, long and sinewy, and rolled to his side to take her into his arms and find her mouth again. He could detect little tremors and shudderings in her body, but she was pliant under his hands and against the length of him.

He ran a hand down her back, slowly curving it around her buttocks, bringing her against his obvious taut, heated middle. Damon began kissing her with such passion and demand that she felt he would absorb her completely within himself. His hands explored sensuously, intimately, slowly, until she wasn't thinking anymore at all but was feeling intensely. Her mind seemed to be spinning wildly in the dark behind her eyelids, and she felt that if Damon didn't hold her, she'd fall deeply into some fantasy abyss. She held tightly to his neck and shoulders.

Damon stopped kissing her and moved her onto her

back. He wanted to see into her face, look at her for a while. His hand touched her left knee and slid up along the inside, gently fingering several raised areas of scar tissue. Dale opened her eyes to see his reaction, but he only smiled lovingly and planted a quick kiss on her chin. His hand followed its own inclination, and Dale's soft expulsion of air and deep sighs told him her sensitive spots. Her skin was warm now, and her breasts were swollen with desire. Under his exploring hand, the very center of her opened and vibrated with longing and tantalizing heat. Her stomach muscles curled and rolled, sending waves of anticipation into her loins and making her willing and ready for him.

Damon knew a headiness and joy he'd never experienced with any other woman. Knowing they'd both waited long enough, he moved to lie over her. He threaded his fingers into her hair and watched the glowing light on her face and her moistened parted lips as they came together as one. He watched her eyes drift and close, the sharp intake of a breath at his complete possession, and Damon knew beyond a doubt with his body and soul that she would forever belong to him.

Dale for her part didn't know about forever, although she hoped it would go on and never stop. She gave unreservedly to Damon and in so doing received as much in return. She experienced and loved the power of his thrusting hips, loved the weight of him on her chest, the playing and exploring of his tongue as he kissed her. She loved the soft rubbing of his thighs against her own, loved fully the differences and rhythms between them. And for the first time Dale felt new meaning to sharing, giving, togetherness, warmth and tenderness.

She wondered what it was about him alone that filled her and released her and made her feel so totally safe and wanted. She only knew she'd come full circle in a wheel lit with bright colors. Magic colors that filled her being with life—and love.

DAMON LAY quietly considering. He felt at peace and complete at that moment of holding Dale securely to his hard body. Even as she slept, the soft breathing tickling his skin, he didn't want to let her go.

With gentle fingers, Damon pushed back the silken hair from her face and looked down at her. Her lashes were like gold threads against the curve of her cheek. Her smooth skin was soft, warm and flushed. Her mouth, just a while before so expressive and responsive, was parted the tiniest bit.

What an incredible mixture she was of woman and child, strength and vulnerability, convictions and doubts. But he had no doubt at all that it was the woman whom he'd made love to and who had returned his caresses with an ardor of her own that was infinitely pleasing. She held back none of herself. It had been so natural, so satisfying, that Damon knew it had been a singularly unique experience, because all the conditions were perfect.

Damon's hand rested on her breast and felt the gentle rise and fall as she breathed evenly. The nipple was richly pink and still erect. He wanted to put his mouth to the breast, but he was afraid of waking her. He settled instead for letting the curved flesh rest in his palm and his thumb rub back and forth over the hard top. When Dale moaned in her sleep and pressed closer to him, Damon reluctantly moved his hand.

It continued a downward journey along her rib cage. A finger explored her navel. He laid his open hand flat on her stomach where the skin was velvet-smooth and gently curved. Suddenly, Damon tried to envision Dale rounded and pregnant, carrying a child. He ran scenarios through his mind of how lovely, how serene and suited to the part, she'd be. A wave of emotion, unfamiliar and frightening, fantastic and pleasing, coursed through him. "Dale," he murmured, aware of the implication for now and the future with her. He was exhilarated. He moved his hand around to her back and held her closer to him. But thinking in terms of the future presented an astonishing list of questions that needed his attention, and he continued to lie awake and think.

After a while, Damon felt her move. Her hand came to stroke his jaw and neck. The fingers moved to his throat and splayed open over his chest, enjoying the texture of skin and hair. She was awake now, but Damon did not move or say anything, enjoying enormously her curiosity.

Dale's fingers brushed and smoothed his chest hair, playing in it. She moved her head and brought it hesitantly closer so that her mouth touched his skin. Damon caught his breath and felt desire waking in him once again. Dale's action was not in itself sexual but was delivered as a singularly sensual treat.

Damon felt her tongue dart out, small and wet, and lick over his male nipple. An incredible shock of newly discovered pleasure snaked through him as he felt her mouth cover the small erect projection. His jaw tensed, and he held himself back awhile longer.

Dale's hand moved down his chest to the hard muscles of his flat stomach. The hand grew daring and moved lower to rub into a thicker, coarser thatch of hair. But then she stopped.

Damon felt his chest constrict. He reached out a hand to grab her wrist, and from Dale there was a surprised gasp as she lay stunned at finding him awake. But Damon only wanted to encourage her to go on and touch where she pleased. He led her hand until it completed its search and then explored on its own. Damon surged against her and after a time shifted position.

"Oh, God," he shuddered, turning to her. And now he bent to take the exact same liberties, his mouth closing in exquisite delight around her breast and his hand searching and finding. Soon they were both lost, clutching each other with sighs and moans and unintelligible words of love and whispering each other's name. They swayed and rocked in a timeless primitive dance.

It had not been an exercise simply for pleasure, although for both of them it had been overwhelmingly satisfying. It had been more an expression of trust, need, care—feelings that extended far beyond the mere sexual encounter. For Damon it had been wonderful to feel consumed by her entire person.

And from Damon's point of view, for the difference between just a momentary release and an emotional and physical commitment, their union had been well worth the wait.

Chapter Seventeen

Dale wasn't sure what it was that brought her fully awake with a tiny start. Her eyes opened wide to scan the room in its dawn light. Maybe it was the sensation of her back pressed against a warm, comforting presence not usually there. In any case, she was alert, even if momentarily confused.

And then, of course, it all came back to her. Every detail was recalled and outlined in her memory with crystal clarity. Every moment spent being swept through a storm of emotions and feelings she'd never known before repeated itself in her mind. It had left her sated, languid and happy. She knew peace, comfort and love. And with it all, and Damon, she had slept the night.

Dale lay for a moment, however, as the full magnitude of her actions and involvements finally dawned on her. Before the previous night, she could conceive of returning to New York with Damon's love a secret all her own that would give her wonderful warm memories and fantasies of what might have been between them. But now that they'd made love, learned to know each other thoroughly, she knew that when she left California, she'd be leaving a tremendous part of herself behind with him.

Damon had always been very honest and clear about wanting her, and he'd won it all. Her body and her heart. But in the background had been yet another player—Jessica. Now Damon had them both.

Despair settled on her, and Dale felt an urge to turn over into his chest and arms and beg him to hold her and not let her go. To want her always. Instead, she cautiously began to move away from the long, hard body behind her, trying to slip out of the bed. She was just about to swing her legs onto the floor when the arm over her hip and waist closed and clamped tightly around her. Dale found herself being hauled back slowly but purposefully over the sheet and once again pressed to Damon's body.

"Where do you think you're going?" The voice was a sleepy, deep, husky drawl. She didn't answer. She was somehow more instantly alert to the taut boldness of him against her back. "It's barely five o'clock," Damon said now, pulling the cover over her again.

"I...I know. I just...woke up," Dale murmured.

Damon let out a sleepy sigh and pressed a kiss to the back of her head. "Did I wake you?"

Dale bit her lip. "No, I was just...suddenly awake."

Damon was quiet behind her for a long time. Suddenly, he gave her a gentle squeeze and let up on the pressure of his arm around her middle. "You're not used to waking up to someone else in your bed, are you?" he asked softly.

"No," she barely whispered.

Damon had already known that. He smiled to himself and pressed another kiss to her head. It felt so good to wake up with her that way, as if he'd been doing so a long time. Dale had been feeling the same thing.

But apparently Damon had other thoughts in mind right now. A hand came up to gently caress and play with a breast. His mouth moved to find her ear and lick languidly around the shell of it, ending with a nibble on her earlobe. A soft sigh of delight breezed out from her lips. Dale was thinking she shouldn't let it happen again. He'd already gotten what he wanted from her. Why not leave her with the little bit of strength she had left that would get her back to New York? Why strip her of everything—even her failing will to resist giving him everything he wanted?

"Damon," she whispered, trying to fight but just more or less lying there in giddy abandonment as his mouth found a sensitive cord in her neck and his hands roamed down to her thighs. But her calling of his name was far less a command than it was a plea. Damon's knee bent, and his thigh came up to cover hers; he pulled her onto her back, his head coming around so that their lips could meet and greet hungrily.

Dale knew if she didn't stop now she was never going to get a second chance and would stop wanting it. Damon released her mouth and worked his way down to a ripe, quivering breast more than ready for his ministrations. Her hand came up to thread fingers through his soft brown hair.

"Damon..." she tried again. This time he heard her. He lifted his head to see her face, loving the ravished look, her parted lips letting expressive sounds out. He grinned.

"Did you want to say something?" he teased confidently.

"Oh, Damon, I...I'm not very...good at this," she managed in a low voice that shuddered. She opened her eyes and blinked at him. Part of what she meant was that she was not very good about taking their lovemaking lightly. But Damon was not considering that. He had picked up on the other meaning.

"I have no complaints about last night," he whispered in a serious, hoarse voice. "And what you don't know—I'll teach you."

Dale looked oddly at him for a long time. She was surprised and pleased to find that his words had a curious calming effect on her. Absently, a hand came up to his bristled cheek and chin. He looked so roguish but was being so kind. Damon turned his head and pressed a kiss into her palm. Then he looked at her again.

"And what I don't know, you can teach me!"

Dale thought her heart would stop. She smiled slowly and lovingly at him and opened her arms to him. There was a bubble of joy, gurgling its way all through her, threatening to burst from her heart and throat. *So this is what I've been missing all these years,* she thought, sighing with deep, rich pleasure as Damon took up his stroking again.

DAWN WAS long gone, and by seven-fifteen the new day was in full swing. Damon and Dale had dozed languidly after making love again, but the second time she awoke, she was able to climb from the bed, separating herself from Damon's warm but limp arm hold around her.

Dale dug out her robe from the armchair, and as she wrapped it around her flushed, awakened body, she tilted her head, smiling down at Damon's sleeping form. The bed coverlet had long since been kicked off and discarded in the passion of the night, but the light sheet covered him just to the waist. His brown hair was rumpled and lay over his forehead. Dale was tempted to brush it back but just stood enjoying him. He still looked rather virile and strong but also young and boyish despite his beard growth. And not caring how silly it looked, she kissed her finger and lightly touched it to his mouth. But the light touch was felt, and Damon shifted sleepily on the bed.

Dale hastily escaped from the room feeling so lighthearted and so young. He had been so wonderful and patient with her awkwardness the night before and that morning. For the time being, everything else—New York, Tai Chin, Jessica—were swept from her mind.

Dale found herself gnawing a fingernail as she stood at the kitchenette counter. Her pleasure in Damon led her to feel particularly romantic and domestic, and she wondered if she dared to tax her skills and attempt breakfast for the two of them. It was hopeless to think she could approach Damon's culinary talents of a week earlier, but she wouldn't completely shame herself. She got the coffee maker going and dug around the refrigerator. She found and sectioned a grapefruit for them. She wasn't sure how Damon liked his eggs, but boiled seemed safe enough. She added toasted English muffins last. She was just hunting out a serving tray to put everything on when Damon called out imperiously with a yawn.

"Dale! Where are you? Is that coffee I smell?"

Dale laughed. "I'm making breakfast. It's almost ready," she shouted back, looking to see if she remembered everything—napkins, knives, butter, sugar. Damon chuckled from the bedroom.

"*You're* making breakfast! *This* I gotta see!" he teased.

"Don't you dare come out here!" Dale said in a panic. "And if you don't stop laughing, I'll send you away without even coffee!" There was more laughter from Damon.

Lifting the tray, she cautiously made her way back to the room, tossing her head to swing her loosened hair from her face. The tray dipped to the cadence of her slightly uneven walk. Damon was lolling against both pillows, his strong arms up and his hands behind his head when she came through the door. At once, with amazing grace and agility, he was sitting up and reaching for the heavy tray.

"Dale, why didn't you call me?" he said impatiently. She tossed her hair again but relinquished the tray to Damon.

"Don't be silly. I've got a lousy knee, but I'm not an invalid!"

Damon moved to put the tray down, and in so doing the sheet left him bare. Dale stood for a silent moment, not in embarrassment—they were certainly far beyond that—but in total appreciation of the strong, healthy body that was his. She felt awed. Then she looked up to catch Damon's eyes, and now she did blush. He silently reached out for her hand and pulled her gently back onto the bed.

Damon wanted to tell her how extraordinarily beautiful she was in the morning, how he loved her wild rumpled hair. He wanted to kiss her good morning but remembered they'd already done that and it had led to other things. He wanted to get past the tight feeling in his chest to let her know no other woman since Madge had ever in his life made him breakfast. He just continued to stare openly.

Dale's blush deepened under his continual gaze, and she laughed nervously, handing him a cup of coffee. "I...I'm not Julia Child, but I don't think any of this will kill you!"

Damon kept his eyes on her and took a healthy sip. He raised his brow. "Good coffee!" he said honestly.

Dale was pleased. But she shrugged her shoulders. "I'm better at other things."

"Mmm" was Damon's seductive comment.

They ate the breakfast in compatible, easy conversation, as if they'd always done so. Damon teased her about her cooking efforts, but Dale took the teasing as it was meant. She returned to the kitchen with their cups for more coffee. Damon followed behind to put the tray on the counter. He walked comfortably from the bedroom to the kitchen stark naked and at ease, and even that had a contentment to it as Dale sensed how completely at home and relaxed he seemed with her.

However, she kept taking furtive glances at the clock, realizing that the morning was advancing quickly into afternoon. But she carried the coffee cups, filled for a second time, back to the bedroom. Damon was back on the bed, fluffing up the pillows behind his back and shoulders. He took his cup from Dale and motioned for her to lean back against him, which she did readily, taking advantage of every opportunity to be held by him.

Her head rested just under his chin, and Damon's free arm circled around her to rest on her stomach. They were silent for a few minutes. Damon finished his coffee first and put his empty cup on the night table. "It's too early to see Tai," he said bluntly.

Dale started. "W-what?"

Damon sighed, getting more comfortable against the pillows. "You're thinking of her, aren't you?"

She nodded. "I . . . I can't help it."

"I know you can't," Damon said softly. "First of all, you like her a great deal. Second of all, you're trying to help her medically. You're caught from all sides, so no matter what you do or where you are, you're worried."

"I suppose." Dale sighed. "I do get so . . . so totally involved. You did say I took it all too seriously."

"Yes, I did say that," Damon admitted solemnly, reluctantly. Now he understood why she did.

"But don't you see? I have to take the children so much more seriously. It's up to me to help them understand all the pain and why it's happening to them!"

"I bet because no one ever took quite so much time with you."

Dale nodded grimly. "It was very hard at times. And very lonely. I used to feel as if I was in pain all the time." She had never admitted so much before, and for Damon it was an indication of how much she'd come to trust him. He was very moved and loved her all the more. The arm tightened around her, and he reached to kiss her temple.

"There's a solution, you know."

Dale frowned. "Is there?"

"Mmm. You should have children of your own." And as he said so, his large hand began to rub rhythmically, erotically, back and forth over her stomach, slipping inside the robe to her bare skin.

Dale caught her breath as much at his words as at his actions.

"Haven't you ever thought of that?" Damon whispered against her temple.

Dale opened her mouth to speak, but nothing came out, and she felt suddenly overwhelmed with sadness. She had. So often and so long ago that having it mentioned again stirred up deeply suppressed feelings that she'd been denying in order to go on with her life. Having children seemed not to be her destiny. Helping children was—and always someone else's. "Yes, I—I've thought of it." Her voice was a mere whisper, and under his hand Damon felt a sudden tensing of her stomach. "There's only . . . one problem."

"What is it?"

"I have neither the prospect of a husband nor someone wanting to be . . . be a father." Her voice was very thin. Damon was well aware of it and suddenly got an insight into another aspect of her that made him want to crush her to him and tell her not to worry, that it was going to be all right.

"That's two problems," Damon whispered. "But who's counting?" He was pleased to see her mouth curl briefly into a smile.

"In any case, they're not that easy to overcome. At least not for me."

"Hasn't anyone ever wanted to marry you?" he asked in sudden curiosity.

Dale grimaced and smiled. "Once."

"And?"

"I said no. I didn't love him. Not even to have children."

"I'm glad to hear it," Damon said sternly, "on both counts." Dale shifted her shoulders to get more comfortable against him.

"Do . . . do you want children?" she asked hesitantly. He could have a ready-made family if he wanted. Dale wondered what he thought of Jessica's children.

The truth was that Damon had not given any thought to having his own children, at least not until that morning. Madge was just not the kind of mother to hint at or demand grandchildren. But Damon was suddenly thinking with some warmth and vivid imagery how fantastic it would be to have a couple of kids that he could teach and watch grow and do things with. Children to love and share with a woman he loved deeply. His hand was still stroking Dale's stomach.

"I'm not sure what kind of a father I'd make. But I'd like to find out if I can be as kind and patient and attentive as my dad was to me and Pete. He was really terrific," he said by way of an answer. Dale liked it. It was honest and thoughtful.

"And while we're on the subject of children," Damon crooned softly, "we didn't give much thought to that last night or this morning. Should we have?"

Dale drew in a sharp, short breath. She'd never given it a single thought, either. But what made her take notice was Damon's use of "we." Not should *you* have or should *I* have but *we*. If anything went awry, they would both be responsible. She swallowed hard, suddenly loving him so very much. She smiled to herself. "No, I guess we weren't really thinking." She hesitated, touching her fingers to the back of his hand. "I'm not taking anything, but we needn't have worried. The timing is all wrong."

Damon didn't respond, only stroked his fingers down her cheek. She let out a sigh. "What are you thinking?" he asked quietly, not wanting her to be sad for a minute.

"Only that Tai's parents are really very lucky. I hope they realize it. She is so special, so very bright, so unique."

Damon's hand on her cheek moved to her chin, tilting her head up and sideways. His mouth hovered over hers. "So are you," he whispered earnestly, so gently that Dale felt a rush of tears begin to well up in her. But before she could concern herself about hiding them from Damon, he kissed her. Crying was now the last thing she had on her mind.

His hand slid down her neck and throat and slipped into the loose neck of her robe to zero in on a breast. It immediately responded to his touch. He deepened the kiss as his fingers stroked and caressed her nipple. The arm that Damon had around her middle pushed her over until Dale was almost sprawled on top of him, their searching mouths still fastened together.

They shouldn't make love again. It was getting late.

She'd never get to the hospital at that rate. With his arms squeezing her to him, with his need so obvious and bold, how could she leave?

But there was a beeping sound, and they separated breathlessly, listening to the unexpected and unwelcome interruption. Damon muttered an expletive and reached across Dale to turn off the beeper. If it went off again, it meant his service was not just trying to reach a doctor but that they needed *him*. A minute later, it went off again.

Dale sat up, quickly getting out of his way so he could reach the phone. She retrieved their two empty cups, then pulled the loosened robe around her still-stimulated body and went into the kitchen. She could hear Damon's deep professional voice now in place of his gentle whisperings of a moment before. She began to clear the breakfast tray and clean up. She could hear him receive information and then follow it up with two calls of his own.

Dale was drying her hands on a paper towel when he finished on the phone and came from the bedroom in the process of wrapping her forest-green towel around his body. His face was alert and serious. "There's been a training accident over at the naval air station on Alameda. It's an emergency."

Dale became alert, too. She nodded, heading back to the bedroom. "Why don't you shower quickly, and I'll get your things."

Damon nodded and went into the bathroom. Dale, in the meantime, gathered all his clothing and laid everything out on the bed so he could dress quickly when he came out. He was finished with the shower in less than three minutes and more or less shaved in another two. With a flash of humor, Dale thought ruefully that he was ruining the edge on her razor!

As he dressed, Dale realized he was dressed formally, as he had been the night before for the fund raiser. "Will you have time to change?" she asked, looking around for his jacket and tie and spotting them on the living-room sofa.

"Just! Luckily, it's on the way." He stuffed the tie in his jacket pocket and checked to make sure he had his beeper, keys and wallet. He looked at Dale with a frown. "I hate to rush out like this."

"It can't be helped. This is an emergency."

"And I wanted to see Tai with you this afternoon. I wanted to tell her her social life is not dead just because she'll be in a cast most of the summer."

Dale stood staring at Damon wide-eyed. Automatically, she held up the jacket for him to slip his arms into, but her mind was racing as all the doubts and questions fell into place in her head. That's it! That's what has been bothering Tai. My God! How could she not have seen it!

The girl wasn't concerned about the additional pain and was not even thinking of whether she'd be skating the following year or not. But she was fifteen years old, and all her friends would be spending the summer going to parties and the beach, dating and just being teenagers, and she would spend all of it in a cast from her ankle to her mid-thigh. She would miss it all. How clearly now Dale remembered what it had been like for herself. How clearly she could recall the awful pain of being left out and alone while everyone else was having fun. It was like history repeating itself. Why didn't she think to use herself as an example and tell Tai everything about her own experience?

"Dale?" Damon questioned when she stood trancelike, staring at him. She blinked. "Are you all right?"

"Yes, yes," she answered. He didn't have the time to worry about her. "I'll tell Tai you asked for her and explain about the emergency. And I'm going to have a nice long talk with her today. I think I know what's been bothering her."

They got to the door. Damon opened it and swung around to face her. He looked over her soft mussed state and smiled, but there was no time to enjoy it. He quickly cupped her cheek and bent to kiss her briefly.

"I hope it's not too serious," Dale said.

"I'll call you later and let you know."

Dale stood on tiptoe and quickly kissed his jaw.

"What's that for?" he asked with a lopsided grin.

"I'll talk to you later and let you know. Good-bye—" And she pushed him out the door and closed it. She thought she heard him laugh as he bypassed the elevator and ran down the stairs.

Chapter Eighteen

"Dale, I'd like you to meet Harry Sullivan. Harry is a synthetics manufacturer. Does a lot of replacement pieces for the medical field. When I told him about your work, he wanted to meet you." Dr. Anders patted her shoulder paternally and left Dale standing in front of a middle-aged gentleman not much taller than herself. He was good-looking in a rough, unchiseled sort of way. He looked like someone who'd worked and fought and possibly connived very hard to get where he was.

Dale smiled graciously at him, as she had done to everyone during the afternoon. But the man made her immediately uncomfortable. First of all, he didn't smile at her; he leered. And instead of speaking directly to her, he had a tendency to direct his comments and questions to her chest. If Dale hadn't been so amused at first by his predictability, she would have been annoyed. Dale also had to admit she was probably dressed a bit out of character; under different circumstances, the man wouldn't have taken her seriously at all.

She was wearing a three-tiered peasant skirt with a ruffle on the bottom. It was black, with an even scattering of small yellow and white flowers. The white voile blouse was also peasant-style, with a drawstring scooped neckline and white embroidery down the front and sides of the long sleeves. She also wore a pair of medium-heeled sandals, and her hair was twisted into a haphazard knot at the back of her head. She looked at least ten years younger than she was.

Mr. Sullivan shook her hand and held on, not allowing Dale to withdraw it politely. She thought it best to humor him and just let her hand lay limply in his, offering no encouragement. When he realized his squeezing of her fingers as a signal didn't move her at all, he finally let go.

"You're not exactly dressed like a doctor," he remarked, flashing even capped teeth in a smile that was theatrically charming. Dale smiled with equal charm.

"I don't always dress this way."

"Good," he drawled, dropping his eye to her neckline, "I'm glad I caught you out of uniform."

Dale may have been mildly amused by the situation. Damon was not. Caution and politeness governed his movements and his proximity to Dale all afternoon at the garden party given by Dr. Anders and his wife. There were mostly professional people there, and the atmosphere was conducive to making "contacts." In general, Damon didn't object to the principle or necessity of such occasions. In the past, they'd done him a great deal of good. He'd never brought Jessica to one because he'd always known she'd have been thoroughly bored with what she called "fusty old crabs talking about their work." But being there with Dale was different. However, he was not happy with the way she'd been surrounded all afternoon, virtually since the moment they'd arrived.

Damon was very pleased and proud to be with her. She could take care of herself. She mixed well with old and young, men and women, drawing smiles and compliments from all around while seeming to be unaffected and easygoing. But he had not had more than a half-dozen words with her since they arrived and she was descended upon. Damon particularly didn't like the slick character she was talking to now as pleasantly as she'd spoken to anyone else. Damon wanted to go over to the man and say, "Cool it, buster—she's way out of your league!" Instead, Damon swallowed his bile, played with the coins in his pocket and tried not to look disagreeable. He turned his attention with determination to the elderly woman who was describing in some detail her bout with arthritis.

Dale had been rather set upon since arriving. Dr. Anders and his wife had been most hospitable, but she'd hoped to stay closer to Damon, since she hadn't seen much of him since Friday morning when he'd received the early-morning emergency call from the naval air station.

Dale let Harry Sullivan go on with his smooth talk and veiled propositioning. But she really wasn't interested. Casually, she let her eyes wander until she spotted Damon talking to an elderly woman with a rather plaintive expression on her face. As if sensing her eyes on him, Damon turned his head to look at her. He smiled in irony and lifted a shoulder. Dale flashed him a bright sunny smile, and after that he thought he would survive the rest of the afternoon.

Resigned, Dale sighed and turned back to Harry, who was still enjoying the soft peachy exposure of her skin above the blouse neckline. But Dale thought she could have put up with anything that day. She'd never felt so completely happy in her life.

ON FRIDAY, after Damon had left, she'd also showered and dressed, put the bedroom to rights and, with a renewed sense of confidence, had gone over to the hospital to see Tai. She'd already been brought down from recovery and was with her parents and in some pain. Dale had first spoken to Tai's parents and then seen to it that Tai was given something to make her more comfortable. Then they talked. And they continued to do so the entire afternoon. Casually, Dale introduced the subject of her own surgery and subsequent years of missed school, dating, varsity games—boyfriends. Tai listened so intently that lunch went unnoticed when delivered. Finally, it was all said, and it was Tai's turn to speak falteringly of her apprehensions. It was a tremendous breakthrough, because Dale recognized that Tai's background and upbringing were not conducive to confidences and the baring of one's soul. But she was still very young and very much in need of reassurances.

By seven o'clock, Dale had still not heard from Damon, so she went out to dinner with Gloria once again before arriving at her complex after nine. The space of the small apartment had changed in that so much of it—all of it—had in some way been shared with Damon. Suddenly, it was too quiet, and it seemed lonely. And her bed, which only that morning had seemed so full, was now strangely empty. Also, to her embarrassment, she ached all over for his touch. Damon had assuaged a need in her that she was afraid no one else would be able to again. She felt absolutely wanton lying in bed, wishing he was there to touch her breast and ease the swollen sensitiveness. She wished that he was there to hold her and kiss her in her sleep. It was horrible to think she might never know another night's peaceful sleep without him. But she did fall asleep.

The phone rang at two-twenty in the morning, and Dale sprang for it. "Hello, Dr. Christensen," she said breathlessly.

"Good morning," Damon said with obvious weariness in his voice. Dale squinted at the bedside clock and groaned in sympathy for him.

"Oh, Damon," she said. "Where are you?"

There was a deep sigh. "I just made it to my apartment. I thought for sure I'd fall asleep at the wheel. I...I just couldn't go much farther." It sounded so much like an apology.

"Are you all right? Were there many injuries?"

He answered her second question first. "About seven, mostly minor. But there was one badly fractured arm and a spinal injury—possible broken back. We had to get him to a mainland hospital."

"And—and you?" she asked with deep compassion.

"I need about twenty hours' sleep and I'll be good as new."

She smiled, resting against her pillows. "Then go get some sleep."

"Where are you?" Damon asked.

"In bed," Dale whispered.

"Oh," Damon moaned, and Dale grinned. Dale knew it expressed his own disappointment at not being there with her. "I need to see you."

Goose bumps rose on her flesh. Her heart sang. "You need sleep more."

He didn't have the strength to argue, but he hesitated. "I'm not so sure."

"I am. I'll tell Gloria to hold all calls for you tomorrow unless it's another emergency."

"How was Tai?"

"Very well. I took your lead and talked to her about the summer. I...I told her about my own surgery, and she's going to be fine."

"Good. I'm pleased to hear it." But he did sound so very tired. "Dale..."

She chuckled softly. "Good night, Damon."

"What will you do tomorrow?"

Dale sobered. She didn't have the heart to tell him she had to see about going back to New York. Her work was, in essence, done. There was no professional reason for her to stay. "Oh, I thought I'd splurge and go shopping."

"Well, don't plan anything for Sunday. I'm taking you to a garden party."

"Oh! To Madge's?" she asked with instant excitement. Damon smiled warmly to himself over her enthusiasm.

"Sorry to disappoint you, but no. Dr. Anders and his wife have invited us."

Dale grimaced. "It sounds official."

He laughed. "It only sounds that way. They're gracious people."

"Then I'd love to go. Now, will you go to bed?"

"If you insist."

"I do!"

Saturday had not been a sunny day and did not inspire Dale to be frivolous and enjoy shopping. But with heavy, reluctant steps she confirmed her flight back to New York. She sent a letter notifying Dr. Lester Wallace of her return and saw to terminating her business in Oakland. She walked around the city a little listlessly, a feeling of depression and hopelessness at war with the joy she'd found with Damon. If only she had some idea how he really felt about her. For the first time in her life, she was in love. Who knew it would also bring such confusion and despair?

"Dr. Christensen?"

Dale swung around, startled, and found Damon's mother smiling gently at her. As she recognized her, Dale's problems vanished, and she returned the smile. "Mrs. Christensen!" she said softly.

Madge laughed. "Madge..."

"Dale..."

They grinned foolishly at each other. "Are you shopping?" Madge asked.

"No, not really. It's less hectic just to look. How are you?"

"Fine, thank you. I'm so glad to see you again."

"Me, too. Are you on your way somewhere? I don't want to keep you."

Madge laughed. "I'm supposed to be shopping, too. Peter is coming for a visit, and I felt obligated to buy a new dress or something. But I don't feel like it. He'll just have to take me as I am. After all, I'm his mother!"

Dale laughed. "I'm sure he'll be so happy to see you he won't notice what you're wearing!"

Madge nodded, eyeing the younger woman, noticing her innate openness but also a curious sadness. "If you're not doing anything special right now, would you consider having lunch with me?"

Dale brightened at once. "That would be fun! I'd love to." She deferred to Madge and let herself be led to a lovely restaurant that looked like a greenhouse. Its cheerful decor more than made up for the overcast day. The two women exchanged commonplace conversation for several minutes, ordering lunch and becoming comfortable, quite as if they'd known each other a long time.

Madge asked Dale about her work, and, still exuberant over her progress with Tai, Dale outlined the surgery and what happened afterward. Madge wanted to know if Damon had been involved, and, blushing furiously, Dale told her the part he played and didn't play because of the fund raiser. Madge watched Dale intently, much more aware of the play of emotions on the young woman's face than she was of Dale's words.

Their lunch was served, each having decided on quiche and salad. "And what will you do now?" Madge asked evenly.

Dale stopped with her fork halfway to her mouth. She put it down again, feeling her stomach knot. "Go back home. I have a practice to see to. Patients to follow up on."

"And what does Damon say to that?"

Dale stared at the attractive older woman whose eyes were the color of Damon's and now held her gaze. "What . . . what would Damon have said?"

Madge smiled kindly. "It would depend on whether or not you've told him you love him."

Dale's eyes widened, and she clenched the napkin in her hand.

Madge gave Dale a sympathetic grimace and patted her hand. "Well, I guess you haven't," she said.

"W-what even makes you say that?"

Madge finished a forkful of quiche and tilted her head. "Because it's true. I think I knew the minute Damon introduced me to you. I don't mean to be forward, but...you had a rather enchanted look about you. It could only have been love."

Dale frowned and stared blindly into her plate. Madge laughed softly and shook her head.

"I'm surprised Damon inspires such a reaction," she teased, but Dale couldn't find it in her to laugh about something that had so plagued her. She took up her fork again and pushed her salad around the plate.

"I—I don't think I'm the only one it's happened to."

Madge raised a brow. "If you mean Jessica, dear, you're wrong. Damon's not in love with Jessica and never has been."

Dale's eyes flew up expectantly, and Madge's face softened at the open look of appeal. She wondered how much she should say.

"And you're the only woman he's ever brought home for me to approve. I suppose that means something," she finished lamely. She was reasonably sure that Damon felt very strongly about Dale, perhaps even loved her, too. But it was certainly not Madge's place to say so.

"I...I'm pleased that he did. I like you very much, Madge; but Damon knows I'm going home. He couldn't have forgotten that." Dale took a deep steadying breath and tried to finish her lunch.

They had a good time getting to know each other better and reaffirming first impressions. Madge felt rather helpless to interfere in her son's business despite her instinctive fondness for Dale. And she hoped that he'd come to his senses quickly. Madge recognized that Dale was strong in her own way, but she was not invincible.

They spent a few hours together, but then Madge had to get home before it got too late. Dale declined a lift to the hospital complex and walked the half mile instead, giving herself more time to think.

Dale debated telling Damon how she felt but knew she couldn't do that. It just seemed too forward and not her way. Her evening was lonely and depressing, and she went to bed early just so she wouldn't have to think anymore. She tossed and turned in the bed until she couldn't stand it and got up to make herself some tea. When the doorbell rang, it scared her so badly that she poured half the hot water on the counter and kitchen floor. Then, hurrying to answer the summons, she stubbed her toe on the leg of the coffee table. She moaned and hobbled the rest of the way, knowing full well who was on the other side.

Her eyes were smarting with tears when she opened the door and Damon stepped in, tall, handsome and dear. His smile quickly became concern when he saw the painful grimace on her face. "What happened?" he asked sternly, closing the door behind him.

"I—I stubbed my toe, and I spilled water all over the kitchen. What are you doing here?" she managed in one breath. She was both overjoyed to see him and angry that the very idea of his being there suddenly made her so clumsy and on edge.

"Did you hurt yourself?" Damon asked, taking hold of her arm.

"Yes!" Dale said disagreeably, feeling as if she were going to cry any minute.

Damon slowly gathered her stiff body against him. "Shall I kiss it and make it better?" he asked in a seductive, teasing voice.

Dale stood still and unyielding, unaccountably annoyed with him. But the image of his kissing her feet was too ridiculous. She started to laugh. Damon grinned at her. He took hold of her chin and tilted her face.

"Or perhaps you prefer if I kiss you somewhere else?"

She looked at him with her bright jade eyes, so happy to see him and terrified by the power he had over her. Dale put her arms around his neck, and Damon obligingly bent to kiss her lips. But after a moment he bent farther to lift her in his arms and tote her off to the quiet seclusion of the bedroom, her tea and sore toe very much forgotten.

AND THAT WAS why she was so happy now, standing in a sunny garden, feeling that the whole world was beautiful. Damon had said he didn't want to go a whole day without seeing her, so he'd come to her the night before. They'd gotten very little sleep at all but hardly noticed.

Dale looked for him once more and again gave him a smile that made him stare in wonder. After they'd awakened that morning, she'd insisted on going to the center. She said she had to for a few hours. Damon hadn't asked why but had simply said he'd pick her up there at twelve-thirty for the ride to Dr. Anders's house. At twelve o'clock, Damon arrived at the center to learn that Dale was with Tai, saying her good-byes. He hadn't given much thought to her leaving.

But that was only the start of reality for Damon. The full force of it hit him once more when he reached Dale's temporary office. The phone started ringing, and automatically he lifted and answered.

"Dr. Christensen...."

There was a hollow silence, and suddenly there was adolescent laughter. "You're not Dale!" came the skeptical voice.

Damon smiled into the phone, very much intrigued. "You're absolutely right. How did you guess?"

"'Cause you don't sound like her! Dale's got a pretty voice. She's a lady!"

"I quite agree. My name is Damon. Who are you?"

"I'm Barry...."

"Hi, Barry. Can I help you?"

There was a pause. "Well, I don't think so. I have to talk to Dale."

"She's not here right now. I could have her call you."

More hesitation. "I don't know," the young voice responded indecisively. "She told me I could call her if I needed to. And she said she'd come back to New York when my casts came off."

Damon came to attention again. "Oh....."

"And she promised she'd be here when I started working with a phys-physical—"

"Therapist," Damon supplied readily.

"Yeah, that's it. Isn't she finished out there yet? She said she'd only be gone a few weeks."

The magnitude of time passing and irrevocably gone occurred to Damon, and he realized bleakly how much he'd again taken for granted. My God! She couldn't go back to New York now. Didn't she know how much he loved her? Of course not. How could she? He'd only realized himself a few days before. And he hadn't said a word to her.

She had a life that had nothing to do with him. Other patients, a home of her own somewhere. Other colleagues—obligations.

"It has only been a few weeks." Damon said to Barry as much as to himself.

"She's gotta come back!" Barry said a little frantically. "I need her! What if something goes wrong? And she promised."

"Take it easy, Barry. Dale wouldn't break a promise. If she said she'd be there, she will."

"But could you tell her I called, just in case? Tell her it's a matter of life and death!"

Damon couldn't help being amused by the youngster's desperate ingenuity.

But when Damon got off the phone, he knew he couldn't do it right away. He needed just a bit more time to work it all out in his own head....

IT WAS NOW getting late in the afternoon. Damon had managed to circulate quite freely among the other guests, but Harry Sullivan was rather tenacious and a little dense. Every time Dale turned around, there he was again.

She continued to smile and be charming, but she could feel her teeth gnashing, and her jaw begin to ache from holding the smile in place for such a very trying man. She didn't care if he had the best facilities in the world for manufacturing what she needed—he was tiresome.

Dale felt a hand—large and most familiar now—slip around her waist. To others, it might seem an innocent and friendly gesture. To Dale, it was personal, possessive and welcome. She looked over her shoulder and smiled with warm eyes at Damon's broad form.

"Darling," he murmured, just loud enough for Dale and Harry Sullivan to hear. Dale stared wide-eyed at him, while

Harry tried to make himself taller. Dale quickly recovered and leaned comfortably against Damon's chest.

"I wondered where you'd disappeared to," she said softly. "Oh, Damon, this is Harry Sullivan. Mr. Sullivan, this is Damon Christensen."

The smile on Harry's face slowly began to fade. "Oh— your husband," he murmured distastefully, shaking Damon's hand with a distinct lack of enthusiasm. Dale struggled not to laugh.

"How do you do, Harry. I'm sure you'll understand if I steal her away from you?"

Harry threw up his arms in total surrender, and his interest in Dale died.

Dale stood next to Damon, giggling like a schoolgirl, "I suppose we should have told him the truth. That was very mean of us."

"No, it wasn't," Damon said caustically.

"I'm very glad you came over, however."

"My pleasure," Damon said, turning a special private look her way. He waved a hand vaguely. "Have you had enough of this?"

Dale sighed. "Yes, I think so."

"Then why don't we sneak away and leave?"

She nodded mischievously. "Why don't we!" She began to move, but Damon tightened his arm around her waist. Dale looked at him with a frown.

"How's our timing doing?" he asked significantly, his voice low and hoarse in her ear. Dale blushed.

"It's fine," she admitted, secretly happy to say so.

"Your place or mine?" Damon asked.

Dale looked at him. "Yours," she answered almost shyly. Damon led her to the door, smiling.

"Then let's get out of here."

IT WASN'T until the next morning that Damon told Dale of the phone call from Barry. He took a chance that the evening and night together loving and whispering to each other in the dark would have the effect of making her think twice about leaving. It didn't. If anything, Dale became soberly alert to the information and a little quiet.

Unreasonably, Damon found himself jealous of a twelve-year-old boy who could command her attention three thousand miles away, even as he was moved and deeply impressed with her total commitment to each of her cases. He just didn't particularly feel like being understanding.

Part of it was Damon's own confusion and inability to deal suddenly with changes in his life. He didn't have as much practice as Dale had had, and she'd begun a whole lot earlier. It all seemed very straightforward and simple to him. He loved her. And he was convinced that she felt strongly for him, because he knew her to be a woman not to take an affair lightly. Therefore, he only had to tell her he loved her and everything else would fall into place. He had sudden confidence enough for both of them, which was just as well, because Dale was convinced now that it was impossible for her to stay, no matter what. She'd made a promise to Barry, and Barry was her responsibility.

For a long time after Damon told her about the call, she lay quietly in his arms, her cheek pressed to his hair-covered chest. His heartbeat was very strong and powerful—and rhythmic. She loved the sound and feel. It was Damon's. Her love and, dear God, almost her life. He *was* strong. He could go on. It was only Dale who wondered miserably how she was going to survive without him. Were her work and her kids ever going to be enough again to fill the painful open void in her heart?

She turned her head and began to press gentle, provocative kisses on his chest, covering his nipple with her mouth, tasting and feeling so she'd remember.

Damon was making his own plans to take her to dinner, perhaps into San Francisco for the evening, where she'd never had a chance to go during the whole month of work. And as her kisses began to stimulate and coax, arouse and make him moan, Damon held her to him in exquisite passion and love, thinking that he'd won.

Chapter Nineteen

In the end, they never did make it to San Francisco. Their only hunger seemed to be for each other. There was a desperation to their lovemaking and a need to repeat it over and over again until they were both so sated and exhausted that a bomb could have gone off and they'd never have noticed.

It was as if Dale wanted to feel and have him in every pore of her. It was as if she were trying in one afternoon to give, take and experience all her love for Damon because it was her last chance. Damon was more basic. He just simply didn't want to let her go. The feel of her soft, lithe body under him sent off skyrockets in his head. He was so overwhelmed with a love and in need of her it began to hurt in his chest. He wanted to keep her right there with him forever. And it was also as if some sixth sense had warned him she was still not his entirely. If he let up for even an instant, she'd slip away right through his fingers.

But in the end, hunger won out. Damon suggested Jack London Square, a remodeled portion of Oakland's waterfront with a number of elegant restaurants. Dale didn't care. As long as she could be with him, she would have been just as happy with the local coffee shop.

Damon showered and changed first, dressing to look impossibly handsome in charcoal-gray slacks, a white shirt and a navy-blue tie with small white dots. With it he wore the infamous navy blazer from New Orleans with its subversive brass buttons. Damon drove her to the complex for her to change. She dressed beautifully and simply. And if they hadn't left soon to eat, they wouldn't have eaten at all that evening.

All other women that Damon had ever known faded from memory. It was as if he'd never known or never wanted anyone else but the woman standing shyly in front of him, unsure of her own attraction to him.

Dinner was an elegant and glamorous affair. Damon ordered champagne, but they were silly with it, toasting New Orleans, Boris Teller, the Oakland Athletics and San Francisco Bay. Damon also managed one "To us," which just about stopped Dale's breathing altogether. They were finishing coffee just as a trio began playing the kind of romantic, slow music meant for dancing. Damon tried to coax Dale into one dance, but she shook her head and blushingly said no. They were standing near the dimly lit entrance to the dance floor, and Damon was standing behind her.

"Just one dance," he whispered.

"Oh, Damon, I can't! My... my knee. And I'll be all out of step."

"There's nothing to step to," he said gently. Holding her waist, he turned her to face him.

"But I—I've never danced before," she admitted, feeling embarrassed.

"I'm not so hot myself," he said with a rueful grin, trying to see into her bowed face. "But I thought we'd just hold on to each other and sway. My feet will be safe—and so will yours!"

He heard her giggle. Damon felt relief at the sound from her. Dale lifted her head to take a hesitant peek at him, seeing that he was sincere about how they would manage, but it was too much for her. She pulled her bottom lip between her teeth and shook her head firmly.

"All right." Damon gave in, briefly kissing her forehead. "Then let's go for a walk."

They wandered aimlessly around the waterfront, feeling no need for conversation as Damon held her hand. Every now and then they'd look at each other and smile. Damon would sometimes just squeeze her hand, and she'd return the pressure. But they were both somewhat pensive, thinking about the same thing—her leaving—each coming to different conclusions as to how to deal with it.

They stood on a breezy pier watching the diamond lights of the city of San Francisco, feeling as if it were all unreal.

Feeling a bit unreal themselves. Damon squeezed her hand again.

"How do you like California?" he asked casually, looking out over the bay.

Dale looked out, too. "It's going to fall off into the ocean," she responded with a perfectly straight face. It was meant to make him smile. But a surreptitious glance at Damon's face showed she'd failed. "Why do you ask?"

Damon shrugged offhandedly. "Just curious to know how it stacks up against New York," he said, squinting against the breeze that further ruffled his hair. Dale watched him affectionately.

"I think California is a pretty state—what I've seen of it." She frowned over her answer. "But I sort of feel you have to be on the East Coast to get anything serious done."

Now Damon did smile.

"Maybe it's all that sunshine and palm trees."

Damon's smile slowly faded. Dale was curious, feeling the tension in his hand and stiff arm. "Could you live here?" he asked calmly, smoothly. But Dale was instantly alert, and her heart skipped a beat. She turned to stare at him a long time.

"I...I don't know. It...would depend," she said, her wide eyes bright with questions and searching Damon's face for a meaning. Damon turned his head to look at her as well.

"On what?"

"On why you want to know."

For a very long breathless moment he studied her upturned face. "Dale, I want you to stay here with me," he said clearly, locking eyes with her.

Dale swallowed hard. A chill ran up her spine. Her heart was sitting somewhere in her throat, and she was afraid to move. Damon took her gently by the shoulders and turned her so that they completely faced each other. He frowned at her paleness.

"Did you hear what I said?"

"I...I heard you," she whispered finally.

Damon bent forward to ply the gentlest kiss from her parted lips. "Don't you understand? I love you."

Dale relaxed inside. She hadn't dared hope to have him

say it. She knew she was probably in love with him the moment she arrived in California and found him waiting at the airport. "Oh, Damon!" Dale breathed out in relief, perilously close to tears. He laughed softly and put his arms around her.

"There's no need to cry."

"I...just didn't think you...could love me." Her voice wavered.

"Dale, I've probably been in love with you since the conference last February. But I'm not always very smart," he said with a derisive little laugh. "I didn't know for sure until last week." Dale clutched him and half sobbed, half laughed into the shoulder of his jacket. "And I wasn't sure how you felt about me. Especially after that stunt I pulled in getting you here."

Dale looked at him as if he were demented. "You mean you couldn't tell? Didn't it show? Your mother knew at once I was in love with you."

Damon chuckled. "So that's what she meant when she said I was blind as a bat!"

Dale joined in his laughter, and then slowly it faded, and they stood enveloped in a silence filled with their love.

"I love you," Damon said again, and cupping her face, kissed her to prove it. Dale leaned into him, accepting it joyously. It was like discovering each other all over again, and it was so wonderful feeling they only needed each other to be perfect and complete. In any case, the euphoria of their love only made it seem that way. Damon felt as if a tremendous weight had been lifted from his mind. Dale did not. The only thing that had been settled was that they loved each other.

Damon settled his arms around her waist, bringing their hips together. He gave her a long, loving scrutiny. "I think I have another name for you," he drawled.

"What's wrong with the one I have?" she said, smiling.

"Nothing," Damon said lightly, pinching her chin. "But it doesn't sound like how I see you sometimes. It doesn't say the way you're special to me."

Dale lowered her eyes and with a complacent smile smoothed the fabric of his shirt with her slender hands.

"Okay." She humored him. "What would you like to call me?"

Damon squeezed her, a hand riding up the side of her torso until his thumb pressed into the soft underside of a breast. His mouth touched her cheek, then moved to an ear. "My love, my darling, sweetheart...."

Dale laughed softly against his throat. "I don't mind any of those."

"How do you feel about Christy?"

Dale's eyes sparkled, and she moved her head to look at him. "Christy!" she murmured. "My family used to call me that when I was a little girl. It was a very special name for me!"

"See what I mean?" He grinned.

Dale reached up a hand to stroke a firm jaw and cheek. "I can't call you by your true name of Michael. You'll always be Damon to me," she whispered.

Damon took the hand to kiss the fingers. "Just so long as I'll always be yours."

They slowly made their way back to the small white sports car. Damon began to talk of his patients from the naval station accident. He had to spend all the next day seeing to each of them and talking to the naval doctors. Dale nodded in understanding. But she wondered when they'd talk about themselves and how to settle the situation looming large and formidable ahead of them. One would think from Damon's cheerful disposition that it was all arranged. If indeed it had been, Dale only wanted to share the information, as well. It was only when she actually found out that she wished she could just have been happy with his love. Expecting anything more was going to be impossible.

Damon had already taken it for granted that Dale would stay in California. Oh, he realized that she'd made a promise to Barry, and he didn't expect her to break it. And although he didn't actually say so, Dale knew he did expect that she'd return to the West Coast and to him.

As he drove her back to the complex, he held her hand, and inadvertently Dale clung to his as if to let go meant losing him again. Damon was asking about whether she wanted to keep his apartment or look for a house. He wanted to know if she wanted a large or small wedding. Dale's stomach knotted, and suddenly she was over-whelmed with sadness, and she fought against tears. He hadn't even asked if she'd marry him yet. There was so much about her he still didn't understand. She took a deep breath and turned to him.

"Damon, but there's my practice and my patients. All my research is in New York."

Damon gave her a brief smile. They were approaching the parking lot of her building. "I would never ask you to give up being a doctor, love, but you can be a doctor here in California and continue with your research."

Dale could feel herself stiffening defensively. "You could be a doctor in New York just as well" was her quiet response. She watched as the smile faded from Damon's face and it grew puzzled. He didn't answer right away but parked and turned off the motor, leaving them in a silence that was now charged and nervous.

He swiveled in his seat to level a searching look at Dale, and she felt her hopes and her heart sink together. "But I want you to stay here."

Dale swallowed, the color drained from her face, her eyes became bleak. She might have known it was too good to be true. She might have known there was a price to pay. Wasn't anything ever easy? Wasn't anything simply a gift, with no questions asked?

Dale shook her head and pulled her hand from his. "My practice is in New York. The people who count on me and need me are there."

Damon looked disbelieving for a second before his mouth hardened. "Dammit! *I* need you!"

"I can't just give it up, Damon. I've worked so hard to establish myself." *And I've already sacrificed so much,* she added to herself. But Damon looked incredulous.

"Does it mean more to you than I do, than our love?"

"Of course not, but—"

"But it's too much of a sacrifice. Is that it?"

Dale's eyes stared long at him, and she forced herself to keep her voice steady and calm. "That's not the point, Damon. The real question is why *my* sacrifice? Why *me*?"

Damon's look of anger slowly faded and was replaced

with a different kind of rigidity. His pride surfaced, his will every bit as staunch and unbending as her own. Damon's resoluteness came out of an uncharacteristic protection of his masculinity, Dale's out of a sense of fairness. It gave her the better position to argue from, but she didn't want to fight with Damon. She wanted only to love him.

"I can't stay here," Dale began, hoping to make him understand. "I can't leave and then come back."

"Even for me?"

"Damon," she said desperately, "not even for *me*!" But Dale could tell he didn't understand. Dale licked her lips and clasped her hands together in her lap. "Tomorrow you must go to see to your patients. Perhaps you will be in surgery all the day after. No matter what, Damon, you'll *have* to do that. Well, I have to return to New York. There's a twelve-year-old boy I made a promise to, and I'll keep it."

There was something about her calm determination that warned Damon she meant it. And the fear that she would actually leave frightened him. "Dale, it doesn't have to be this way!" he said impatiently.

She shook her head vigorously. "I came here because of you. I...I didn't realize it at first, but it's true. But I'll have to leave now for the same reason!"

"I'm not sure I understand. But I do know we can work this out!"

"It's going to be a lot harder than you think."

"Why?" he asked angrily.

Dale smiled sadly. "If you knew me better, you'd know why."

"And you're not going to tell me, either."

Dale looked directly at him, her eyes memorizing his face—his anger of the moment had hardened his mouth and jaw, and his eyes were blazing. "I love you, Damon. But I'm not going to make it easier for you." She reached across then and gave him a light kiss on his mouth. As she moved away, his hand curved to her face, holding her still.

"I can't believe you're going to do this!"

"I can, and I will." And she struggled to get out of the car.

Dale hurried forward to get into the building, praying he wouldn't follow her. He actually got out of the car, too, and called her name once. But Dale never responded. She wouldn't have been able to. Long before she'd ever reached the door, tears were streaming down her face.

DALE SPENT the next morning with Tai even though they'd already said good-bye. The young girl was in much better spirits, resigned to a lost summer. Dale cleared her few things from the temporary office, seeing to it that all of Damon's files were returned to him, hoping that the water blotches on the outside dried before he figured out they were tearstains. She carefully removed Tai's calligraphic autograph to take home and frame. She spent the afternoon writing a final report and prognosis and recommendations for follow-up to her surgery. She turned in her photo ID and beeper and spent two lonely hours in the cafeteria drinking coffee and coming to the conclusion that she was definitely out of her mind.

Some people spend a lifetime looking for love, and if they're lucky, they find it. Well, Dale had never considered finding love, so she'd never even looked. Yet it had happened. She and Damon had literally stumbled into each other's arms, and he had given her precious moments in time. He had also slowly stripped away her absolute need for a show of strength and purpose, her ideas of being secure and independent, to expose beneath a woman, soft and young and vulnerable, who was desirable to him.

So then, what was she doing to herself? Why in the name of her stubborn pride was she risking losing the one man she could love forever? Right at that moment Dale wasn't even sure why she had to go back to New York. Was it to show self-will? Was it for Barry? Or was it that she'd been so used to having to be strong she didn't know how to lean or compromise or decide the most important things in her life anymore?

Gloria could not persuade her to come to dinner. She sensed that Dale was trying to work something out that had to do with Damon. So she didn't persist.

Walking very lethargically as she left the hospital, perhaps for the last time, Dale encountered Dr. Anders. He expressed tremendous gratitude and admiration for her and hoped there'd never be another urgency to bring her so far from home again. Dale's throat constricted, and she gave him a quavering smile. Dr. Anders patted her hand kindly and left her.

He had not missed the emotion at play within the young woman, and although he could hardly be called a gossip and was unaware of the underlying speculation by his staff concerning Damon and Dale, he, too, hoped the young man was not going to let Dale get away from him.

From the apartment Dale called Barry and, keeping her voice playful and light, told him she'd be back in New York by the end of the week. She couldn't help responding to his whoop of joy. Then she called Madge Christensen, because she couldn't imagine leaving without letting the other woman know how much it meant meeting her and how she'd miss her.

Not daring to ask what had happened, Madge only asked Dale if she was sure she was doing the right thing. Was it what she really wanted?

Dale laughed in a broken voice. "No, and I'm not sure of anything anymore!"

There were at least a thousand questions Madge wanted to ask, but she only said, "I'm very sorry that you're leaving, Dale. But I want you to know I'll always be here if you ever need someone to talk to, and I hope you and Damon can work this out. I hate to see you both unhappy."

"Oh, Madge! It's so unfair!" Dale said contritely. Madge's heart went out to the young woman.

"My dear, love is *never* fair. *We're* the ones who must be fair!"

She made Dale promise to get in touch with her as soon as she reached New York. It was in Madge's mind not to let Dale forget for an instant that her heart was not really in New York but wherever Damon was.

And then, for no particular reason that Dale could think of, she found herself calling Boris Teller in New Orleans. She thought that perhaps she would tell him of her success with Tai and how wonderful the opportunity had been to work under such unusual circumstances. She was going to tell him she was on her way back to New York to start the next phase of work with young Barry.

Dale heard his dear voice say hello. She opened her

mouth to speak and promptly closed it again. She tried once more.

"Boris...." She sounded squeaky and thin. "It...it's me, Dale."

And then she burst into tears.

Chapter Twenty

The rain outside the patio doors poured in a steady, hard
stream, as if making up for lost time. It purged Madge's
garden of dust, bugs and dryness and brought with its deluge the promise of new blossoms and sweet air. Something
good would come of the day. Damon did not think so. It
was just another element in the last few days he'd had no
control over that had left him feeling both annoyed and
helpless.

There'd been no need for him to continue with the injured naval men; the cases had officially been turned over
to their own medical personnel that afternoon. Damon was
free to consider his own problem—how not to lose Dale. It
had taken Damon time to see that it was because of his ego
that he had been unable to believe that she'd even consider
returning to New York. It was his hurt pride that had suffered at knowing she could readily place other obligations
over him. But it had also taken two nights without seeing
her, and Madge's prompting, to make him realize what
damage his own ego and pride could do.

Still not able to see or speak to Dale, Damon had descended upon his mother again to bellow about the injus-
tices of his life. Madge had been unmoved and almost
without sympathy for her younger son.

"I don't understand her!" Damon had ranted in exasperation.

"There's nothing difficult to understand," Madge had
informed him, sitting comfortably on the sofa while Damon paced in his torment. "All Dale is asking is honesty
and fairness. And she is exactly what she seems."

"So is Jessica!" he said in total irrelevance.

Madge chuckled. "Silly man—but you've never been in love with Jessica."

Damon let out a sigh. That was certainly true, and the two women were in no way alike. He'd never known anyone like Dale, who got so much simple pleasure out of simple things. Who was so undemanding and so accepting. Whose very presence rejuvenated him and made him feel whole and good. The idea of not having her made his future prospects appear bleak and ordinary.

Dale had him lock, stock and barrel; hook, line and sinker; heart, body and soul. The sad irony was that Damon was willing to bet she didn't realize it. Madge shook her head at her son's bewilderment.

"Damon, it's not that complicated. I have no doubt that Dale loves you. And it's not often we find anything in our lives worth fighting for. She's worth fighting for. You'd be a fool to lose her!"

Damon turned angrily to his mother. "Do you know what she said to me? She didn't want to make it easy for me!"

Madge had to laugh at his indignation. "Good for her!"

"Dammit, Madge! *She's* the one who's leaving! If she loves me, how could she!"

Madge laughed again. "Because you probably didn't give her a choice. Stop being so selfish, Damon! Do you have any idea what it must have cost her to say no to you? She loves you. And she loves her work. She's been sure of *that* a lot longer. You say you love her—and your work. But what would *you* have been willing to give up?"

"But I never expected her to *not* be a doctor," Damon argued.

"Only that she be a doctor here, on your terms!" Madge countered. "You wanted her to make that decision after a month here and on the strength of her love for you. Come on, Damon. Give the poor woman a break!"

Damon paced and thought, ruffled his hair, sighed and paced some more. Madge had never seen him so unsettled. Damon had always been strong and self-possessed—and focused. It was intriguing and wonderful to see he'd found someone who could have such importance and meaning in his life. But only if his stubbornness didn't stand in the way.

Madge sighed woefully. "Damon, you're ruining my carpet and wasting your time here. I think you should go find her and work this out. And give her my love."

Damon turned hollow eyes to his mother and began shaking his head. "I tried reaching her this afternoon. The hospital said she already checked out of the apartment. She was on a three o'clock flight to New York."

DALE'S CONVERSATION with Boris Teller had been very much like that of a daughter seeking comfort and advice from a father. And Boris, very much on the order of an indignant father, could only think of getting his hands on Damon's neck and wringing it thoroughly. But he did his best to soothe Dale.

He had, of course, been delighted that his young protegée was in love. And if she had been in a less tumultuous state, he would have told her she had him, in part, to thank. But she really was too devastated to appreciate the humor. Boris had sighed and tisked and shushed, lamenting the foolishness of the young and secretly thankful that he himself was all done with that. It amazed him to realize how often we each are our own worst enemy, afflicted with too much pride and making life more difficult than it need be. Pride never kept anyone warm on a cold, lonely night. But Boris also knew, thank goodness, from his own experience, that love can lead to illogical thoughts and, at times, hopelessness. Perhaps it was just as well. Without a hurt or a bit of worry, the heart would be a very hollow organ.

Boris hoped his confidence in Damon Christensen had not been misplaced. And he assured Dale that it was not the end of the world. She was to do, for the moment, what she had to do—keep her promise to Barry. Afterward, she could do what she wanted to—love Damon Christensen and make a life with him.

THURSDAY MORNING Dale called Frances McCann to tell her she was back. Thankfully, no questions were asked about California or Damon. Frances said she was ready to begin work the following Monday with Barry; if he progressed well, she could send him home to his parents in three or four weeks to continue therapy in New Orleans. By Thursday afternoon, Dale had seen Barry herself and was touched by his obvious joy and relief at seeing that she'd returned as promised. Dale did an admirable job of masking her own disappointments and sorrow. She gave Barry the Oakland A's shirt and the autographed ball. She watched as he sat stunned and open-mouthed in disbelief at the gifts. He promised he would work twice as hard, and Dale knew deep inside her that the child was going to be everything he wanted to be. She could almost believe it had been worth coming back—almost.

On Friday morning, Barry's casts were removed. At six o'clock that evening, Dale arrived at her house and roamed restlessly from room to room, touching things that were familiar and for the first time feeling how lonely and empty the house was. She ate only half her dinner and listlessly went to bed and cried herself to sleep for the fourth night in a row.

On Saturday morning, she weeded her neglected garden and spoke to her father long distance. She walked a half mile to the beach and a half mile back, and it was only just noon. Dale wondered how she was going to survive not only the weekend but the next few weeks alone. In a frightening moment of thinking her life would never be the same again, she wished she'd never met Damon Christensen.

At one o'clock, the mailman rang her bell. He handed her an armful of journals that had been held at the post office for her return.

"It's going to take you six months just to read the last four weeks'!" he teased.

Dale gave him a wan smile and brushed strands of hair from her face back into her haphazard ponytail. "That's all right. I'm going to have plenty of time for reading," she said sadly, and moved to close the door.

"Oh! By the way—" The mailman pulled a small yellow envelope from his breast pocket and handed it to Dale. "I also have this for you. It's a hand delivery. Have a good day, now. And welcome home!" he said, backing out of the door.

Dale turned the envelope over and saw the name "*Christy*" written in clear letters and underscored. Her mouth dropped open, and her heart lurched into her throat. Dale jerked the door open.

"Wait! Please, wait!"

The mailman turned back. Dale fumbled with the flap of the envelope and tore it open frantically. A pewter coin fell out into her shaking hand. She stared at it in disbelief.

"Where...where did you get this? Who gave it to you?" she asked the puzzled mailman, trying to keep hysteria out of her voice.

"Why, the gentleman at the end of the block. He got out of a cab and asked me if I thought you were home, and I—"

Dale began to rush toward the corner near her house. There was no cab and no one standing. She turned back to the mailman. "Are you sure, Mr. Gallagher?"

"Sure I'm sure! I gave him the envelope to write on myself! Try up at the other end!" And so saying, he waved and continued on his route.

Dale's heart was suddenly pounding, and her ears were ringing. Her hands were sweaty, and she wiped them nervously down the legs of her jeans. Slowly, she began walking the other way, her left knee beginning to tremble.

Dale came in line with the front of her house and stopped and turned her head. There stood Damon, tall, solemn and real, right on her doorstep. Dale stood staring in wonder, fright and joy. He was really there.

Damon had not been sure how he was going to approach her. He had no idea what he would have done if she wasn't even there. But the appearance of the mailman had given him a plan, and it had worked. He'd watched Dale rush after the mailman, seen the agitation in her as she inquired about the envelope. And Damon found that he could only stare at her as she ran to the corner in search of him, just as he stood staring now that she had walked back.

She was standing full in the sun, and the unruly wisps of hair around her head were yellow-gold strands that gave her an odd bright glow. Her eyes were wide, and her expression seemed to indicate a battle going on within herself. One of the things Damon so loved in her was the dual ability to be so open and innocent while fiercely defending what she most believed in. It pained him tremendously to think that he may in some way have changed any of that in her. He loved her desperately—just the way she was.

Dale was afraid to move. Her knee was trembling badly now. For an insane moment she wondered what Damon's reaction would be if she suddenly fell right at his feet! She took a deep breath and took a few hesitant steps forward. Then she had to stop. Damon, standing with his hand in his pocket, saw her falter and immediately started forward to meet her. She took one more step right into his open arms. Damon squeezed her so hard she thought her ribs would snap in two. But she circled her arms around him and held as tightly as she could.

"Damon...." She barely whispered his name.

"I'm sorry. I'm sorry," he moaned emotionally against her hair. From her quaking body he knew she was crying.

"What... what are you sorry for?" she mumbled.

"For letting you go."

They stood like that for perhaps a minute before Damon pulled away and led her back into the house. He picked up his brown leather suitcase and followed her inside. When the door was closed, and Damon had put down the suitcase, he once again took her willing body into his arms. His hands rode up and down her back and sides, refamiliarizing himself as he kissed her neck.

"I love you," Dale heard him whisper hoarsely.

"Oh, Damon." She sighed with relief, pressing closer. After a moment he looked into her face. Dale watched his jaw working in tension as he took a shuddering deep breath.

"I never used to think much about my life, where it was or where it was going. You do what you have to, day to day, and enjoy it if you can. All of that was perfectly okay until I met you."

Dale looked lovingly at him, but her stomach muscles tensed and fluttered. "What happened after you met me?"

"Everything!" Damon said unequivocally. He opened his mouth as if he would dare to try and explain in detail. In the end, he shook his head and repeated, "Everything."

The back of his hand stroked her soft cheek. "I know I never thought one way or the other about being happy until I met you. I know I am very unhappy without you. I know I could continue being a doctor on the West Coast with my life relatively carefree and smooth. But only if I'd never met you." Damon tightened an arm around her waist, his other hand raising her chin. "Dale, I need you to be part of my life. It will be pointless otherwise. And I don't even have the strength to try without you."

Dale bit her lip to control her chin but could do nothing about the tears filling her eyes. Damon began kissing them away, catching one at the corner of her mouth, enticing him to kiss her fully and completely. He pulled her tightly into his arms. "God, I needed to feel you against me. *Something* had to be real in this long, awful week!"

Dale laughed shortly, knowing exactly how he felt.

"I came to stay," he said. "I'm going to take a temporary staff position in Manhattan. We'll stay on the East Coast as long as you want."

Dale stared at him, both happy and confused. "But what about California and your programs at Oakland Central? What...what about your apartment...and Jessica?" she finished weakly.

Damon kissed her to silence her, his light eyes looking over her face. "The most important thing to me in California was my work—and Madge, of course. But as someone reminded me once, I can be a doctor anywhere!"

Dale bit her lip and colored over, but Damon only smiled at her.

"My programs at Oakland will begin without me. They have two good people in the city to fill the gap. I can always go back, if *we* decide to do that. But I just don't have for the moment the same kind of medical commitments that you do."

Dale couldn't believe she'd heard correctly. "You—you'd do that for me?"

"Yes, I would. You drive a hard bargain, lady!" he teased, bringing a hand up to stroke her neck. Dale was aghast.

"I didn't mean it to be that way!"

"I know. But I think it's just as well. As for the apartment, Peter's going to hang around for two or three months, so I left word with Madge for him to go ahead and use it while I'm gone. By the fall we should know what we're doing.

"And as for Jessica, I wish her every happiness in the world. Period. But it's you I love and want."

"You've made an awful lot of decisions in just a few days," Dale murmured with an admiring light in her eyes.

Damon sobered for a moment. "Yes, I have, but why did you have to make it so hard?"

"I didn't want to. But you never asked me what I wanted to do. I had to come back." She rubbed her cheek against his chest and felt his arms tighten. "But I hope you don't think it was all too much trouble."

Dale could feel him chuckle. "It wasn't exactly trouble, my love. More like unmitigated torture!" His voice drawled in memory. "But you're worth it to me."

Damon looked over her shoulder and noticed her suitcase just inside the entrance. It was obviously packed, and he frowned at the implication. "Why is your suitcase by the door?" he questioned in a low voice.

Dale didn't answer at once. She stole a look at his handsome face, the fawn eyes watchful. "Barry starts his therapy on Monday. He won't need me again for a long time. I kept my promise. But I . . . I love you, and I thought I'd fly back to California on Wednesday. I was going to see if you—"

Damon didn't give her a chance to finish. He kissed her into silence, forcing her mouth open so that he could explore and ravish, making her respond to his love. Her breasts were flattened against his chest as her back arched, and she groaned in sudden awareness of him. "You were going to see if I still wanted you," Damon said huskily against her mouth. "Hell, yes! I do. During that infernal plane ride east I wore myself out wondering what *I* was going to do if you'd changed *your* mind!"

"Then . . . you must be tired . . . from the . . . flight," Dale managed in a fast-weakening voice as Damon continued to kiss her and caress her body.

"Exhausted."

"Wouldn't you like to . . . rest?"

He groaned, pulling her hips to meet his. "I plan to. But first I want to see the house." He began unbuttoning her blouse, pulling it from her jeans, nibbling at her bottom lip.

"Damon," Dale said in breathless surprise. "Not now!"

"Yes, now. Let's start with the bedroom."

Dale giggled joyously as he peeled the blouse off her arms and reached for the fastening to her bra.

DALE SIGHED deeply, completely content. She snuggled into Damon's side, her head against his hard shoulder. Their legs were still intertwined, and their bodies were sleek, damp and tingling. Damon laid a hand on her stomach and slid it all the way to cup a full, still-quivering breast.

"Will you marry me?" he whispered against her temple.

Dale's eyes closed, and she smiled softly. "Yes," she answered without hesitation. "I hope you don't mind having a doctor in the family. The hours are awful and often unpredictable!" She could feel his jaw contort with his smiling.

"I won't mind if you won't." Dale moved her arm across his chest, and they held on to each other.

"Damon, we—we don't have to stay in New York. You may not even like it here!"

"I'd like wherever you are," he murmured thickly, then let out a sigh. "Maybe we should compromise and split the difference. Pick someplace neutral in the center of the country."

Dale laughed and wrinkled her nose. "Do you think they need orthopedic surgeons in Kansas?"

There was a long pause, and then Damon chuckled. "I think we'll have to give that idea some more thought!" He squeezed her to him.

"Damon, I—I really wouldn't mind California, you know."

Damon rolled on his side toward her, a large hand splayed over her hip and thigh. "We'll see," he said. "Do you realize how easy this is going to be? We won't have to change initials on luggage, linens, underwear—"

"Damon!" Dale laughed in shock.

"I won't have to change my name. You won't have to change yours. No need to invite anyone to the wedding, because they all think we're married, anyway."

Dale smoothed the hair on his chest. "I think you've been planning this all along."

"If I wasn't so slow in the beginning, I should have been," he said caustically, his hand boldly sliding over her curved bottom. Dale planted a kiss on his jaw. She reached a hand to comb through his hair.

"Frankly, I think the only reason you want to marry me is so I'll cut your hair for you."

"You're absolutely right," he agreed readily in his deep voice, raising a brow at her.

"Damon," she murmured, fingering the hair over his ears, "I do believe you're getting gray."

"I can believe it," he responded ruefully. "After what I've been through, I'm surprised all my hair hasn't fallen out into my lap!"

Dale laughed in real amusement against his chest, trying to imagine Damon bald. Never! He had wonderful hair. "Poor darling, have you suffered?" she asked thoughtfully. Damon stroked her back slowly, pressing his thumb absently along her spine, creating a sensation that caused Dale to squirm. He let out a sigh.

"Probably no more than you. Very likely a good deal less." He looked into her bright-green eyes. "But I was miserable all the same." Damon lowered his mouth to hers, and it was immediately apparent that neither of them had had enough of the other. Their mouths and tongues locked and played. Damon shifted until he was half lying over her. He kissed her eyelids and forehead tenderly.

"Madge said she'd like to be at the wedding but would understand if we—couldn't wait."

Dale blushed. "I would really like Madge to be there."

"I thought you would," he said lovingly.

"And my dad."

"Are we going to be able to arrange all of this in two weeks?"

Dale laughed, stroking his cheek. "Is that all the time I get?"

Damon groaned, pressing his taut, aroused middle against her and playfully biting her lower lip. "You're lucky I'm giving you that much time!" Then he considered Dale seriously. "Although I did give her a choice. Either being at the wedding or with us when our first baby is born."

Dale held her breath and stared with glowing eyes at him. "Our first baby?"

"Mmm...." He wove his fingers into her hair. "I always

thought it would be a crime against humanity for someone as loving as you not to have your own babies—no more borrowing from your cases but your very own." He began to nuzzle her neck and throat. "Ours," he said into the skin.

Dale's arms circled his neck, and she moaned deep in her throat with the budding of desire throbbing within her. "If... if we keep this up, humanity is going to have an addition pretty quickly."

Damon stroked her thigh. "Mmm, since I plan on being the only contributor to the cause, it's fine with me."

Dale's response was completely lost and forgotten as the campaign began.

EYE OF THE STORM

MAURA SEGER

A powerful
portrayal of
the events of
World War II in the
Pacific, *Eye of the Storm* is a riveting story of how love
triumphs over hatred. In this, the first of a three-book
chronicle, Army nurse Maggie Lawrence meets Marine
Sgt. Anthony Gargano. Despite military regulations
against fraternization, they resolve to face together
whatever lies ahead.... Author Maura Seger, also known
to her fans as Laurel Winslow, Sara Jennings, Anne
MacNeil and Jenny Bates, was named 1984's
Most Versatile Romance Author by *The Romantic Times*.

Get this book FREE!

Mail to:
Harlequin Reader Service

In the U.S.
2504 West Southern Ave.
Tempe, AZ 85282

In Canada
P.O. Box 2800, Postal Station A
5170 Yonge St., Willowdale, Ont. M2N 6J3

YES! I want to be one of the first to discover **Harlequin American Romance.** Send me FREE and without obligation *Twice in a Lifetime*. If you do not hear from me after I have examined my FREE book, please send me the 4 new **Harlequin American Romances** each month as soon as they come off the presses. I understand that I will be billed only $2.25 for each book (total $9.00). There are no shipping or handling charges. There is no minimum number of books that I have to purchase. In fact, I may cancel this arrangement at any time. *Twice in a Lifetime* is mine to keep as a FREE gift, even if I do not buy any additional books.

154-BPA-NAZJ

Name	(please print)	
Address		Apt. no.
City	State/Prov.	Zip/Postal Code

Signature (If under 18, parent or guardian must sign.)

AMR-SUB-2

This offer is limited to one order per household and not valid to current Harlequin American Romance subscribers. We reserve the right to exercise discretion in granting membership. If price changes are necessary, you will be notified.

Readers rave about
Harlequin American Romance!

"...the best series of modern romances
I have read...great, exciting, stupendous,
wonderful."
— S.E., Coweta, Oklahoma

"...they are absolutely fantastic...going to be
a smash hit and hard to keep on the
bookshelves."
— P.D., Easton, Pennsylvania

"The American line is great. I've enjoyed
every one I've read so far."
— W.M.K., Lansing, Illinois

"...the best stories I have read in a long
time."
— R.H., Northport, New York

"The stories are great from beginning to end."
—*M.W., Tampa, Florida*

"...excellent new series...I am greatly impressed."
—*M.B., El Dorado, Arkansas*

"I am delighted with them...can't put them down."
—*P.D.V., Mattituck, New York*

"Thank you for the excitement, love and adventure your books add to my life. They are definitely the best on the market."
—*J.W., Campbellsville, Kentucky*

Names available on request.

ARQ-2